JUST A LITTLE HEARTACHE

MERRY FARMER

JUST A LITTLE HEARTACHE

Copyright ©2020 by Merry Farmer

Cover design by Erin Dameron-Hill (the miracle-worker)

ASIN: B08BX16B2C

Paperback ISBN: 9798573439099

Click here for a complete list of other works by Merry Farmer.

If you'd like to be the first to learn about when the next books in the series come out and more, please sign up for my newsletter here: http://eepurl.com/RQ-KX

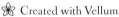 Created with Vellum

CHAPTER 1

LONDON – SEPTEMBER, 1890

*N*iall hadn't let the letter out of his sight since the moment he'd received it. Or rather, in the week since Lily Logan had handed the letter to him in the middle of a particularly chaotic rehearsal, it had lived tucked in the inner pocket of his jacket during the day and on the table next to his bed through the night, even when it was too dark to actually see it. He felt its presence at all times, in stillness or in chaos. And the rehearsal for his latest show was utter chaos just then, since the curtain was set to rise on *Love's Last Lesson* in just over a fortnight. But all Niall could think about as he rushed from the hall to the dressing rooms—where he'd been approving a change to the lead actress's Act Two costume to comply with the woman's vanity—to the wings on stage left so that he could deal with yet another catastrophe, was the letter burning against his heart.

"But sir," the harried director, Mr. Abrams, argued from a small platform set up over a few rows of seats in the house, "you are addressing this song to the chorus of royal courtiers. You cannot deliver it downstage with the chorus behind you."

Niall skittered to a stop just past the wings on stage left, already rolling his eyes at the battle unfolding in front of him.

"The audience has come to see *me*, sir," Everett Jewel, the star of the production and a legendary actor in his own mind, snapped back to the director. Even though they were merely rehearsing, Everett was in full costume and make-up—although he always seemed to dress in full costume and make-up, whether he was on the stage or strolling through Hyde Park. His back was straight and he looked as indignant as Niall had ever seen him.

"The audience has come to see Mr. Cristofori's work," Abrams shot back, narrowing his eyes at Everett.

"I can assure you, the crowds are already gathering outside the theater to see me," Everett continued to argue. "Or did you not see the line outside the stage door after rehearsal yesterday."

"I'm convinced you pay them to fawn over you," Abrams grumbled.

Niall winced as Everett's back shot even straighter and his kohl-rimmed eyes flared. Unsurprisingly, Everett's partner, Patrick Wrexham, was only a few feet away, leaning against the proscenium, where he had been watching the rehearsal with a copy of the script and a pencil in his hands. Niall sent a look Patrick's way, wondering if the former police officer would need to step in to break up yet another fight between Everett and Abrams. Patrick only answered Niall's questioning look with a shrug and a half-grin as though it were just another day with Everett.

"Haven't you read my reviews, man?" Everett strode a few feet to the right, as if delivering a stirring monologue. For all Niall knew, that was what Everett thought he was doing. "Have you not seen the likenesses of me printed in the papers? And you dare to suggest I have to pay my adoring public?"

"Is he serious or is he just winding Abrams up again?" Niall murmured to Patrick, moving to stand shoulder to shoulder with the burly man as they watched the argument pick up steam.

Patrick shrugged. "A little of both. He didn't sleep well last night."

"Nightmares again?" Niall asked. He knew enough about Everett's horrific past to know there were nightmares.

"At first," Patrick replied with a self-satisfied grin.

Niall answered that grin with a knowing chuckle. He also knew enough about Everett and Patrick's relationship to know Patrick Wrexham was the best thing that had ever happened to London's hero of the stage and that Patrick knew exactly how to deal with the peacock.

"This is Mr. Cristofori's show," Abrams argued on, pointing to Niall and alerting Everett to his presence. Everett spared a cheeky smile and a nod for Niall, but Abrams went on with, "You, sir, are but an instrument used to convey his work—a tool, if you will."

"I'll show you a tool, you—" The rest of his insult was drowned as Everett began to unfasten his trousers and several of the stunned chorus girls standing behind him gasped, either in fright or in expectation.

"Everett," Patrick barked, barely moving from where he leaned. When Everett glanced his way, shoulders dropping slightly, Patrick shook his head.

Everett cleared his throat, face going pink, and refastened his trousers before anything untoward could be revealed. Once that was done, he rolled his shoulders and tilted his chin up. "Perhaps we should ask Mr. Cristofori where he thinks I should deliver the outstanding solo he's written expressly for me, which is custom tailored to satisfy the tastes of my adoring public?" He arched one eyebrow and glanced from Abrams to Niall.

Abrams crossed his arms and looked to Niall as well.

"How can you live with a man who believes the sun shines out of his arse?" Niall muttered to Patrick.

Patrick chuckled. "He knows that arse belongs to me."

Niall laughed before he could stop himself. But at the same time, a pang of longing squeezed his chest. He'd had a love like that once. He'd been able to make ribald jokes and back them up with long, sleepless nights. He'd once

4

had someone who looked at him the way Everett was looking at Patrick now, like nothing else mattered but him, and he'd been able to return those looks, those kisses, those touches.

All that was gone now. All he had left was the letter that practically screamed in his pocket, right over his aching heart.

He cleared his throat and pushed forward to the center of the stage. Once at Everett's side, he turned to study the chorus, then pivoted forward to judge the distance to the audience. He walked down to the apron of the stage, glanced back at the chorus again, then gauged the distances to both of the wings. Finally, he strode back to where Everett stood, chin still tilted up, and motioned to three of the chorus girls.

"Cheat your way downstage," he instructed them. "That way Everett can stand closer to the audience for the number without looking as though he's ignoring the chorus entirely."

The girls rushed to take up their new places. Everett preened as though he'd scored a victory. Abrams scowled from his platform in the house.

"Do you have a problem, Mr. Abrams?" Niall asked.

"Only that I thought you'd hired me to direct this production," he answered.

Niall smiled reflexively. It was what he always did when faced with a confrontation where he knew he was right but didn't want to offend anyone. "So I did, Mr. Abrams. Because you are the best there is. However, I do have directorial experience, and Everett is right, in part, when he says that the audience is coming to see him as well as my work."

Everett crossed his arms and smirked at Abrams as if to say he'd told him so. At least, until Niall turned to him and murmured, "You're not helping, and stop being such a pillock."

Everett dropped his arms and sighed. Abrams shifted his weight from foot to foot, looking as though all he really wanted to do was get on with things.

"Can we finish the number?" Niall asked, glancing from Everett to Abrams and back. "We have to clear off the stage in a few minutes so that Gerald and the others can finish with the set anyhow."

"Whatever you say, Niall," Everett answered with a smile and a pointed look to Abrams. Niall suspected Everett had used his given name as proof that he was personal friends with Niall, whereas Abrams was hired help.

"Behave," Niall told him in a low voice as he moved to leave the stage. "Or else I'll have Patrick punish you later."

"Ooh, yes please," Everett cooed in a particularly fey manner, winking past Niall at Patrick.

Niall shook his head as he left the stage. "Make sure he doesn't get arrested before opening night," he told Patrick as he passed.

"If it hasn't happened by now...." Patrick let the rest of the sentence fade.

Niall chuckled and moved on, heading back to the theater's workshops to put out whatever other fires had started with his production before it was too late. His grin over Everett's antics and Patrick's understated adoration faded before he'd made it to the hall. The letter in his pocket demanded his attention once again, as if it were literally on fire. He thought about it every spare second of the day. Whenever the necessities of his production, on stage and off, or essentials, such as sleeping and eating, weren't at the forefront of his mind, the letter was.

He'd read it so many times that he didn't need to take it out of his pocket to remember the words.

"*Dearest Niall. I will be blunt. Since seeing you again after such a long and bitter separation a fortnight ago, my life and my world have utterly fallen apart. I don't know how to explain the heaven and hell that my life has been for the last ten years—heaven because it has brought me three wonderful children, whom I love more than life itself, and hell because I have been forced to spend those years without you. Oh, Niall, I was so wrong to pretend that you didn't matter to me and that what we shared was nothing more than the folly and experimentation of youth. Not a day has gone by when I haven't remembered you with a smile...or more. Seeing you again after so long only proved to me that my self-inflicted wound of a decade ago has not only failed to heal, it has only gotten worse.*"

"Oh! Mr. Cristofori! Mr. Cristofori!"

Niall nearly jumped out of his skin as Martin Piper

seemed to leap into his path out of nowhere, he'd been so lost in remembering the letter.

"I've been looking everywhere for you," Martin went on, his words rushed and his color high. "I wanted to ask you about this line of dialog in Act One, right before the ballroom scene."

Martin's arms were filled with prop swords, and a small, wooden shield was fastened over one of his arms. He held the script in his right hand and something that looked like a rubber bat in the other. Combined with the man's perfect oval face and large, hazel eyes that looked perpetually startled, Niall had a hard time determining whether the man was coming or going.

"What do you need to know?" he asked all the same.

"This is my first speaking, singing role, you see," Martin said in an almost apologetic voice, as if Niall hadn't been the one to cast him as Everett's page, one of the secondary leads. "I want to make sure I get it right. I've always wanted a life on the stage, but all I've done so far is work with props. I've done that in theaters all across England though, but never for very long at a particular theater. I have no idea why—" Two of the swords slipped out of his arms as he attempted to fumble his way closer to Niall in the midst of his ramble to show him the script. "Oh, dear."

Martin bent to pick up the swords, which caused him to drop three others and the rubber bat. As the man turned to retrieve a sword that had bounced out of his reach, he knocked into a small table containing the remnants of someone's tea, sending a teacup crashing to the floor.

"Well, that wasn't supposed to happen," Martin said, whirling the other way to reach for some of the shards of teacup. Another of the wooden swords fell out of his arms, and he kicked the bat against the wall. He grunted and seemed to reassess what he was doing, then reached for the bat, knocking the table again and toppling a discarded glass of water as he did.

"Martin, Martin, stop!" Niall told the man, grabbing his arm and hoisting him upright. "You're going to bring the entire theater down if you don't stand still for three seconds."

"That happened once," Martin replied, wariness in his eyes. "At the Community Playhouse in Durham. I was responsible for changing out the stage during inter-mission and—"

As he spoke, he leaned over to pick up a few more swords. The few he'd managed to get back in his arms spilled to the floor. This time, Niall bent to help pick them up. As he did, the letter fluttered out of his pocket and landed near the shards of teacup and spilled tea. Throat squeezing with irrational levels of fear over ruining his precious missive, Niall snatched at the letter.

"What's that?" Martin asked with a curious smile as they both straightened. Martin held so many wooden swords and in such an awkward manner that he looked like an overgrown hedgehog as he eyed the letter. "It must be important, the way you jumped at it."

"It is important," Niall said, flustered, tucking the letter back in his jacket pocket, hands shaking.

"Who's it from?"

Niall eyed the man warily. "An old friend," he said. "Lord Selby." He didn't know what prompted him to give Blake's name to a man he'd only come to know recently. There was no way Martin could possibly know the nature of his connection to Blake, though even if he did, like almost everyone else in the theater world, he wouldn't care. In fact, Niall had seen Martin ogling some of the male dancers from the ballet that the Concord Theater shared an alley with during breaks. But that didn't mean Niall was ready to spill the whole sad story of his shattered love affair.

"Oh." Martin seemed satisfied enough with the cryptic answer. "Friends are lovely, aren't they?" Before Niall could answer, Martin breezed on with, "Anyhow, about this line." He managed to hold the script up enough so that Niall could see the scene in question. "Do you want me to be serious or comedic with this line? Or with the whole part. I mean, I would never want to steal focus from *the* Everett Jewel, but it strikes me that quite a bit could be made of this part."

Niall's mouth twitched into a grin. Martin would never be competition for Everett in terms of leading man material, but as a comedic performer, Martin was perfectly capable of stealing shows, whether he knew it or not. That was precisely why Niall had pushed to have him cast in spite of Abrams's hesitation.

"Make the most of it, I say," he told Martin, resting a hand over his heart to make sure Blake's letter was secure. "Go ahead and challenge Everett's standing as the star of the show."

"Oh, I could never be the star of any show," Martin went on, eyes round.

"I wouldn't be so sure of that."

Niall gave the man a friendly smile and would have slapped his shoulder in encouragement, if he didn't think it would cause Martin to drop wooden swords all over again. Martin truly was the clumsiest man Niall had ever known, but he was also far, far more intelligent than anyone gave him credit for.

Not unlike Blake when they'd first met at university.

Another pang hit Niall's heart as he walked on. He remembered the way Blake had smiled modestly whenever Niall complimented him in those early days, remembered the bright and youthful energy in Blake's eyes. He remembered the warmth of Blake's smile and the way his lips had tasted the very first time they'd kissed, remembered the way his heart had sped up, the bittersweet fear that they two of them would be caught. He remembered the perfection of Blake's arms around him, the joy that had infused every part of him as their bodies entwined. He remembered the sounds of surprise and pleasure Blake made when he was worked up and the explosive way he cried out when he came.

Suddenly, the cramped hallways of the theater were too much for Niall. He changed direction, telling himself that costumes and set decoration and whatever other problems his production had could wait. He needed to get away from the closing walls of the theater, from the reminders of everything he'd lost.

He found the nearest door leading outside and burst into the balmy September afternoon. The heart of London buzzed with activity in the middle of the day. Carriages rolled up and down the streets of Covent Garden, men and women going about their business dodged tourists who stood marveling at the theaters and restaurants packing the streets. More than a few working girls—and rent boys—watched them or called out, carefully hawking their wares. It was the world Niall had immersed himself in after university, the world he felt most comfortable in. Yet, he felt the need to get away from it more strongly than ever. He needed to be alone with his thoughts, which had been suspended in the past ever since receiving Blake's letter.

"And now the unimaginable has happened," the letter went on. Niall recalled every word. *"Annemarie has uncovered the truth at last. She puzzled out who and what I am and where my heart truly lies. And she has taken the children. I am beside myself. I don't know where they have gone. I haven't been able to eat or sleep in days. It feels like the last of my soul has been ripped from my body. I am terrified that Annemarie will take the children to her father's home in America, in which case, I may never see them again.*

"I don't know what to do, Niall. I don't know who else

to turn to who will fully understand the position I am now in. I need you, more than I have ever needed anyone. I knew it the moment I saw you again. Please, Niall, please come to me. Please forgive me for turning my back on you by helping me now. I don't think I can go on without you. Yours, truly, Blake."

Yours. Truly. Niall swallowed the lump that formed in his throat, hopping onto an omnibus that would take him to Park Lane. Those two words, so common in ending correspondence, were everything Niall had ever wanted to hear from Blake but had long ago given up on. Blake should be his, but he wasn't. Their love should be true, but it had proven to be otherwise. And now here he was, standing at a crossroads as Blake begged for his help. Begged in the most painful, desperate language Niall could imagine.

He pondered it all as the omnibus rattled on. What was he supposed to do with a plea like that? Everything within him longed for Blake and had for more than a decade. The man was his other half. He'd known it from the moment he laid eyes on him. But Blake had hurt him. No, it was more than that. Blake had fatally wounded his heart. Niall hadn't been the same since that horrible spring day. The sight of Blake's regret-filled, hazel eyes, their long lashes, and the deadness of his look would haunt Niall until the day he died. Even his brief reunion with Blake almost a month ago now in Leeds had left Niall feeling raw and unsettled. Blake had been affable enough when Niall had taken Everett and Patrick to

Leeds in an effort to thwart Blake's brother, Montague, Lord Castleford, who had been part of a notorious child kidnapping ring. The time he and Blake had spent together had been short and brittle, but it had been the first time the two of them had laid eyes on each other in a decade, and it had ripped the wound open all over again.

The omnibus stopped at Hyde Park Corner, and Niall got off. He walked the rest of the way to the discreet door of The Chameleon Club lost in thought, barely nodding to the attendant at the front desk when he entered. He didn't have any particular business at the club, but he always felt a level of comfort there. The Chameleon Club was a formal and discreet establishment for gentlemen like him, owned by The Brotherhood. It was a place where there was no judgement, and where help was often just a conversation away. Niall didn't have any particular expectation of help, although, he thought to himself with a wry grin, he wouldn't say no to some of the club's excellent pastries and tea.

He was just helping himself to a scone in the dining room—which was quiet as usual on a Thursday morning, but not entirely abandoned—when none other than John Dandie approached him, a young, awkward-looking man with blond hair, like he spent his time out in country sunshine, trailing behind him.

"John, what are you doing here?" Niall asked, taking his scone to one of the empty tables in the vast room.

"Hadn't you heard?" John asked. "I've moved back to London. I'm opening a new law office."

"Not rejoining David and Lionel?" Niall asked, referring to John's former law partner, David Wirth, and David's new partner—in every sense of the word—Lionel Mercer.

John grinned. "That would have been awkward, considering all the water under the bridge between David and I. I'm setting up a new practice. This is Cameron Oberlin, the clerk I've just hired to manage the place."

"How do you do?" Young Mr. Oberlin nodded uncomfortably, bobbing a quick bow and glancing around, as though ghosts would pop out of the walls at any moment.

"Cameron is a country lad," John said with a friendly grin, thumping the young man's arm. "He's not used to the idea that there's a safe place for our sort in the big, noisy city."

"I see." Niall shook the man's hand before sitting. "You'll get used to it soon enough."

"But what about you?" John took a seat at the table with Niall, gesturing for Mr. Oberlin to do the same. "I saw you as you walked in. You looked as though you had the weight of the world on your shoulders. You still do."

Niall sighed and reached for the teapot and a teacup from the center of the table, where the service was already set. Instinct told him to keep himself to himself, but he'd known John for ages. Known him at university, in fact. John knew Blake as well. In fact, John and David had had front row seats for the bliss and the heartache back then that drove Niall to distraction now. If ever there was someone Niall could confide in, it was John.

All the same, he didn't trust himself to actually talk about it. Instead, he paused in the middle of pouring his tea and took Blake's letter out of his pocket. He stared at it for a moment, then gingerly handed it over to John.

"What's this?" John asked, taking the letter with a concerned look. As he opened it and scanned through it, Niall finished pouring his tea. He poured for John and the decidedly intimidated Mr. Oberlin as well. When John finished reading the letter, he blew out a breath, folded the letter and put it back in its envelope, and handed it back over to Niall. "Judging by the date, you've had that in your possession for some time now."

"A week," Niall admitted, voice hoarse. He took a sip of tea.

"So what are you going to do about it?" John asked, taking up his own teacup.

"I don't know," Niall said, sipping tea to avoid giving more of an answer.

"I've heard all about Blake's current troubles," John confessed. "Gossip travels fast in our circles."

"It does," Niall agreed, setting his teacup down. His stomach twisted a little too much for him to drain his cup, like he would have if it were whiskey.

"It sounds to me as though Blake could use a trusted friend right now." The look in John's eyes said something far different than his words. It said that Blake could use his old lover back.

"I don't know if I can," Niall sighed. "He hurt me, John. Ten years, and I still haven't recovered."

John reached across the table and patted Niall's hand. "The heart is the most difficult organ to heal, but it's better than leaving it broken."

Niall glanced at his friend. John was right in theory, but in practice, forgiveness was much harder. Niall didn't know if he was capable of it. He'd invested too much of himself all those years ago and had paid a steep price for it.

"What exactly happened between you and Blake anyhow?" John asked. "I mean, I know about Annamarie and everything the late Lord Selby demanded of Blake, but what happened between the two of you?"

Niall swallowed the lump in his throat, his whole body throbbing with bittersweet memories. He took a deep breath and said, "It's a long story."

CHAPTER 2

YORK – 1880 – TEN YEARS EARLIER

The room Niall had been able to commandeer for auditions for the play he'd written over the winter as the last project of his final year at university wasn't all that he'd hoped it would be.

"It's too small," he muttered to John and David as they helped set up chairs for their fellow students at the back of the room, who had come to audition. "It doesn't even come close to approximating the stage in the auditorium."

"At least it has a piano." John nodded to the instrument in the corner.

"Why wouldn't they let you hold auditions in the auditorium?" David asked, taking two chairs to the table that had been dragged into the center of the room for Niall.

"I'm just a student, and Professor Carroll is giving a lecture there this afternoon," Niall answered with a sigh.

"That old windbag?" John snorted a laugh. "Lecturing about his trip to Egypt last autumn again, is he?"

"For your information," a young man with sandy-brown hair piped up from the cluster of hopefuls at the back of the room, "Professor Carroll is a great explorer and Egyptologist. His excavation work in Thebes has garnered international attention."

"Yes, of course, and I respect him highly for it," Niall answered the young man graciously, then turned a scolding look on John. "Professor Carroll's lecture is more important than auditions for a student play."

"Yes, but aren't you performing this as part of commencement festivities next month?" David went on, taking a few chairs to the front of the room, which had been designated as the stage area.

"That's the arrangement I have at the moment," Niall said with a wary sigh.

In fact, it had taken a minor miracle and the intervention of Professor Ballard from the English department to convince the committee in charge of commencement ceremonies to allow Niall to stage his original musical play during the most public week of the university's year. Few of the men on the committee had wanted to take a chance on a green playwright. Even fewer had loved the idea of an all-male production of a show with explicitly female parts, particularly as it was a love story.

Truth be told, Niall was anxious about the production himself. Not just because he was the only person he knew with a voice high enough to perform the lead female role. If and when he was able to stage the play in London, he would most definitely cast women in the female roles. Seeing as there was a dearth of women in attendance at university—and even if the place had been crawling with female scholars, none would have dared to audition—if Niall wanted his play produced, he would have to fill the leading lady role himself.

"At least they didn't force you out into the green for your auditions," John said, crossing the room to inspect the piano. It was a simple upright that stood in one corner. John tapped a few keys, proving that the instrument was in tune, at least. "That was sporting of them."

"This *is* the choir room," Niall said, going to the table to organize the sides he'd had made up for auditions into piles designated by scene. "Gentlemen, if you'd care to come forward and sign your name to the audition list, then take some of these scenes to study, we'll begin the audition momentarily."

The dozen or so fellow students who had come to audition gathered around the table, putting their names down and taking sides, all while murmuring to each other. Niall moved to the piano, where David and John were picking out simple tunes and flirting a little too obviously.

"The two of you had better watch your step," Niall warned them. "The walls have eyes, and you know how difficult life can be if the wrong people get wind of who you are and what you like."

"I'd like to see them try to cause trouble for us," John said, sending David a fond look. David was too busy playing the piano to notice. "Besides," John went on. "If anyone asks why David and I are thick as thieves, we'll just tell them it's because we're working together to start a law practice in London after graduation."

"So you're going through with those plans?" Niall asked.

"Yes," David answered, proving he was paying attention after all. "So when you eventually relocate to London to launch your fabulous career as a playwright and theater impresario, we can all still be friends."

"Well," Niall replied with a wry grin, turning back to his table. "At least we can still be friends."

It was nice to share a laugh with men that he did, indeed, consider his friends. Friends had been few and hard to come by for Niall. Aside from being raised in a quiet section of the English countryside, where most of his peers were more interested in the latest in farming equipment or crop rotation techniques when he was up to his eyeballs in Shakespeare and Moliere, few of the other lads had wanted to play with the slender, effeminate boy whose voice didn't seem like it would ever change.

It wasn't until he had secured a place at university

and found himself amongst his own kind—in more ways than one—that Niall had begun to flourish. He'd made friends, put on a few needed pounds of muscle, learned to play cricket—though he would never be any good at it —and his voice finally dropped…a bit. And for a change, he was celebrated for his skill with a pen instead of teased for it. With graduation right around the corner and the excitement of his planned move to London to pursue the theater as a career—mad as everyone thought he was for it —Niall felt as though his life were just about to begin.

"Thank you for coming out to audition, gentlemen," he addressed the small but growing crowd of hopefuls who were waiting to audition for his play. He could hardly believe that anyone would be interested in something he'd written, let alone forgoing other activities to take part in it. "A few of the roles have already been filled, but plenty of major parts are still in need of casting, including Siegfried, the male lead."

"Who's playing Greta, then?" a tall man standing near the back of the room asked with a cheeky grin.

"Please say it's one of the Miller twins," another hopeful added, causing a round of laughter. The Miller twins were buxom sisters, daughters of the university's bursar, whom half of the student body had their eye on.

"I'm afraid I'll be playing the role of Greta," Niall laughed along with them. "All roles will be filled by university students."

"No girls?" the tall man asked, no longer amused.

"Not this time."

The tall man grumbled something, thrust the pages of script he'd taken off the table at the man standing closest to him, and stomped out of the room.

Niall's brow flew up as he fought not to be offended. "I guess I'm not pretty enough for him," he said, feigning a hurt look.

The others laughed, which went a long way to ease the tension that had been growing in Niall's shoulders. He gestured for the remaining hopefuls to take seats at the back of the room as John helped himself to a chair at the table where he sat.

"If it's girls you're looking for," the man who had defended Professor Carroll said, "we've got some staying at our house. They've been there all summer."

Niall did his best to hide his grin over the man's eagerness to share the information as he shifted through the papers on the table. "Is that so?" he asked, not really paying attention. He needed to start the auditions so that he could get on with things, cast the play, and start rehearsals. His future life depended on it.

"Not just any girls," the defensive man said from somewhere behind Niall's shoulder. "The Cannon family from New York has been staying with us for most of the summer." When Niall didn't reply, the man went on with, "Their family is practically American Royalty. Mr. Cannon has made a fortune on the railroads. His daughter, Annamarie, is rumored to be the catch of the year. We've become quite friendly."

"Lucky for you." Niall scanned the list of names of

men auditioning, then turned to the defensive man. "Your name, sir?" he asked.

"Ian Archibald." The defensive man came forward, his hand outstretched. "At your service."

Niall took Ian's hand and shook it, sizing him up as quickly as he could. Ian wasn't bad-looking with his sandy-brown hair and green eyes. His face was just a bit squat, and he had more of a look of the country bumpkins Niall had grown up with stuffed into a suit rather than the sort of elegance John Dandie had, even lounging in a stiff, wooden chair, as John was now.

"I see your name is on my list of auditioners, Mr. Archibald," he said, nodding to the front of the room. "Let's see how you sing."

"Yes, sir." Ian nodded, then strode eagerly to the front of the room, where David still sat at the piano, ready to accompany.

Ian leaned in to say something to David, who nodded, then launched into the stilted strains of a tune that had been popular in their fathers' time. Niall took a deep breath and rested back in his chair. This was it. His very first auditions for a show that he had written and would direct and star in. Perhaps it was only a student production at an out-of-the way university few people cared about, but to him, it was the beginning of everything.

And by the time Ian made it through the first verse of his song, Niall had started to wonder if it were the beginning of a thousand troubles. It wasn't that Ian couldn't sing. His voice was passable, if a little pitchy. Ian certainly had confidence, though his manner was confrontational, daring Niall not to enjoy his performance, instead of engaging.

"Thank you," Niall said once he was done. "Have a seat, and once we run through everyone's songs, I'll call you up to read."

Ian nodded, looking a bit disappointed, perhaps that Niall hadn't praised him or handed him the role on the spot, and headed to the chairs at the back of the room.

"Michael Hollister," Niall read the next name on the list.

A new candidate for a part leapt up from his chair at the back of the room, handing sheet music to David, before taking his place and beginning his song. It was all Niall could do not to wince. The man was terrible. He could barely carry the tune, let alone do justice to the words he was singing. And the next man to audition was just as bad. And the next.

Niall exchanged a look with John after the fourth off-key, muddy singer to assault their ears. Neither said a word, but their looks conveyed everything. More than a dozen men had come to audition, and while some had the range to play one of the secondary roles, the only one who came close to having the talent to play Siegfried was Ian. And if he were honest, something about Ian Archibald made Niall cringe at the thought of playing opposite him. There was a kiss written into the play, after all.

"Right," Niall sighed, trying to hide his disappointment after the last audition, turning to face the hopefuls at the back of the room. "If that's the last of you, we can move on to reading scenes, and—"

"Am I too late?"

The man who dashed into the room was out of breath, his unfashionably curly hair tousled as though he'd run through the wind to reach the choir room, his face splashed with pink and hazel eyes bright. He was the most beautiful man Niall had ever seen in his life. He lifted what had to be a satchel of books off of his shoulder as he strode into the room, approaching Niall's table, chest heaving as he caught his breath. He walked with an easy manner, smiling as he did, seeming to bring sunshine into the room with him.

"I'm not too late, am I?" he asked again.

Niall shook himself, realizing he'd been staring, dumbstruck, at the man. His lips were the most fascinating shape Niall had ever known. He instantly wanted to touch them, to kiss and explore them.

That thought startled him to full attention. Not only was the man built like an athlete in a way that radiated masculinity, Niall knew him. At least, he knew him from afar. Any student at the university would be hard-pressed not to know who Blake Williamson, Marquess of Stanley, future Duke of Selby, was.

"You're just in time," Niall answered, his voice going high and soft. He cleared his throat, forcing himself not to sound like a complete ninny, and went on with, "We were just about to start readings, but if you have a song to perform for your audition, we'll do that first."

"I do," the man said with a breathless nod. "Let me just put my things down and catch my breath."

"Take your time," Niall said, giggling.

When Blake turned away from him, heading to the back of the room to set down his satchel and remove the light coat he wore, Niall grimaced at himself. Giggling? Was he actually giggling at gentlemen now? Hadn't he just told John and David to be careful about being so obvious they were found out? Niall didn't have the first clue about whether the future Duke of Selby was like them, even. Although by the look of him and the way he commanded the room as he walked over to the piano, he was far too powerful and sure of himself to be that way. It was a terrible loss.

Niall had to blink himself out of a near stupor of observing the man as Blake said something to David that caused David to get up from the piano.

"I hope you don't mind if I accompany myself," Blake said. "It would be a shame to waste all those piano lessons."

"I don't mind at all. Go right ahead," Niall said, fighting tooth and nail not to giggle again. He'd been lucky enough to hear Blake sing and play at a student event at Christmas, and was well aware the man had talent.

Blake nodded at him, their eyes meeting for a moment. Blake's smile widened and their gaze held just a fraction longer than Niall would have expected before Blake glanced down at the keys. A few pretty chords sounded, then Blake launched into the lilting strains of a popular ballad.

His voice was magical—a clear, melodious tenor. Even John sat up straighter as the song went on. Blake sang with emotion and vitality. His playing was just as good, far better than David's had been. The intensity of feeling that the song demanded shone through in Blake's face. Niall was absolutely captivated. His heart seemed to expand and squeeze in his chest simultaneously. His blood pumped faster, sending heat through him in the most inconvenient way. He should have been alarmed that his cock responded to the sound of Blake's voice, but he was too mesmerized to care.

Before Blake finished the song, Niall had already cast him as Siegfried. But there was a theatrical protocol to observe, even though it suddenly felt like a waste of time.

"Thank you, that was wonderful," he said, doing a poor job of keeping the excitement out of his voice as Blake finished and stood from the piano. "If you'd like to have a seat, we'll do a few readings."

"Down, boy," John whispered to Niall as he followed Blake with his eyes all the way to the back of the room.

"Ssh." Niall swatted John to get him to behave, then cleared his throat and fussed with the papers in front of him to calm his overwhelmed nerves. "Right, let's start with Mr. Archibald and Mr. Foreman reading scene three."

It took every last ounce of patience Niall had to grind his way through the hour it took to give everyone who had auditioned a chance to read scenes. He would have leapt at the chance to get up and read with Blake himself, but after his initial reaction to the man, he didn't trust himself not to act like a complete idiot around him. Then again, since there was no way on earth that he *wasn't* going to cast Blake to play opposite him, he would have to drag himself back out of the clouds to at least be able to talk to him, and soon.

"Thank you, one and all. I've seen everything I need to see," Niall announced as Blake and Ian finished reading a scene together. "I'll post the cast list on the community board tomorrow morning."

"Brilliant," Ian said, bringing his script back to the table as the room erupted into noise and scraping chairs as everyone got up to leave. "That will give me plenty of time to share the good news with Annamarie Cannon and her father before supper tomorrow. We've all been invited to dine with Lord Masterton at Brickley House, you know."

"How very lovely," Niall said, no idea who Lord Masterton was or what the significance of Brickley House could be. Then again, he wasn't entirely sure where London was or what the significance of Buckingham Palace was as his gaze settled on Blake's bright smile.

"You know the Cannons?" Blake asked Ian, his dark brows shooting up.

"They've been staying with us this summer," Ian answered with an arrogant tilt of his chin.

"I'm impressed," Blake said.

Niall suddenly wanted to murder Ian. No, that wasn't right. Blake was just being kind. That had to be it. Everything about Blake Williamson radiated kindness and good nature. The way he smiled at Ian was simply polite. Although it could be argued that the way he smiled at Niall was merely polite too. Niall prayed it was more than that. He prayed Blake felt the same instant kinship that he did.

"I know who you are," Niall blurted once Ian walked away to fetch his things.

Blake's smile widened for a moment. "I'm sure everyone knows who I am, thanks to my father," he said, his expression settling into a familiar smile.

"No, I mean I heard you play that concert at Christmas," Niall went on, losing his battle to remain calm and mature. "Your playing, that is. And your singing. I'm, er, familiar with your work."

"You're just saying that." Blake tilted his head down slightly, bashfully.

Niall's heart came close to exploding in his chest. "No, I mean it. I loved that concert. You're incredibly talented."

"Yes, well, talent in a future duke isn't considered much of an asset," Blake said. "I have a feeling Father isn't going to allow me to indulge in the arts for much longer after I graduate. That's why I was sincerely hoping to land a part in your play. It would be a last hurrah, so to speak."

"You have the part," Niall blurted before Blake was completely finished. "The part of Siegfried is yours."

As soon as the words were out, Niall felt like he might be sick. Or that he'd already been sick all over Blake's shoes. The effect was the same. At least the rest of the men who had come to audition had already left the room, and John and David were too busy flirting over by the piano to have heard his nonsense.

Blake blinked in surprise, then burst into a smile. "Are you certain? You want to offer me the part?"

Niall forced himself to unclench and stop behaving like a moon-eyed schoolgirl. "You were far and away the best singer who came out today," he said in a more conversational tone. "Trust me. You didn't see what I had to work with earlier."

"I did have the impression that not everyone was up to scratch," Blake said with a look that made Niall feel as though it were the two of them against the world.

"You're the only person in the world who I can see playing Siegfried," Niall said, relaxing even more. Blake was human. He had to remind himself of that. He wasn't some god sent down from the heavens to bless Earth with his presence. Although Niall wouldn't have been at all surprised to find out he was. "I want you," he said, then made a wordless sound of embarrassment and went on with, "I mean, I want you for the part. You're perfect for the part. You're the only one who could do it any justice."

"Then I happily accept." Blake's smile was warm and forgiving. He moved past Niall to fetch his satchel and coat. "Who do you have playing Greta?"

"Um, me?" Niall followed him, trying not to think of himself as a puppy. "I hope you don't mind," he rushed to add.

"Not at all," Blake said with a gracious laugh, straightening from where he'd picked up his satchel. "I think it would be amazing to play opposite the man who wrote the play."

Niall's mouth hung open, but he couldn't think of a thing to say to a compliment like that. Best of all, Blake didn't seem at all uncomfortable with playing opposite another man. Though he still didn't think that Blake was an invert like him.

"Rehearsals start tomorrow afternoon," Niall said at last, no idea what else to say. He was highly aware that John and David had stopped flirting with each other and were now watching him and Blake with a little too much interest.

"Fantastic," Blake said, putting on his coat and looping his satchel over his shoulder. He paused, an idea lighting his face. "You know, I have a spare ticket to that concert at McQueen Hall tonight. Do you want to come?"

Niall nearly choked on his tongue. "That's the most exclusive concert the university has seen all year," he said.

"I know." Blake's eyes lit with mischief. "I bought two

tickets, but I haven't been able to find anyone to go with me. Are you interested?"

Niall was more than interested. His hands and feet were swiftly going numb with excitement, and he was having a hard time catching his breath. "I am definitely interested," he said.

"Then come along," Blake said, gesturing toward the door. "I'll even buy you supper afterwards."

The corners of Niall's vision went black for a moment. The most handsome and talented man he had ever met was offering to take him to supper and a concert. And no, it didn't mean anything. How could it, considering they'd only just met? But that didn't stop Niall from racing back across the room to gather his things with shaking hands and shove them into his own school satchel. Across the room, John winked at him and David nodded in encouragement. Niall's face heated at his friends' gestures, but he hardly had any brain left to think about it. All he knew was that he was about to have the night of his life with the man of his dreams.

CHAPTER 3

"*I* was lucky enough to hear Octavia Righetti when she sang in London two years ago," Blake said as he and Niall strode across campus on their way to McQueen Hall. The spring evening was balmy and fragrant with roses that were just beginning to bloom in overflowing garden beds between the august buildings. "She has the voice of an angel."

"She does?" Niall studied Blake's rapt expression. Everything about him, from the sensual shape of his mouth to the way the late-afternoon sunlight lit his face with a golden glow had Niall's heart beating faster.

"Absolutely." Blake glanced to Niall with a bright smile that seemed to make his eyes warmer and kinder. There was so much life in those eyes, so much emotion, even though the two of them were merely walking to the concert. Perhaps it was Niall's imagination, but Blake's gaze seemed to linger on him for a moment, dropping to his mouth, before he went on with, "She was the talk of the season on her last tour. I'm amazed that the university was able to convince her to perform here."

"You've been to London?" Niall cursed himself the second the question flopped past his lips. Not only was it a beat behind where their conversation had gone, he was certain it made him look like a rube.

But Blake laughed, his eyes crinkling and his smile widening. "Of course I've been to London," he said. He swayed closer as they walked and nudged Niall with his shoulder. "Haven't you?"

Niall's entire arm tingled where it'd made contact with Blake's. He wanted to lean closer to Blake and return the gesture, but knowing him, it would come off as clumsy. "I haven't," he confessed. "All of my money has gone toward tuition." He cursed himself again for bringing up money and making himself look like a pauper. Blake was in line to be a duke. His family probably had more money than the royal family.

"But it's where you're heading after graduation, isn't it?" Blake asked. "I mean, a playwright as talented as you must be in London. Every theater in Drury Lane will be clamoring to produce your plays."

A flush of pleasure filled Niall from head to toe as they turned a corner and started down the promenade that would take them to McQueen Hall. He wanted to slow his steps so that he could make their walk last forever.

"How would you know if I'm talented?" he asked

with a self-deprecating laugh.

Blake looked genuinely surprised at the question. "I saw the play you wrote last spring."

Niall's brow flew up. "That was just a lark some of the underclassmen put on for fun."

"And it was brilliant," Blake said, his smile genuine as he met Niall's eyes again. For the second time, his gaze lingered longer than Niall expected. "And I saw you at the cabaret in the fall," he went on.

Niall was out of ways to express surprise. His brow was already up, and he was certain his eyes bulged. "My part in the cabaret was miniscule," he said. And how could he have missed spotting Blake in the audience? The crowd hadn't been that large.

"Your part might have been small, but your presence was extremely notable." Blake's gaze dropped to Niall's mouth again before he snapped his head forward as a pair of students passed. He dodged out of their way, which caused him to bump gently into Niall.

Niall raised his hands reflexively to protect himself and keep Blake from stumbling. The result was that he grabbed Blake's arm before he could stop himself. He was reluctant to let go as they moved on past the other students, but he knew he had to. The signals he was receiving from Blake were confusing at best. There was most definitely an instant rapport there, but whether it was merely friendly or something more, Niall had absolutely no idea. He let his hand brush against Blake's as he let go and continued on, though, watching Blake carefully to see how he would react.

"You have no idea how much I'm looking forward to being in your play," Blake said as they climbed the stairs of McQueen Hall. The door was open, so they walked through into a semi-crowded lobby that echoed with other conversations. In spite of that, the genuine emotion remained in Blake's expression. "I've wanted to try my hand at acting for as long as I can remember, but this is the first time I've ever been brave enough to audition."

"I'm sure you're always brave," Niall said as Blake paused in an empty spot to one side of the door. He wanted to slap a hand over his face. How was it possible that he could write line after line of witty prose, but he couldn't fasten together two sensible words to have a conversation with a handsome, intelligent, well-mannered, beautiful, warm, gorgeous....

He lost his train of thought when Blake laughed bashfully and lowered his head. "I'm not brave," he said, a slight pinch of shame in his eyes. "Not by a longshot." He lifted his head slightly, appearing to study Niall's face. Something softened in his eyes. It made Niall's heart run riot in his chest and his trousers feel embarrassingly tight.

"Lord Stanley. I thought that was you." An older gentleman who was dressed far more fashionably than Niall could ever hope to afford to dress strode toward them from across the lobby. He stretched out a hand to

Blake as he came near. "Of course, I shouldn't be surprised to see a young man like yourself at Miss Righetti's concert." He winked as he took Blake's hand.

"Lord Fairport." Blake greeted the man with an open smile, seeming suddenly far more mature than his years. "It's good to see you again. And I wouldn't miss a concert like this for the world."

"I'm surprised you aren't accompanying Miss Righetti this evening," Lord Fairport went on. He glanced to Niall. "This one never misses an opportunity to accompany a beautiful woman singing." He chuckled and lifted one eyebrow knowingly.

Niall's heart sank, even as he drew on every bit of his acting prowess to seem amused by the comment. So Blake fancied women after all.

"Lord Fairport, allow me to introduce you to my friend, Mr. Niall Cristofori, a playwright with an astounding future in front of him." Blake stepped closer to Niall, touching a hand lightly to his back as he presented him to Lord Fairport.

Every bit of Niall's awareness shifted to that touch, and his heart soared again. He nearly fumbled Lord Fairport's hand when the man offered it to shake. "Pleased to meet you, my lord."

"And you, sir. Any friend of Lord Stanley's is a friend of mine," Lord Fairport said, shaking Niall's hand briefly, then letting it go. "Although Stanley here has so many friends that I'm beginning to lose track." He laughed.

Niall's heart sank all over again. It was as though he were riding in a train that kept speeding up, then abruptly slowing down.

He was spared having to come up with anything clever to say as the doors at the far end of the lobby were opened and the men and women waiting in the lobby drifted into the auditorium.

"Forgive me, gents," Lord Fairport said with a short bow. "The wife gets a bit tetchy when I loiter too long before these things."

They said their goodbyes and Lord Fairport strode off, leaving Niall and Blake to make their way into the auditorium at a slower pace.

"He's a friend of my father's," Blake explained. "They went to university together. Which is encouraging, really."

"Oh?" Niall glanced to him, both for an answer to whatever thought Blake had started and to try, once again, to judge his character.

"I like the idea that lifelong friendships can be formed at university," Blake said, his smile widening as he met Niall's eyes. That softness and brightness were back in his expression, as though nothing made him happier than being in Niall's presence. "Don't you?"

The man was going to be the death of him, that much was certain. He was just too charming, too perfect. And Niall couldn't make heads or tails of him.

"Come on." Blake touched his hand lightly once

they'd handed their tickets over to the man at the door and made their way down the aisle between chairs that had been set up facing a piano at the front of the room. "I bought us excellent seats."

There wasn't a chance in Hades that Niall would be able to pay attention to a single note of the concert. The brush of Blake's fingers against his hand was one thing, but the fact that he'd spoken as if he'd intended all along for Niall to accompany him to the concert was enough to keep his spirits soaring for weeks to come. Us. He'd bought *us* excellent seats.

Which was a preposterous idea, considering they'd only met that afternoon. Then again, Niall remembered and admired Blake from a previous concert, and Blake had apparently known and admired him for over a year. The whole thing was a blissful dream. Not to mention the way Blake's gaze seemed to linger on him when they spoke.

But as the concert continued, Blake watched Miss Righetti sing with the same sort of absorption. Not only that, he seemed highly appreciative of the unknown young lady Miss Righetti asked to sing with her. Niall supposed it was possible Blake shared the same appreciation of both men and women, but he had yet to truly establish whether Blake had any interest at all in men—or rather, in him—to begin with.

His roiling discomfort and confusion over the issue only got worse when the concert was over.

"That was fantastic," he said, leaning close to Niall

and seeming to guide him through the crush of people, all leaving the auditorium at once. He rested his hand on Niall's back again with a familiarity that usually came after years of friendship. "Miss Righetti has such a command of her higher register, don't you think?"

"She was certainly singing through the notes instead of into them," Niall said. It was probably a stupid observation, but Blake seemed to be impressed by the technical comment as they reached the lobby.

But before Blake could comment, he was distracted by a call of, "Lord Stanley. That *was* you I saw sitting in the front."

Blake's hand remained on Niall's back for a moment as they both turned to see a tall, middle-aged gentleman waving to Blake from the center of a small cluster of elegant people.

"Sir Richard." Blake burst into a smile and waved to the man, then tugged Niall's sleeve to pull him toward the crowd. "Fancy seeing you here this evening."

"I have to entertain my guests somehow," Sir Richard replied jovially. "Allow me to introduce Mr. Douglas Cannon from New York, his lovely wife, Abigail, and his charming daughter, Annamarie. And you know my son, Edward, of course."

"Good to see you again, Edward." Blake shook Edward's hand, then proceeded through a round of introductions to the Americans.

Niall felt completely and utterly out of his depth. Although he did know Edward Archibald, at least on sight. The unassuming young man was a classmate, though Edward was apparently bound for a political career, whereas Niall's course of study was geared toward his future on the stage.

He blinked as a few pieces fell together. Archibald. Ian Archibald had auditioned for him that afternoon. And he'd mentioned the Cannons of New York. As soon as the connection was made, Niall had to hide a grin. Ian had been uncommonly proud of himself for knowing the wealthy Americans, and now Niall could see why. They were every bit the New World aristocracy that nobs in England were falling all over themselves to become acquainted with.

"Thank you for the invitation, sir, but I already have plans for the evening," Blake said, drawing Niall's attention back to the conversation he'd drifted away from. Apparently, there had been an invitation to supper that Niall had nearly missed.

"Some other time, then," Mr. Cannon said. "It's not every day that a railroad worker like me gets to meet a future duke."

Everyone involved in the conversation laughed, but Niall failed to see the joke. He didn't like the way Mrs. Cannon casually fanned herself as she studied Blake either, as if he were a piece of meat or a pawn on a chessboard.

"Enjoy your evening, then," Blake said, gallantly extracting himself, and Niall, from the conversation. "I'm sure my father will be in touch with you soon."

They turned to make their way out of the lobby.

"You could have gone with them, you know," Niall said as quietly as he could and still be heard over the chattering crowd lingering in the lobby and just outside on the steps.

"I already said I'd take you to supper." Blake shrugged. "And I'd much rather wile away the evening in a cozy pub than sit around some over-decorated table in a stuffy old townhouse."

"I seriously doubt that," Niall laughed. "Those were important people." He glanced over his shoulder in time to see the Archibalds and the Cannons stepping out into the spring evening.

"I'm with an important person," Blake argued, nudging Niall's arm as they picked up their pace.

Niall's heart fluttered into a confused mess. He thanked the growing dark for hiding the blush he could feel coming to his face. "I'm not *that* important."

"You absolutely are," Blake argued, his smile accented by the colors of evening. "You're a future famous playwright. Someday, I'll be telling everyone I meet that the two of us are friends."

"But we've only just met," Niall said, stilted, yet hopeful.

"It doesn't feel like we've just met," Blake said, pointing across Niall to indicate that he should turn down a side road. Niall knew there to be several pubs along that particular street, but more importantly, the gesture forced them much closer together. "It feels like we've been friends for ages."

"Yes, it does." Niall had to agree. Though if they'd known each other for ages, he might have a far clearer picture of where the night and their friendship was headed.

Blake picked one of the smaller pubs for their supper, one that was hundreds of years old and contained numerous quiet alcoves with low ceilings and beams that concealed them from plain sight. The barmaid seemed to know him—a detail that had Niall's heart momentarily sinking again—and brought them tankards of good beer as soon as they were seated at a particularly cramped and cozy table. So cramped, in fact, that their knees were squashed against each other under the table, no matter how they sat—something that had Niall soaring with possibility again.

"So how did you become involved in theater?" Blake asked once they had thick meat pies in front of them. He shifted slightly forward as he ate, which forced their knees together even more intimately.

Niall could hardly taste the food he put in his mouth. "I can't remember a time when I wasn't involved in some sort of theatrical production," he replied, pretending not to be so excited his cock was straining against his trousers. "Apparently, my first role was that of our infant Lord in a Christmas tableaux the local rector organized when I was only a few months old."

Blake laughed, everything about him inviting and open. "Somehow, I'm not surprised."

"That my introduction to theater happened when I was a baby?"

"That you are God," Blake answered with a flicker of one dark eyebrow. "Aren't all playwrights?"

Niall's heart beat in double-time. "Good heavens, Lord Stanley, that's sacrilege."

"Is it?" Blake's expression grew more mischievous. "Really?"

"Just don't let the rector hear you say it," Niall flirted in return. Actually flirted. He must have been out of his mind.

But then Blake said, "There are plenty of things that I would never tell the rector," with a look of such heated teasing that Niall was in serious danger of unmanning himself right there at the table.

Niall had to take a long swig of beer to steady himself. So Blake was game after all...wasn't he? He could have meant something else by his comment. There wasn't a single thing in the man's way of carrying himself or speaking that hinted he was anything but straight. In Niall's experience, men like him always had a tell of some sort.

He gulped his beer, then put the tankard down with an awkward clunk and asked, "When did you start playing the piano?"

He was certain the question came out sounding too confrontational, but Blake shrugged and looked deliciously bashful for a moment before answering, "I can't remember. Like you, I was a child prodigy."

"I bet you were."

Niall wanted to slap a hand over his mouth at the way the words came out. Flirting was one thing, but he was in serious danger of getting the both of them into a world of trouble. Especially when Blake grinned as if Niall had implied a thousand inappropriate things.

"Piano lessons were part of my early education," Blake said, using his fork to toy with the crust of his pie. "I should count myself fortunate that Mama read something about the importance of a musical education when she was young. My brother, Montague, and I were given lessons in every instrument you can imagine, as well as singing, from a young age. Montague never took to any of it, mind you. He claims to detest the sound of music. I suppose I got his share of a love for music along with my own."

"So you love it, then?" Niall put down his fork—his stomach was too filled with butterflies to eat much anyhow—and leaned his elbow on the table, propping his head in his hand as he watched the interplay of lamplight on Blake's angelic face.

"More than anything," Blake sighed with feeling. "I don't just play the piano, you know. I sing, of course, and I play the violin as well, and the cello, guitar, lute, and clarinet. And I compose."

The man could have slowly unbuttoned his jacket and waistcoat and peeled off his shirt and Niall wouldn't have been as aroused as he was by that list and those words.

No, that was a blatant lie. Blake undressing in front of him would have been the very height of arousal. And to think that the perfect man composed his own music as well.

"Niall?"

Niall sucked in a breath and jerked straight. He'd been staring and lusting, and Blake had caught him at it.

"I thought I'd lost you there for a moment," Blake went on, his grin knowing and teasing.

"You'll never lose me," Niall blurted before he could think better of it.

Blake's grin grew, and his eyes flashed with something heated beyond words. "I'll hold you to that, you know," he said.

You can hold anything to me, particularly your delicious body.

Niall cleared his throat and sat straighter. "I have to cast the rest of the play," he said, blinking his way back to business. "I have your part and my part settled, but I told everyone else I'd have the cast list posted tomorrow morning."

"I could help you, if you'd like," Blake said, sitting straighter himself. The shift in position meant that their knees slipped even more intimately together and their legs entwined.

"I'd like that," Niall said, surprised he was able to

form thoughts at all. "A second opinion is always a good one."

"Agreed." Blake turned to wave to the barmaid, who was just visible from their cozy alcove. "Two more beers for my brilliant friend and I," he said, then glanced to Niall. "I think we're in for a long night."

CHAPTER 4

*N*iall had never been so eager to get to a rehearsal in his life. Only two days had passed since his supper with Blake, but Niall felt as though it had been a lifetime since he last talked to him, since he last feasted on the sight of his kissable lips and sparkling eyes. They'd sat for hours at the pub, casting the play and discussing details of the script and the songs. Blake had read through all of the scenes Niall provided prior to auditions, but he didn't know the whole story, so Niall told it to him.

By the end of the evening, Niall was left with the feeling that he knew bits and pieces of Blake well, just like the sides he'd handed out to those auditioning for the show, but he didn't know the whole story. He was certain Blake had been flirting with him...right up until Blake winked at the barmaid, making her blush, as he paid for their meal. Niall had gone home replaying every word that had been spoken between the two of them. He'd examined every look and every smile in his mind, attempting to decipher them. And then he'd beat himself off while imagining what it would feel like to have more than his knees entwined with Blake's.

He still blushed when he thought about how good it had felt to do that as he approached the door leading backstage in the auditorium, where the play would be staged and where rehearsals were being held. There was absolutely nothing out of the ordinary about frigging oneself during university. Everyone did it. But it was somehow intimate and dangerous to envision a particular object of affection, someone who was now an integral part of his life, while doing so. Whether Blake would be horrified or flattered to be the subject of his fantasies was another story.

The debate raging in his head and his groin was halted as soon as he opened the backstage door and heard the strains of a haunting and unfamiliar piano melody. It was rich with emotion and went straight to Niall's heart. So much so that he closed the stage door quietly behind him and crept as softly as he could past the heavy, black curtains in the wings and out to where the piano stood on the far downstage corner.

Unsurprisingly, Blake was the one playing the passionate song. Niall's breath caught in his throat as he watched Blake's slightly bent head, took in the pinch of emotion in Blake's expression as he played. It had to be an original composition. Niall had never heard anything like it before. The style was entirely new. It was the most beautiful thing he'd ever heard.

When one of the floorboards creaked under Niall's foot as he crossed the stage, Blake fumbled his song and jerked straight. His eyes went wide, as though he'd been caught doing what Niall had done to himself the night before, but when he saw it was only Niall who spied on him, he let out a heavy breath and relaxed.

"I thought I'd been caught," he said, standing quickly from the piano bench and skirting his way toward center stage.

Niall shook his head and shrugged. "Why would it matter if you were caught playing what I assume is an original composition?"

Blake sent him a guilty look and rubbed the back of his neck where his curling hair brushed his collar. "My father doesn't know that I was cast in this play," he said. "He doesn't really approve of my musical interests either."

Prickles broke out along Niall's back. He pretended to be casual as he crossed to the narrow set of stairs leading from the stage to the house, where a table had been set up for him for the rehearsal. Though nothing in Blake's manner or expression said as much overtly, Niall had the distinct feeling that Blake's father wouldn't approve of his attraction to other men either. If, indeed, Blake was attracted to men. Niall still couldn't figure that out.

"Were you planning to invite your family to the

performance?" Niall asked as he removed his school satchel from his shoulder and put it on the table. A second, worse thought hit him, and he pivoted to face Blake, eyes wider. "Would he pull you out of the production at the last minute if he discovered you were in it?"

"He wouldn't approve, but he wouldn't force me to quit," Blake said, following him to the table. "So you don't have to worry about that."

"Oh, I'll worry about that," Niall said, opening his satchel and taking out his copy of the script. It already had copious notes scribbled all over it in pencil—everything from blocking to how he wanted certain lines delivered. "I will worry about everything having to do with this play and its performers until the final curtain call is finished."

"You don't have anything to worry about."

Blake's deep voice came from only a foot or so behind Niall. He'd approached so close while Niall was busy at the table that when Niall turned around, they were almost in each other's arms. It was a bloody shame that Niall had his script clenched in his hands, almost like a shield between the two of them. That was the last thing he wanted to convey to Blake, especially when he could smell the scent of the man's shaving soap. Blake had missed a spot on his jaw, close to his ear, proving that his beard probably grew in with lightning speed if he didn't shave every day. Niall caught himself wondering what a day's worth of stubble would feel like against his chest or his inner thigh.

Hard on the heels of those thoughts, the door at the back of the auditorium opened, and a group of underclassmen who had been cast in the chorus burst into the room. Blake stepped back from Niall so fast that Niall thought he would stumble over the chairs. Blake cleared his throat and waved to his new castmates as a few more entered the room.

"Stanley," one of them, Morton, called out as soon as he entered the room. "Fancy seeing you here. Brilliant goal yesterday, by the way. That goalie didn't stand a chance."

In an instant, whatever spell had been cast between Niall and Blake vanished. Niall remembered the football game he'd heard about the day before and assumed that was what Morton was talking about. Of course Blake would be enough of a bloke to score a winning football goal. The way he walked over to the particularly rough and tumble men Niall had cast to play the swordsmen in his show, thumping them on the back and being congratulated in kind was as obvious a sign as anything that Blake wasn't like him.

He sighed, shook his head, cursed himself for a fool caught up in wishful thinking, and set about organizing his notes for the rehearsal. More and more of his cast arrived, and Niall did everything he could to stop himself from gazing longingly at Blake as he laughed and chattered away with the blokey blokes.

"I still can't believe you cast him in the lead," Ian grumbled to Niall almost as soon as he entered the auditorium and deposited his things in one of the empty seats.

The comment served to alert Niall to the fact that he was staring at Blake even though he'd told himself not to, and that Ian was bitter about the casting.

"Blake has the best voice," he explained with what he hoped looked like a casual shrug as he took his script down to the stage and mounted the steps. Ian followed behind him. "Some of Siegfried's songs are technically complicated. But you did extraordinarily well at the audition yourself. That's why I cast you as Reinhold."

"So you're saying that if Blake hadn't swooped in at the last minute to steal the role, it would have gone to me?" Ian asked, crossing his arms.

Niall paused when he reached the center of the stage and looked over his shoulder at Ian. The man's nose was thoroughly out of joint. "It's best not to think about what could have been."

He faced forward, ostensibly looking at his script, but peeked at Blake and his rambunctious friends as he did. The group was thoroughly enjoying whatever noisy conversation they were having now, but in the midst of the revelry, Blake glanced Niall's way. It could have completely been Niall's imagination, but Blake's eyes seemed to take on that particular soft warmth they had in the pub the other day.

Niall's heart thudded against his ribs, particularly when Blake's gaze shifted to Ian standing by Niall's side and his mouth went tight. Niall blinked, forcing himself to concentrate. Ian was saying something. But the possibility that Blake was jealous of another man talking to him was too good to be true. Literally. It couldn't possibly be true. More likely, *he* was jealous of *Blake* getting along so famously with the sort of men who would never be caught dead socializing with him and had only auditioned for the play because they thought girls would fawn all over them for treading the boards.

"...wouldn't have time to rehearse all day for the lead role anyhow," Ian was saying. Niall faced him fully, forcing himself to block Blake out of the line of his vision and out of his thoughts, if such a thing were even possible. "Our special guests require constant attention." Ian grinned like a cat who had a canary.

"Oh. Yes. I'd forgotten about your guests," Niall said, glancing around the stage and wondering if he needed to bring on anything to serve as set pieces or to mark up the floor that early in the rehearsal process. "Are they coming to see the show?" he asked by rote.

"Of course," Ian said with a sniff. "Although, if you're lucky, I could introduce you to the Cannons earlier than that."

"I've already met them," Niall said, half distracted. Blake and the blokes were moving down the aisle toward the stage.

"You've already met them?" Niall turned back to Ian to find him drooping with disappointment.

"Yes. At a concert the other night," Niall said. "Blake —that is, Lord Stanley—introduced me."

Blake was in the process of leaping onto the stage with exceptional physical prowess. Niall's train of thought was completely derailed as he imagined the power Blake must have in his legs and torso.

"Let's get this rehearsal started," Morton said in a booming voice, draping an arm around Blake's shoulders once they were all on the stage. "We've got a passel of loose women to woo tonight."

They all laughed, including Blake. Although Blake's smile was somewhat tight as he met Niall's eyes. At least, Niall thought his smile might be tight. It was hard to tell. Everything about the man was hard to tell. The Blake who had been so filled with emotion as he played a piece of his own composition and the one who laughed along with his mates as they fetched their scripts and spread out across the stage were two entirely different men.

"We're only rehearsing Act One today," Niall said, taking charge of the rehearsal as more cast members arrived and clambered onto the stage. "We'll run through the opening number first, then the Act Once finale, then scene four, and then the chorus is free to go. It will just be the principles after that."

Running a rehearsal wasn't new to Niall. Running one with a chorus of rowdy university students wasn't new either. He'd long ago worked out exactly how he needed to speak and even move to command the attention of men who wouldn't normally have given him the time of day. Morton and his lot were a handful all the same, particularly as they rehearsed the scene four number in which his character, his female character, was introduced to the hero. The play was a ridiculous melodrama set in medieval Germany that involved a bride, Niall, who was kidnapped by a band of rowdy knights, Morton's chorus, led by Ian's character, Reinhold, to marry a depressed prince, Blake. It was love at first sight for the prince, but he had to spend the rest of the play convincing the bride of his worthiness before she would consent to the marriage and seal it with a kiss.

"Come now, Siegfried," Ian read his line, dragging Niall across the stage to Blake. "Have you ever seen a woman as lovely as this?"

Behind them, Morton and his chorus snickered.

"A lady indeed," one of the blokey blokes muttered.

"Not as sweet as the one old Blake was dandling on his knee last month," Morton said in return. "But close."

They all burst into ribald laughter. Niall's face burned hot, though he couldn't figure out if Morton's lot were taking a dig at him or the woman Blake had supposedly been with, or because the fact that Blake had been toying with a woman proved he would never be interested. The burst of self-conscious confusion was so bad that the aura of authority Niall had worked to present crumbled.

"Are you going to wear a wreath of flowers in your hair, like sweet Flora had, Cristofori?" another of Morton's crowd teased, sending a pointed look Blake's way.

Niall wanted to disappear into the floorboards.

Until Blake silenced his friends with a serious look. "Gentlemen, we have a rehearsal to get through. We can save the pub-talk for the pub, can't we?"

"Look who's gone all twitchy," Morton said with a teasing grin. "Embarrassed, are you, Stanley?"

"Only over your bad behavior," Blake replied. Somehow, he managed to be dead serious while also grinning, as though he were in on the joke with the others. His shoulders dropped a bit and he went on with, "Let's show Cristofori the respect he's due."

As quickly as Niall's spirits had soared over the way Blake defended him, they sank at the use of the name Cristofori instead of Niall. There wasn't time to dwell on it, though. Blake was right about one thing—he had a rehearsal to run.

"From Reinhold's line again, if you please," he said in his most authoritative voice.

Somehow, they made it through all of the Act One chorus parts. Morton and his friends settled down and learned their blocking as Niall directed. They practiced the songs a time or two, and Niall was surprised at how swiftly they'd learned them. All the same, Niall was relieved when they finally left and it was just him, Blake, Ian, Paul, the man playing Hilda opposite Ian's Reinhold, and Gregory, the man playing the king, left to run through the remaining scenes in the first act. And since the play wasn't a full-length production, they were able to get through the scenes quickly.

The only problem with finishing the rehearsal in

record time was that it would mean Niall and Blake would part ways sooner. Niall scrambled for a way to stop that from happening.

"I have some extra time, if you want to run lines," he told Blake as subtly as he could as Paul and Gregory left the stage to fetch their things.

"You aren't going to study?" Ian interrupted, as though the offer had been directed to him.

"Study for what?" Blake asked, moving toward the piano and sitting on the bench. He launched right into playing a light-hearted, popular tune.

"Don't tell me you haven't heard about the prize Professor Carroll and the Classics department is offering," Ian said with a smug look.

"I think I did hear something about that." Niall gathered up a stray script someone had left on the stage and drifted toward the piano, wanting nothing more than to listen to Blake play.

"I wouldn't be surprised if you hadn't heard about it," Ian went on. "Apparently, you have to apply to take the exam Professor Carroll is giving in order to win the prize. Only the top students are being allowed to sit it."

"Applying to take an exam?" Niall shared an amused grin with Blake. His heart jumped into his throat when Blake returned the grin with a sparkle in his eyes. He'd missed that intimate sparkle throughout the rehearsal.

"The prize is outstanding," Ian told them as they all gathered around the piano. "I've seen it. I got an exclusive, early look at it."

"What is it?" Blake asked, switching from his light-hearted tune to a more ponderous one that subtly underscored Ian's cocky attitude.

"It's a medallion," Ian said. An inexplicably mischievous grin spread across his face.

"Medallions are often prizes in academic competitions," Niall said, frowning slightly.

"True." Ian leaned in closer. "But there's something Professor Carroll doesn't know about this medallion."

Blake switched tunes once again to play something filled with mystery and importance. "What doesn't he know?"

"He had the medallion made by a local artisan using one of the artifacts he brought back from his expedition to Egypt," Ian said, lowering his voice dramatically.

Blake played quieter to match. "Why is that special?" he asked.

Niall was having a hard time not laughing at the way Blake teased Ian without Ian seeming to know it. It wasn't cruel teasing, which only made it more endearing.

"The center of the medallion contains a carved scarab beetle," Ian all but whispered to them, eyes alight. "I've seen it, though, and it's not the one Professor Carroll thought he handed over to the man to make into a medallion."

"It isn't?" Niall's frown deepened. "Shouldn't someone tell Professor Carroll?"

"No, of course not," Ian scoffed. "The scarab in the

prize medallion is invaluable. It's inlaid with gold. It must be thousands of years old."

"Then someone should definitely tell Professor Carroll," Blake said, sitting back a bit and returning to the light-hearted song he'd begun the conversation with.

"I would think that a man who lectures on Egyptology and who has been to the pyramids would know the value of the artifact he was giving away as a prize in an academic competition," Niall said.

"I found out that his assistant handed over the scarab to the medallion maker," Ian said. "I doubt Carroll will ever clap eyes on the thing. Which is why I intend to win it."

"You do?" Niall eyed the man skeptically. He had no idea about Ian's academic prowess, but he seemed confident enough.

"I have top marks," Ian said, as though he could read Niall's mind. "I can't think of anyone who stands a chance of scoring higher on this exam than me. I'm sure to win it, and all things considered, this is the kind of prize that could make a man's fortune."

"It's that valuable?" Blake asked, pausing his playing.

"Yes." Ian nodded.

"They why don't we take the exam too?" he asked Niall, grinning from ear to ear.

Ian's smug look dropped. "You can't do that. The deadline to apply for the exam was yesterday."

"I'm on good terms with Professor Carroll," Blake said with a shrug. "He'll let me apply, even if the deadline has passed. I'll tell him to let you apply too." He stood and walked around the piano to stand next to Niall.

Ian scoffed and shook his head. "You think you can get everything you want just because you'll be a duke someday."

Blake had the good sense to look sheepish, even though he said, "It's a fact. I didn't make the rules." He grinned sideways at Niall as he spoke.

Niall had to raise a hand to his mouth to stop himself from snorting, but it was the way Blake looked at him that had him flushing with heat down to his toes.

Ian narrowed his eyes, glancing between the two of them. "You can't do it," he said. "It's past the deadline."

"We'll see." Blake nodded, then turned to Niall, effectively shutting Ian out. "We need to pay a visit to Professor Carroll."

Ian grunted, then threw up his hands and turned to go, muttering to himself.

As soon as he had his back turned, Blake's expression changed. The softness was back in his eyes, but with it was a strange, new tension that pinched his shapely lips and flushed his cheeks. "I should have asked if you wanted to compete for that silly prize," he said, his voice lowering to a golden register. He reached out to brush Niall's sleeve.

Niall's throat squeezed, and it felt as though the temperature in the room had risen by at least ten degrees. "I don't think I'm smart enough."

"I'm sure you are." Blake broke into a smile, brushing Niall's sleeve again. "You're brilliant."

The first touch could have been explained away as an accident. The second, coming so soon after the first, could only have been deliberate. Especially since Blake's hand lingered on Niall's sleeve. His hazel eyes were downright molten when they met Niall's.

"I could help you study," he said, lowering his voice to an almost obscene level.

"Y-you could?" Niall had trouble breathing.

"It's the least I could do for making extra work for you while you're trying to mount a play."

The word "mount" seemed to stand out in vivid colors, carrying an entirely different meaning, to Niall's overheated ears. The invitation couldn't possibly mean what he thought it meant, could it?

"Come over to my place tomorrow night," Blake went on, nearly causing Niall's eyes to pop. "It's a little bit against the rules, but Father insisted I have my own flat just outside of the university's campus. I hardly ever have anyone over, so it would be the perfect chance for me to play host."

"I—" Niall's mouth dropped open as he attempted to answer, but didn't seem to want to shut again. Blake was definitely propositioning him. Absolutely. Why else would he invite him to his private flat in the evening?

"You can bring Ian along, if you'd like," Blake added a moment later, though there was definite teasing in his eyes.

Or was there? Maybe he didn't mean their study session to be anything more than studying after all. Niall was completely and utterly confused.

Then again, there was only one way to find out what was truly going on.

"It sounds delightful," he said, his words coming out too breathless and too high-pitched. There was no way he would be able to recover from the embarrassment if all Blake wanted after all was to study. "I'll see you tomorrow, then."

CHAPTER 5

*N*iall's heart was in his throat the following evening as he made his way off-campus to the address Blake had written on a scrap of paper. Between grinning at the absolute neatness of Blake's handwriting—the way it mirrored every writing primer he'd ever seen, with just a hint of a forward slant—and the unexpected refinement of the neighborhood he found himself in, Niall was buzzing with expectation.

"Oh, good, you found the place." Blake greeted him at the door to his second-floor flat with a luminous smile.

"You gave excellent directions," Niall said, his mouth growing dry. Not because of the opulence of the flat that Blake invited him into with an extended hand, but because Blake was dressed in shirtsleeves, his waistcoat unbuttoned. His hair was slightly damp, as though he'd bathed recently, and was a riot of curls.

"It doesn't look like student accommodations," Blake

went on, speaking just a bit faster than usual. "Any time I've had someone over, they've had a hard time finding the place."

"Do you have people over often?" Niall's brow lifted even as his spirits sank into trepidation.

But Blake answered a quick, "No." His cheeks colored, and he glanced bashfully down for a moment before peeking up at Niall through his dark lashes.

Niall's knees wobbled and he fumbled his satchel as he removed it from his shoulder. He could scarcely draw breath as he took in the full extent of the flat, its lavish furnishings, cozy fire, surprisingly fine art on the walls, and an upright piano against one wall. A small dining table was laid out with a bottle of wine and two glasses as well as a plate containing various dried fruits and cheeses.

Nothing about the arrangement felt like a mere study session. Niall's heart ran wild in his chest. Blake was interested in him after all.

As soon as the joyous thought entered Niall's brain, Blake stepped away from him, shut and locked the flat's door, and crossed the room with purposeful strides toward the table.

"I don't know what your strengths and weaknesses in the Classics are," he said without looking at Niall as he fetched a small stack of books from a shelf near the table. "I do well with Greek and Latin, but my History leaves something to be desired." He pulled out one of the chairs at the table before circling around to have a seat in the opposing one, gesturing for Niall to sit as he did.

It took Niall a few seconds of working his jaw soundlessly as he stepped unsteadily toward the table to form the words, "I'm good at History. And Literature, obviously."

He cringed inwardly. Blake must think he was a moron.

Instead of giving any indication of that, however, Blake smiled and gestured for Niall to sit again. "Sounds like we make a perfect pair," he said as Niall flopped into the offered chair. "For studying, that is," Blake corrected himself quickly, face flushing an even darker and more charming red. "We each have what the other lacks."

"Perhaps Professor Carroll would let us take the exam together as one," Niall said with a strained laugh.

"Wouldn't that be nice." Blake laughed along with him.

His gaze lingered on Niall for far longer than it should have, his hazel eyes seeming to glow with fondness as he studied Niall. There was something about Blake's scrutiny that made the hair on the back of Niall's neck stand up, as though Blake were trying to figure out what he made of Niall and hadn't quite come to a conclusion. In fact, if Niall wasn't mistaken, there was a hint of strain beneath the warmth in Blake's look, something akin to worry.

Niall blinked and sucked in a shallow breath. Blake wasn't afraid that he'd attack him or behave inappropriately, was he? Who he was and what he preferred wasn't exactly a secret at the university. Niall had enough of a standing among his fellow students and society that his nature was largely ignored, but there were always one or two people who treated him as though he were a rabid dog just pretending to be tame.

"I bought wine," Blake blurted after the silence dragged on for a painfully long time. He snatched up the bottle on the table, which looked to have already been opened. "It's good wine too, French wine. Burgundy is my favorite, but this is a tasty merlot that I think you'll like." He poured gracelessly into the two glasses waiting on the table, splashing a bit of red onto the crisp, white tablecloth that Niall had only just noticed, in a way that would stain it irreparably.

"I'm not choosy when it comes to wine," Niall said, alarmed at how gruff his voice sounded. "Spirits, on the other hand, I'm extraordinarily particular about. I've tried my hand at mixing a few original concoctions now and then, and I've gotten quite good at it."

Now he was the one rambling. Niall wanted to roll his eyes at himself. At the rate they were going, they wouldn't study at all. They'd just sit there acting like boobs. And unless Niall worked up the nerve to ask a few pointed questions, he would never be able to determine just what Blake was and how he felt about him.

"Right," Blake said after taking a long swig of his wine and opening his Latin book. "There's no telling what might come up." He paused, his eyes shining. "On the exam." He cleared his throat. "So we should start with languages. I know Professor Carroll is a stickler for conjugations."

"Aren't we all sticklers for conjugations?" Niall said with a wry grin, then hid the lame attempt at a joke by downing half of his wine in a few gulps. He had the distinct feeling he was going to need it to get through the night, and he hoped Blake had more stowed away somewhere.

Latin proved to be more of a distraction than he would have accounted for. As soon as they began studying in earnest, Blake grew incredibly serious about academia. It didn't take Niall long to realize that, as intelligent as he knew he was, he was outmatched by Blake's intellect. But as the study session progressed, Niall began to notice that Blake's attention was easily scattered.

"That's odd," he said with a pinched grin as they reviewed the plot and key motifs of *The Iliad*. "Did you get your inspiration for Siegfried and Greta from Homer?" He leaned forward slightly, reaching for the wine bottle to pour himself a second glass.

Niall glanced from Blake's hand on the bottle to the nervous shine in Blake's eyes to his reddened lips, then back to his eyes. "Classic literature is full of tales of women who have been stolen from someone or another and given to men who don't deserve them to serve as wives and concubines."

"Concubines." Blake chuckled. "That's a fun word. It implies all of the fun and none of the commitment."

Niall arched one eyebrow, wondering if one glass of wine had been enough to make Blake drunk or if he was babbling because he was nervous. "You don't like commitment?" he asked.

Blake's face pinched as though he'd said something wrong. "I adore the idea of commitment." He glanced briefly to Niall once he finished pouring, but didn't seem to be able to hold his gaze. "It must be wonderful to find someone who you want to spend the rest of your life with, grow old with, experience the joys and sorrows of life with. Who wouldn't want to commit to something like that?"

He took a long drink from his refreshed glass. Niall watched him, sensing something was wrong. His heart beat faster. There were far more facets to being the sort of man he was than deciding who to go to bed with. If Blake really was like him, commitment, even on an emotional level, could be a serious problem.

As if Blake could read Niall's thoughts, he rushed on with, "The trouble is who one is expected to spend the rest of his life with. From where I'm sitting, the rest of my life seems like a very long time." He met Niall's eyes with a devastating seriousness. Niall read his expression as the proof he was looking for that Blake wanted him. Until he turned around and said, "As a student, of course. And as a future duke. I'll be extraordinarily lucky if I'm allowed to choose my own wife." He punctuated his comment by taking a long drink—or rather, by lifting his wineglass to his mouth in a way that hid his face.

Niall watched him intently for a few more seconds before sighing and saying, "I'm not sure that being a concubine was as fun as you make it out to be. None of those poor girls had any more choice in the matter than you do. It's astounding how little choice we actually have in whom we love." He fixed Blake with a gaze meant to bore into his soul. Come hell or high water, he was going to determine Blake's nature by the end of the evening, even if it killed him.

"You're right about that," Blake said, avoiding looking directly at him. He finished half his glass of wine and put the glass on the table with a sigh, then clapped both hands to the table top. "Enough of these dusty old classics. I don't think I can sit at this table for another second. Why don't we take this opportunity to run lines for your play instead?"

Niall's brow shot up, and he watched as Blake leapt restlessly out of his chair and paced across the room to fetch his script. "If that's what you want to do," he said, rising slowly, then pushing his chair in.

"Do you have a copy of the script?" Blake asked, retrieving his and flipping through its dog-eared pages.

Niall grinned. "I wrote it. I know it by heart."

"All of it?" Blake's expression brightened as he and Niall met in the center of the room in front of a comfortable-looking sofa with spindly tables at each end.

"All of it," Niall laughed. "Although, to be fair, that's probably also because I've been directing the production myself and starring in it as well."

"Do you have ambitions of being a director once you make your scintillating debut on the London stage?" Blake asked mischievously.

"Not if I can help it," Niall answered. "I'm much better suited to squirreling myself away in a tidy flat, scribbling and bringing new ideas and new worlds to life."

"If anybody can do it, you can."

Blake stopped rifling through his script for a moment and let his shoulders drop as he smiled at Niall. There was an unmistakable fondness between them, a camaraderie that Niall had never experienced with anyone. Blake was wildly different from him in so many ways. He was a sun to Niall's moon. He was exuberance and charm, whereas Niall was cleverness and ambition. But underneath that, Niall felt as though somehow their souls matched.

Blake cleared his throat, then said, "Where do you want to start?" in a rough voice.

Niall shrugged, pretending the electric charge between them wasn't about to set the room on fire. "Wherever you feel you need the most rehearsing."

Blake nodded, grinned, and took a small step back, focusing on the script again. "I'm good with memorization, so I think I have most of it down already. Of course, since I started at the beginning, I'm less certain about the end."

"Then let's work on the final scene," Niall said.

"Right." Blake nodded, leafing through to the back of

the script. "Perfect. Siegfried has vanquished his rivals and won Greta's admiration."

"My heart rejoices to be the bride of such a valiant and noble prince," Niall recited the line, raising the timbre of his voice for the woman's part.

"And mine to be a bridegroom as well as a prince now," Blake said, speaking the line first, then checking the page to make certain he'd said it right. He inched closer to Niall. The spark between them seemed to grow. At least, until Blake cleared his throat and rocked back to deliver the next line. "Reinhold, I was wrong to censure you for stealing a bride for me." He pointed to the spot where Ian would have been standing if they were on a stage. "You will be showered with riches and honors for your part in this."

"And you will have my eternal gratitude," Niall said, studying Blake carefully. He was still anxious, still restless.

He moved closer to Niall, lowering his script and gazing deep into Niall's eyes as he said, "Come, my darling. Let us celebrate our union instead of denying it. Let all the kingdom celebrate with us."

Niall's breath caught in his chest. If ever there were a way to prove definitively how Blake felt about him, this was it. He thanked God that his earlier self had written the next bit of the play the way he had, then recited, "My lord and my master," then took a huge stride forward that brought him right up against Blake.

The action of the script called for a kiss. Heart in his

throat, Niall obeyed his own stage direction to the letter. He clasped either side of Blake's face and slanted his mouth over Blake's with all the daring he could muster.

For one, terrifying moment, Niall thought everything he'd guessed about Blake was dead wrong. Blake went rigid, sucking in a breath as Niall kissed him with the full force of the desire that had been building in him since the moment he'd first clapped eyes on him. He felt a shudder run through Blake, heard his script drop to the floor. Blake's lips were soft beneath his, but remained firmly closed.

Niall pulled back, shame burning in his cheeks and disappointment feeling like it would grind him to a pulp. "I'm sorry," he whispered hoarsely, letting his hands drop. "I—"

Before he could get another word out, Blake sucked in a sharp breath and launched toward him. He clasped the sides of Niall's head and brought his mouth crashing over his in a kiss that startled Niall and robbed him of all sense. Better still, Blake groaned deep in his throat as he kissed Niall furiously, as though his emotions were so intense that he couldn't keep them in check for another second.

"Niall," Blake sighed, kissing him harder. He brushed his tongue along the seam of Niall's lips until they parted, then slipped inside to taste Niall with an even deeper sigh.

As soon as Niall realized his arms were flailing uselessly in shock at the intensity of the kiss, he reached for Blake, embracing him and digging his fingertips into the broad plane of his back. "Yes," he sighed before he could stop himself, then returned Blake's kiss passionately to hide the madness that was rising up to consume him.

Blake clasped Niall close in turn, the heat of his body sizzling against Niall's. Blake's breath came in sharp, shallow gasps as he alternated between kissing Niall's lips and brushing his lips and teeth along Niall's jaw. He kissed his way to Niall's neck as well, leaning into him so forcefully that Niall stumbled backward. He backpedaled all the way into the piano, sitting hard on the keys and causing a riot of discordant sound.

Blake laughed breathlessly at that as he pushed Niall's unbuttoned jacket off of his shoulders. His hands fumbled with the buttons of Niall's waistcoat a moment later, then tugged the hem of Niall's shirt out of his trousers. Niall was certain he had died and gone to heaven as Blake's dexterous hands spread across the bare skin of his sides.

It was proof that Blake wanted him and more, and it made Niall bolder than he'd ever dreamed he would be. He mirrored Blake's actions, pulling his shirt up so that he could touch Blake's sides and stomach. He wanted so much more than that, though, and fumbled with the fastenings of Blake's trousers.

Blake gasped audibly as Niall reached in to stroke his already hard cock. Feeling how hot and alive and thick Blake was had Niall's own prick jerking to be freed in his trousers. He explored Blake fully, hungry beyond measure, cupping his balls and learning everything he could about how Blake felt and reacted to his touch. The slickness of pre-cum at Blake's tip said more than words ever could about how ready Blake was for everything Niall wanted from him.

And he wanted everything.

He somehow found the strength to push against Blake, flipping their positions so that Blake sat hard against the piano keys with another discordant blast. Niall leaned into him, making quick work of the fastenings of his own trousers, then guiding Blake to handle him. Blake complied eagerly and breathlessly, nearly sending Niall over the edge with the first stroke. It felt so unbelievably good to have Blake's hand on him, exploring the way he'd just done, that Niall whimpered at the sensation.

He wasn't going to last, but somehow that only spurred him on. He kissed Blake mercilessly as the pressure built within him. Their open mouths were hungry for each other, but better still, Blake seemed hell-bent on making Niall come. His touch felt so good that Niall wouldn't have been able to stop himself if he'd tried. He came with a shattering force, moaning into Blake's mouth in the middle of a kiss and spilling into his hand. Blake gasped, his eyes going wide for a moment.

Those gorgeous eyes narrowed with hazy passion, then closed entirely as Niall sank to his knees. He might have been loose and dazed after coming, but he wasn't done yet. He drew Blake's trousers down to his thighs, then took his thick, hard cock in hand, positioning it how he wanted it. And he wanted it desperately. He kissed and licked the slickness from Blake's head before unapologetically drawing the whole thing into his mouth.

Blake groaned with pleasure and gripped the edge of the piano hard, sending more discordant notes soaring. Niall reveled in the intensity of Blake's pleasure and abandoned any semblance of politeness or decorum to suck him like there was no tomorrow. He loved every second of it, even though Blake's size took some getting used to. His own discomfort was nothing to the desperate pants and sounds Blake made. Niall made merciless use of his tongue and moaned himself as he sent Blake rocketing toward the edge. Blake came with a profane cry as Niall swallowed him reflexively.

It was all so good that once it was over, Niall rested his forehead against the firm muscles of Blake's abdomen as he caught his breath. The scent of musk and salt filled his senses. Blake's skin was hot and damp under his hands where they rested on his hips. For a moment, neither of them moved as they gasped and fought to regain their wits. The only thing that stopped Niall from kissing his way up Blake's belly and chest to capture his lips again was the dawning awareness that, even post-orgasm, Blake was as tense as a tiger.

That realization caused him to lean back and glance up at him. Where Niall hoped to find a look of sated adoration, Blake looked horrified. Niall swallowed tightly and pushed himself unsteadily to his feet. He was already taller than Blake by a bit, but with Blake seated on the piano keys, he almost towered above him.

"It's all right," he panted, caressing Blake's face with both hands. "We didn't do anything wrong."

Blake continued to breathe shallowly, staring at Niall as though the world had just come to an end. Anxiety swirled through Niall, killing all of the satisfaction of the moment. He studied Blake with a wary heart, praying he hadn't just ruined everything. But no, the storm of emotion in Blake's eyes wasn't terror over being attacked by someone who had forced him to do something against his will. The fear went much deeper than that.

"It's all right," Niall repeated, brushing his fingers through Blake's hair, his heart breaking for the confusion Blake must have been feeling. Without needing to be told, Niall could guess that he'd just opened Pandora's Box for Blake. "You're going to be all right."

He leaned in, kissing Blake softly, his heart feeling too big and too full for his chest. His adoration for Blake had reached a whole new level. He wasn't the hopeful supplicant, begging for a piece of Blake's affection anymore. He was the one with more experience who needed to guide a lost soul through the darkness and into the light.

But as soon as he rocked back to check how Blake was feeling, Blake cleared his throat and said, "I think you should go," in a hoarse voice.

Niall jerked back, stung. Blake's gaze dropped below

Niall's waist, where his half-erect cock was still on full view. Something about the look was accusatory, so Niall returned it by staring blatantly at Blake's prick. The sight of it only filled him with longing and uncertainty, though. He took another step back and fastened his trousers, tucking his shirt in. What should have felt like a moment of victory and closeness had turned into an even worse sort of uncertainty than anything Niall had felt before.

"I'll go," he said, turning away. He moved to fetch his things.

"I don't mean to be—" Blake started, but didn't finish.

Niall buttoned his waistcoat and jacket, then shoved his school books into his satchel and slung it over his arm. By the time he turned back to Blake, Blake had straightened himself and sat on the piano bench, which he'd pulled out from where it'd been tucked, staring at the damp spot on the cuff of his shirtsleeve. Niall's face flared hot, knowing he'd caused the dampness.

He wanted to say something, wanted to soothe Blake and make everything all right again. He also wanted to shout at Blake for being blind to his own desires. He couldn't form words to express either thought, though, so he did the only thing he could do and left.

Only when he was outside in the cool, spring air, striding fast across the university's campus on the way to his lonely dormitory room, did the guilt set in. He should have talked with Blake first. He should have been brave enough to ask outright what Blake wanted instead of pushing things. The farther away from Blake he got, the more acute his guilt.

By the time he made it back to his room, he knew what he had to do. Without missing a step or wasting a second, he threw his satchel aside and sat at his desk, reaching for a sheet of stationary.

"*My dear Blake*," he wrote, then paused. Using Blake's name along with the things he knew he had to write would spell disaster if the letter were somehow intercepted. For Blake's sake, he couldn't take the risk.

"*Dearest B*," he wrote on a fresh piece of stationary. "*I'm so sorry that I pushed things beyond the point where you were comfortable tonight. But I couldn't keep my feelings for you a secret any longer. I have to be honest, considering what happened between us just now. I have wanted you from the moment I first saw you. And I mean that in deeper terms than kisses and passion. My soul feels as though it has known yours through many lifetimes. We fit together in so many ways, as the last week has proven. Yes, I am filled with a burning desire to know you in every way and to enjoy so much more than what we did tonight. But I was wrong to thrust those things on you without asking first.*"

He raised an eyebrow at his own phrasing, but his passions were too deeply engaged to stop.

"*Please accept my deepest apologies, not for what we did, but for how we started. My sincerest hope is that we can continue to so much more from here. I will never forget the intensity of your kiss. Your taste will be in my mouth always. I've had a glimpse of heaven, and now it is a dream I won't ever be able to leave behind. Say you want me too and I promise you we will find a way to enter heaven's gates together. Yours passionately, N."*

As soon as he was finished, he made sure the ink was dry and folded the letter, stuffing it into an envelope and scribbling the address of Blake's flat without writing his name. Once that was done, he launched away from his desk and out of his room, searching for one of the hall boys who ran errands for the occupants of the dorm.

"Deliver this right away and there will be an extra shilling in it for you," he told one of the lads when he found one.

"Yes, sir." The boy took the letter and the coin Niall gave him and rushed off.

Only when Niall was back in his room, stripping off his clothes and catching a faint hint of Blake's scent on him did he wonder if he'd just made a crucial mistake. Blake might reject him entirely. That would be humiliating enough, but they still had a play to produce.

$\mathcal{N}$iall was deliberately late to rehearsal the next day. His heart beat in his throat as he approached the auditorium. He broke out in a sweat at the sound of his cast chatting and laughing. He would recognize Blake's laugh anywhere, and it was definitely a part of whatever merriment was going on in the auditorium. The thought of facing Blake after what had passed between them and after the letter he'd so rashly sent was enough to have Niall breaking out in hives. He paused just outside of the auditorium door to catch his breath and steady his nerves. It didn't help that he'd hardly slept a wink the night before either. He was exhausted, his nerves were rattled, he had a rehearsal to run and a play to produce, and his heart was on the line.

With one final breath, he gathered his courage and marched into the auditorium.

"Sorry I'm late," he told the full complement of his

cast as he strode down one of the auditorium's aisles to the table set up for him near the front. "I was studying and I lost track of time." He nodded to Ian, glanced at the bits and pieces of the set that had been built since the last time he'd visited the auditorium, and waved to the accompanist, who sat at the piano on the stage. Only after he'd done absolutely everything he could think of to occupy his attention did he dare to peek at the group of men where Blake stood.

"Don't worry, it happens to the best of us." Paul came forward to clap Niall on the back as he slipped his satchel off his shoulder and set it on the table.

Niall didn't have the first clue what Paul was talking about. Blake talked and laughed with Morton's group in the front corner of the auditorium, looking as though he didn't have a care in the world. He was perfectly groomed and slouched over his seat with casual ease. When Morton and the others stood to make their way to the stage for rehearsal, Blake followed with perfect elegance and grace.

Niall remembered the way Blake's hips felt in his hands, the way his skin smelled and his prick tasted. He remembered the enthusiasm in the way Blake had kissed him and the joy he'd felt at the plaintive sounds Blake had made when he came close to coming. When the accompanist played the first few notes of the opening number of his play, Niall remembered the clash of sound when Blake had gripped his piano's keyboard as Niall sank to his knees.

At last, Blake sent the briefest of looks in Niall's direction. In a flash, Niall could see that his casual demeanor and joking with the other men was a façade. The intensity in Blake's eyes was enough to shake Niall to his core. But he had a rehearsal to run.

"Are we going to tackle Act Two today?" Paul asked, still standing by Niall's side.

"Hmm? Oh. Yes." Niall cleared his throat.

Paul narrowed his eyes slightly, then glanced to the stage. Niall's face was already hot, but he felt as though it heated even more when a flash of understanding dawned in Paul's expression. Paul grinned slightly, then stepped away from Niall. "All right, then," he said, starting toward the stage.

A burst of frustration hit Niall. Paul clearly thought he knew something, but there was nothing to know. Nothing that had been stated, at least. It didn't matter how desperately Niall wanted there to be something for Paul to smirk about, he couldn't, with all honestly, say there was anything between him and Blake. Except for everything. Everything unspoken.

"Time is wasting," Niall said, using every last one of his acting skills to pretend that nothing was wrong and that he was in full control of the situation as he took his script from his satchel and started toward the stage. "We need to make certain we've mastered the blocking for Act Two as well as the choreography for the finale."

"If you can even call it choreography," Morton said, elbowing Blake, who stood next to him.

Niall swallowed the rush of jealousy that accompanied the grin Blake sent Morton in return. He had a job to do. It didn't matter that that job involved playing opposite the man he'd fellated the evening before, a man he wasn't sure returned his feelings, a man he might just have humiliated himself for. His responsibility was to his cast.

"Let's start by running through the Act Two opening number." He nodded to the accompanist, who launched into the cheery number.

Slowly but surely, Niall's back unclenched, allowing him to make actual progress in directing his cast through the second act. It was a relief how fast Morton and the other chorus members had picked up their songs. He didn't even mind Morton inventing choreography of his own to accompany them. The more of them that were dedicated to the show the better, as far as Niall was concerned. And who knew? Perhaps Morton had a secret desire to choreograph, though Niall would have been shocked beyond belief if it turned out that Morton was an invert.

Rehearsing the scenes between songs turned out to be the most challenging part of the rehearsal, particularly the scenes Niall and Blake played with each other. As they came closer and closer to the scene that had unraveled with an entirely different ending the evening before, Niall's palms grew sweaty and his heart refused to settle.

"Reinhold, I was wrong to censure you for stealing a bride for me." Blake crossed the stage to clap Ian on the shoulder, a move that took him farther away from Niall instead of closer, as they'd rehearsed several days before. Ian reacted too strongly, but rather than stopping to tell him to stop being a ham, Niall let Blake continue, panic growing in his gut. "You will be showered with riches and honors for your part in this."

"And you will have my eternal gratitude." Niall's voice cracked on his line. He cleared his throat, moving closer to Ian as well and using him as a shield between him and Blake.

"Aren't the two of you meant to be saying this whole part over there?" Ian asked with a frown, scanning through the penciled notes in his script.

"It felt more natural to cross to Reinhold for this line," Blake told Niall.

Their eyes met and held for the first time since the rehearsal had started. It was as though lightning cracked over the stage. Niall couldn't breathe. The intensity of feeling in Blake's eyes bored into his soul, but whether that emotion was fear or anger or passion, Niall couldn't tell.

"It's just that I have written right here that you do that part over there," Ian said, pointing with the pencil in his right hand to the other side of the stage.

"If it feels more natural to be here...." Niall started, letting the sentence fade.

"I'm not sure I trust my instincts when it comes to what feels natural," Blake said, still holding Niall's gaze.

Niall could have murdered him on the spot. Aside

from the fact that he *would* say something with such deep meaning while Ian was standing between the two of them, it was an abdication of responsibility.

"You're going to have to decide that for yourself," Niall said, stepping away and turning his back to Blake.

Blake cleared his throat and delivered the line, "Come, my darling. Let us celebrate our union instead of denying it. Let all the kingdom celebrate with us."

Niall turned back to him, sucking in a breath and wondering whether Blake would dare to kiss him on the stage, in front of everyone else. All he did was march past Ian to stand directly by Niall's side, studying his script as though it held the answers to every question in the universe in its pages.

"And that's where we kiss," Blake said without looking up.

"My hero," Niall said, his jaw clenched.

The accompanist dove into the opening bars of the final song that would end the show. Morton and his chorus shifted into place and Niall crossed to sweep Blake into the position the two of them were supposed to have for the final number. The other, minor characters moved into place as well.

In the midst of the burst of movement, Blake pulled something flat out of the pocket of his jacket and slipped it subtly into Niall's pocket. Without meeting his eyes or acknowledging what he'd done, Blake took Niall's hand and moved to center stage as he began to sing.

Niall could hardly remember the words to the song

that he'd written. Blake had slipped a letter into his pocket, he was certain. He wanted to read it so badly that the corners of his vision blurred. Morton made a few suggestions about choreography for the finale that Niall agreed to without truly noting what they were.

As soon as the final strains of the finale faded and the cast dissolved into applauding themselves and chattering, Niall wanted to bolt out of the room to read Blake's letter. Rehearsal was far from over, though.

"Excellent," he said, feigning a smile as he peeled away from Blake and moved to the front of the stage, where he could address his cast as a whole. "Morton, I like what you did with the dancing bits. Why don't you run through that again while the rest of us take a quick break?"

The chorus members glanced to Morton, then followed his instructions as they shifted into positions. Blake pretended to be interested in what they were doing as he moved to the end of the stage, then hopped down and took a seat in the house to watch. Gregory moved to sit with him, attempting to start a conversation that Blake didn't seem particularly interested in. Blake's glance kept cheating over to Niall as he walked to the stairs and descended into the house.

They were on opposite sides of the auditorium, as far away from each other as they could get. Anyone stepping in to observe for the first time would think they had no interest in each other and no connection whatsoever outside of the play. But as Niall reached for the letter in his pocket, he knew better. He held his breath as he unfolded the neat sheets and began to read.

"*Dearest N.*" His stomach did a somersault at the tenderness of the greeting.

"I found out something that you're definitely going to want to know," Ian said directly at Niall's side.

Niall gasped and flinched away from him, clapping the letter to his chest. He hadn't noticed Ian descending from the stage right behind him. The man leaned far too close to him now. "What did you find out?" he asked, dreading the possibility that Ian knew something about him and Blake.

Ian's smug grin grew twice as crafty. "That medallion that Professor Carroll had made as the prize for the Classics exam," he said. "He really did send the wrong scarab to the craftsman. I checked up on it myself."

Niall blinked at him, no idea what he was talking about. "Oh?" he asked out of politeness.

"Yes." Ian's eyes flashed with avarice as he pivoted to stand just in front of Niall, blocking Blake from his view. "I had a long conversation about it with Miss Annamarie Cannon last night. She's fascinated with Egypt, you know. I told her all about the value of the scarab and how whoever wins that medallion would be able to sell it for a small fortune."

"I still don't see how an expert like Professor Carroll would be careless enough to let go of a priceless artifact," Niall said. What he wanted to say was, "Get the hell away from me, you fool. Can't you see I have a love letter to read?"

"I'm going to win that prize," Ian went on. "And I'm going to win Annamarie Cannon's heart as well."

"Best of luck to you," Niall said as dismissively as he could without being overtly rude.

"So your little friend, Lord Stanley, had better be on his guard."

It took Niall a moment to remember that Blake was Lord Stanley, a marquess, a one-day duke. As far as Niall was concerned, he was the man who had kissed him like his life depended on it the night before. He was the man who had penned unknown treasures that he held in his hands right then and there.

"I'm sure he will be," Niall said with a tight smile. "Now, if you will excuse me, I...I need to find a water closet before we start the second half of rehearsal."

He pushed away from the wall, charging up the aisle to the hall and hoping Ian wouldn't follow. Out of the corner of his eyes, he spotted Blake turning his head and following him with his eyes. That only caused Niall's gut to clench harder.

He was lucky that there was a private room directly across from the auditorium. He dashed into it, shut the door behind him, and moved to the window so that he had enough light to read Blake's letter.

"*Dearest N. I should be the one to apologize, not you. I don't know where to begin to describe my feelings earlier. I can't sleep for thinking about it and replaying every glorious moment in my mind. I never should have sent you away so callously. I shouldn't have sent you away at all. But if we're being honest with each other, which I think we must be at this point, I was so shocked by everything that I wasn't thinking straight.*

"The truth is that I've wanted you as you've wanted me from the moment you proved to be so wonderful at auditions. I've wanted to kiss you and to hold you in my arms, run my fingers through your hair, and taste your skin, from the moment you smiled at me as I sang and played."

A strangled sound of victory erupted from Niall's lungs and tears of joy stung his eyes.

"But you have to understand," Blake went on, *"these feelings are entirely new to me. I won't lie and say I've never been attracted to men before. I have. I always have been. I had resigned myself to never do anything about it, though. My plan was for that attraction to be something distant, at the back of my mind, to be ignored. I even fancied I could force myself to be normal and feel those same feelings for women, to the point where I've acted on it in order to fit in. But the moment your smile warmed me and your wit enthralled me, I knew pretending was a hopeless cause.*

"Everything we did earlier this evening was a revelation for me. Nothing has ever felt so good as kissing you and touching you. Nothing has ever aroused me more than knowing that we could do anything and no one would stop us. I cannot begin to describe the power and pride I felt

when you came in my hand, or the agonizing bliss of your mouth bringing me to orgasm. I'm hard all over again thinking about it now.

"*But I'm also terrified, and I know you could sense it. I have so much at risk when it comes to love. I've known since the cradle what my life is supposed to be. I know that I can't have what I truly want, and what I truly want is you. Or rather, I know that the odds are stacked impossibly against us. I can't stop thinking about you, though. I can't stop wanting you, aching for you. If I don't kiss you again soon, I'll go mad. If I don't follow this passion wherever it leads, I'll be the worst sort of coward imaginable. But I'm lost and frightened. I don't know what to do. Help me to do the right thing. Yours, B.*"

Niall was panting and tears streamed down his face as he finished the letter and pressed it to his heart. Blake wanted him. He'd been right all along. He'd enjoyed what they'd done the night before. But he was conflicted. Niall felt the pain of Blake's words as though it were his own pain. The world Blake came from and the expectations that had been heaped on his shoulders were a world away from his own circumstances. He could hardly blame the man for being confused and anxious. But Blake wanted him. That was all that mattered.

He folded the letter carefully, tucking it into the inside pocket of his jacket, then splashed a bit of cold water from the jug on the table under the window over his face. As he headed back to the auditorium, he was certain he looked a mess. At least he could blame it on the same thing every other student at the university could blame red, puffy eyes and distraction on—studying and the strain of looming exams.

"Sorry for the delay," he announced as he strode back into the room. He thought about adding an excuse for his absence, but opted against it as he strode to the stage with renewed vigor. "Let's run through the last couple of scenes. Chorus members, if you're satisfied with your dance, you're free to go."

Morton and his friends wandered slowly off the stage, laughing and shoving each other, completely oblivious to the deeper drama happening right next to them.

Blake did a poor job of concealing his expectation as he climbed onto the stage, forgoing the stairs in favor of looking athletic, staring heavily at Niall as he did. Niall couldn't wipe the smile off his face as he went to retrieve his script before taking the stairs onto the stage. He stole only furtive glances at Blake, not trusting himself to spend any more than a fraction of a second looking at him. He'd give them both away if he did.

As it was, he didn't do a good enough job of acting to fool everyone.

"Is there something between you and Stanley?" Paul murmured to him as he helped Niall rearrange the furniture on the stage that was standing in as set pieces.

"No," Niall answered, a little too quickly and too vehemently. He laughed nervously, intending to cover his slip, but likely only making things worse. "What makes you say that?"

"It's just that the sparks between you are palpable," Paul continued with a teasing grin, speaking low enough that no one would overhear.

"They are not," Niall argued. When Paul's expression turned flat and doubtful, Niall rushed on. "We're playing opposite each other. That's all. Blake is a brilliant actor. If you're sensing anything at all, it's acting. There's no need to go blurring the lines between what's real and what's imaginary."

"If you say so." Paul clearly didn't believe a damn thing Niall said.

Niall shook his head, wondering if he could end up believing it himself if he tried hard enough. It would be safer for everyone if every fiber of his body didn't long for Blake, if he didn't want to abandon rehearsal to drag Blake back to his flat so that he could show him the sort of pleasure two men could really feel with each other. He was hungry for the unfettered sounds Blake had made the night before, and he wanted more of them. They were the best music Blake could possibly make.

"Let's start from the beginning of Reinhold and Hilda's scene," he said, taking charge with a confidence he hadn't felt since rehearsals started. "Right before Greta interrupts them."

That night, he took pen to paper with more enthusiasm than he ever had in his life.

"*Dearest B. You cannot imagine the joy that filled me*

when I read your letter earlier. Feeling passion is one thing, but knowing that passion is returned, however exciting and unnerving it might be, is pure bliss. And pure bliss is what I want to make you feel in every way.

"I want to kiss you until you sigh my name aloud, until you can't think of anything but my mouth on you. I want to explore every inch of your body, drive you mad with arousal like you've never experienced before. I want to teach you things that you've only ever dreamed of, like the pleasure there is to be had in having your earlobes nibbled or your nipples licked. I want to leave marks on the tender flesh of your inner thighs that only you and I will know about. I want to suck your balls and tease your arsehole until you're so mad with desire that you burst. I want to be the one to open you up for the first time and feel your breathless pants as you learn what it feels like to be filled.

"And then I want to lie, tangled and sweaty, with you, whispering secrets and laughing over nothing deep into the night. I want to share my heart and my dreams with you and hear everything you want to say to me in return. I want us to have secrets that no one else could possibly guess at, our own little world that no one else can touch. Say you want these things too, and I will move heaven and earth to give them to you. Yours eternally, N."

CHAPTER 7

*T*he letters continued for weeks, though a few of the dozens stood out in particular....

"MY DARLING N. THERE IS NOTHING THAT I WANT *more than to unravel the mysteries of the love that dare not speak its name with you. I don't know if you are aware of how beautiful and desirable you are. There is a grace in the way you move that makes me hungry for you. The spark of intelligence in your eyes captivates me. I am fascinated by your neck, of all things, and want to kiss and bite it. I had only a glimpse of what it would feel like to explore your body with my hands the other night, but I want more. I want to learn every inch of you, discover what makes you shiver and sigh. I want your scent on my sheets and your laughter in my heart.*

"There. I can write as beautifully as you when I put my mind to it. Though I'm certain it took me ten times as long to compose those words as it does for you to write the same to me. Don't ever stop writing your beautiful words for me. They are like sweet tarts that melt in my mouth—as I hope you will someday soon—and fill me with happiness, which is especially important as it's been so impossible for us to find time alone together. I have never cursed my schooling and social schedule so much in my life.

"I'm sorry for pretending to ignore you at Professor Carroll's study group earlier. I panicked when John Dandie hinted that there might be anything other than friendship and a professional relationship between the two of us. And then I saw Ian fawning all over you yet again, and jealousy got the better of me. I know there could never be anything between you and Ian. He's not like us, and he has his heart set on wooing Miss Cannon. But seeing you give even the slightest bit of attention to another man strikes a dark chord in me that I'm still confused by.

"We'll sort this out soon, I'm certain. Until then, I count the minutes until our next rehearsal, and I may just have to relieve myself while thinking of you after sending this letter off. Yours in passion, B."

"DEAREST B. FORGIVE ME FOR LAUGHING OVER THE idea of you being jealous of Ian, or any other man, where I am concerned. You can rest assured knowing there is no one else who has captivated my heart or who I want as desperately as I want you. I'm the one who should be jealous after seeing you accompanying Miss Cannon at the musicale Lady Fairport hosted this evening. Everyone was captivated by your playing, especially Miss Cannon. The way she smiled at you and flirted is everything I wish I could do publically, but we both know how impossible that would be.

"Your voice truly is the most sensual thing I've ever heard. There is a trueness and a resonance to it that goes straight to my soul...and other areas that are unmentionable and inconvenient in public. I could listen to you sing all day. I could listen to you sigh with pleasure and moan with bliss and call out my name as you come too. You have no idea how wicked it makes me feel to imagine all of the things I plan to introduce you to as soon as possible to cause those delicious sounds. You won't be able to think of anything or anyone else for the rest of your days.

"I have to admit, it's become rather fun in this last week to pretend there is nothing but professional courtesy and platonic friendship between us. It almost makes up for our utter lack of ability to sneak off together for more than a handful of minutes. Stealing looks is as entertaining as stealing kisses. Though we really should be more careful. We were so nearly caught with our mouths plastered together this afternoon that I couldn't stop shaking for a good half hour after we went our separate ways. I long for us to finally find an evening when neither of us has other obligations so that we might take this where it has been heading all along.

"Until then, I think of you constantly, I dream of you, and I abuse myself mercilessly while imagining what I plan to do to you. Deliciously, N."

"BELOVED N. WE ARE MOST CERTAINLY GOING TO END up in a sticky situation if we can't find a night to spend together soon. And I mean that in every way you can imagine. My laundress gave me a funny look the other day as I requested clean sheets for the fourth time in one week. And I'm relatively certain Gregory was smirking at the state of my trousers in rehearsal today. I'm afraid if we don't find satisfaction soon, the fire between us will spill over and our secret will be revealed.

"To that end, I've canceled my plans to dine with the Archibalds and Cannons yet again tomorrow night. Three times in less than a fortnight is more than enough, if you ask me. Mrs. Cannon is an absolute delight, but I'm not sure I like the way Annamarie has been sizing me—or rather, my title—up like a piece of meat. Or the way Ian has taken to glaring at me, like I've snatched away his toy.

"The only person I want eyeing me like a piece of meat is you. The way you look at me drives me mad with desire. Every time I catch you with the same look in your eyes as you wore before sinking to your knees on that glorious night weeks ago, my blood runs hot. I want you on *your knees again, and I want to do the same to you. My mouth waters thinking about the possibility. I want the full experience of loving you and being loved in return.*

"Tomorrow evening, after the exam. We'll make some excuse to go off to supper together. I could even have food waiting at my flat, though it won't be what I want to eat first. Say you'll be with me and we can be together the way I've wanted for so long, the way we should be for eternity. Carnally, B."

NIALL COULD HARDLY SIT STILL FOR THE DURATION of the Classics exam. He couldn't concentrate on the words on the page Professor Carroll had given to each of them. Writing was most definitely his talent, but every word that dripped from his pen as he vainly attempted to conjugate Latin verbs and write essays on Aeschylus felt stupid. He bobbed his leg up and down rapidly to expend some of his pent-up energy, but his thoughts would only go in one direction.

Blake had cleared the way for the two of them to be together that night.

He glanced up from his examination paper, knowing the whole thing was a lost cause, and peeked sideways. Blake had casually taken a seat at the desk beside his for the exam. They'd exchanged banal pleasantries before Professor Carroll delivered the exam, chatting about the play with John and David, and Ian. Not a soul would have had the first clue where he and Blake intended to end their day by anything in their behavior, although Niall had had to force himself not to look directly at Blake through the entire conversation.

He looked now. Blake was the picture of perfection with his face screwed up in concentration. His shoulders were hunched slightly and his mouth was pressed in a firm line as he scribbled away on the sheet in front of him. His lithe hand flew like the wind, making Niall marvel at the man's powers of concentration. Niall couldn't wait to feel those hands on his skin, to brush his own fingers through Blake's thick hair, to kiss his lips until they softened and parted with a moan of pleasure.

A sharp hiss on Niall's other side snapped him out of his increasingly carnal thoughts. He shifted to peek at Ian, who scowled at his exam paper as though it were a mortal enemy. Ian had bragged about scoring highest marks on the exam and winning the prize. Niall doubted the Egyptian medallion was worth a fraction of the amount Ian seemed to think it was, but he was well aware of the pride involved in winning. The medallion was a symbol of superiority that Ian was determined to claim.

"Eyes on your own exams, gentlemen," Professor Carroll scolded at the front of the room.

Niall sucked in a breath and focused on his own work once more. The jolt of being called out—if Professor Carroll was, indeed, singling him out or if others were engaged in the same curiosity—was enough to push Niall through the rest of the examination time. When Professor Carroll finally ordered them to put their pens down, Niall was satisfied that he hadn't completely embarrassed himself. He'd done all right. But the exam was the very last thing he cared about.

"Good old Carroll was trying to fool us with those irregular Greek verbs," Ian boasted as they all gathered their books and satchels and headed to the hall once the exam papers were collected. "I'm certain I translated every one of them perfectly, though."

"Then congratulations are in order," Blake told him with a smile that Niall would have sworn was genuine, if he didn't know better.

Niall and Blake walked shoulder to shoulder down the crowded hallway, brushing up against each other every few steps as they dodged fellow students exiting their exams or rushing off to study sessions. John and David kept their distance, several strides behind. The two knew full well what Niall and Blake had been up to for the past few weeks, and Niall suspected they found it hilarious. Just to show them, Niall kept as close to Blake as possible, risking exposure by touching Blake however he could. It would have been a perfect overture to what Niall knew was coming if Ian hadn't tagged along with them, keeping up at Niall's other side.

"I thought it was devilishly clever of Carroll to include those questions about Thebes as well," Ian blathered on, strutting like a peacock and smirking at Blake, as though Blake couldn't possibly have been ready for the questions. "I'm glad I thought to reread the papers Carroll published about his excavation last year."

"They were far more useful than I expected," Blake agreed.

Ian looked momentarily crestfallen. "You read them too?"

Niall fought to hide his grin as Blake shrugged and said, "Of course. Anyone with any sense reads the papers a professor has written before sitting an exam for a prize he's offering."

Blake looked so cool and calm as he spoke that Niall's heart bounced around his chest. Not only was he handsome and clever and a beautiful singer, Blake could tease a clod like Ian and come off sounding magnanimous.

"I'm certain you'll tell Miss Cannon all about it at supper this evening," Ian grumbled as they passed through the main doorway and out into the unseasonably warm spring day. The sun was shining as it dipped toward the horizon, the roses that had been planted just outside of the building filled the air with gorgeous scent, and everything was green and fresh.

And Blake made it all a thousand times better by saying, "I'm sorry, but I'm not going to be able to make it to supper this evening. I've already sent a note to your mother."

Ian scowled for half a second before his expression brightened to something akin to joy. "You won't be there?"

"No," Blake said. "Other plans." His hand subtly

brushed Niall's, though there was no way Ian could have seen it.

Niall nearly missed a step as his heart thumped and his body heated.

"That's a shame," Ian said, sounding as though it were anything but. "I guess I'll have Miss Cannon all to myself then."

"Looks like you will." Blake smiled at Niall, mischief dancing in his eyes.

"Your loss," Ian snorted. "You know she and I have been getting particularly close lately."

"I'm happy for you," Blake said genuinely.

Ian narrowed his eyes slightly. "She's almost as much of a prize as Professor Carroll's medallion, you know."

"So I've been told. And I'm certain you'll win both." Blake nodded to him, then veered slightly to the right, where a path cut through two of the university's main buildings and headed off campus. "Best of luck to you," he said to Ian. "And Niall, I have a question about the days we're rehearsing next week. Walk with me?"

"Certainly," Niall said, playing his part and looking surprised by the invitation.

Ian frowned and walked on. There wasn't a shred of suspicion in his expression. Niall was certain he and Blake were about to get away with everything.

Blake picked up his pace once they were away from the center of campus. "I almost feel sorry for Ian," he said in a low voice, darting a glance this way and that to assess whether anyone was paying any attention to them. "He wants to win the medallion and marry Miss Cannon so badly it's alarming."

"I know what it's like to want things so badly it's alarming," Niall murmured, unable to keep the grin off his face.

"So do I." Blake lowered his voice to a near whisper.

He grabbed Niall's hand and launched into a run. Niall gasped and then laughed as he stumbled forward, clutching his satchel so it wouldn't fall off his shoulder, and matching Blake's pace. They must have looked like two children dashing along the path, past the cricket pitch, and through the gate that separated the university from the rest of the town. Niall couldn't stop giggling as they ducked and dodged their way around townspeople going about their business or heading home from busy days at work.

He thanked God that Blake's flat was only a handful of blocks from the university. They mounted the stairs to the second floor two at a time, and by the time Blake unlocked his door and grabbed Niall by his necktie to pull him inside, they were already red-faced, sweating, and out of breath.

Blake threw his satchel off his shoulder, letting it drop to the floor as Niall did the same, closed and locked his door, then spun to launch himself at Niall. Their bodies met in an awkward crash as Blake grabbed Niall's face and their mouths collided. Niall groaned deep in his throat, though the sound came out high-pitched and needy, and stumbled backward with the momentum

Blake had started. He kept reeling back until his calves hit the edge of Blake's sofa and they tumbled clumsily across it, but Blake kept kissing his lips, his cheeks, and his neck.

"I want you," Blake growled, nipping at Niall's earlobe as if he knew what he was doing, which Niall suspected he didn't really. "I've wanted you more and more with every letter you sent me. I've saved every one and read them all dozens of times. I want everything you described in those letters and more."

Niall blinked and laughed and panted as Blake tore at the buttons of his jacket while kissing and licking his neck, as he'd said he wanted to do in his letters. "Everything?" he managed to say as he gripped the back and side of the sofa for purchase. "I'll give you everything and then some."

"Good." Blake lifted himself above Niall enough to push at his jacket and waistcoat as though he wanted them gone, then sat up to remove his own jacket. His heated gaze remained fixed on Niall the entire time as he shrugged out of his coat and loosened his tie. "I've been dreaming about being naked and sweaty with you for over a fortnight now."

Niall sighed unsteadily as he toed off his shoes and unbuttoned his cuffs. "I'm tired of just imagining what you look like naked," he said, feeling bolder and fiercer with each passing second.

He could hardly catch his breath as he peeled off his shirt and unfastened his trousers. Blake was undressing at a faster rate than he was, and when he tossed his shirt aside, revealing a perfect, muscular chest with a dusting of dark hair that narrowed to a line that disappeared beneath the waist of his trousers, Niall momentarily forgot what he was doing or where he was.

The look of pure lust in Blake's eyes did nothing to straighten out his thoughts, nor did the way Blake surged into him, knocking him back against the arm of the sofa. Blake kissed him hard, bruising his lips and thrusting his tongue into his mouth as his hands spread across Niall's sides, exploring. Sounds of pleasure that Niall hadn't known he could make ripped out of him as Blake stroked his belly and chest, teasing his nipples. It was so much so suddenly, and it was so good that Niall was in serious danger of losing control within seconds.

That danger only grew more acute as Blake's mouth left his to trail across Niall's neck to his chest. Blake hummed and groaned as if he were the one receiving pleasure instead of giving it as he kissed and licked his way to one of Niall's nipples. The sensation was so amazing that Niall gasped and arched into him, grabbing the back of the sofa with one hand and burying his other in Blake's curly hair.

Blake didn't stop there, though. His hands made quick work finishing with the fastenings of Niall's trousers, then pushing them down. Niall let out a stran-gled sound of bliss as his cock leapt free, straining up against Blake's touch. The intensity of the pleasure he felt was so powerful that he trembled as Blake cupped his balls and brought his mouth to the tip of Niall's prick.

Blake barely had it in his mouth when Niall gasped, "I can't. I'm not going to—"

It was already too late. He came hard in Blake's mouth, arching and moaning as he did. Blake swallowed, his eyes wide, then broke away, panting.

"I'm sorry," Niall panted, going hazy in the post-orgasmic glow, but still pulsing with arousal. "You're just so perfect."

"It's fine," Blake whispered, sliding his way up Niall's body to kiss him. The musky taste of his mouth kept Niall's senses reeling. "You're fine. We're fine." Blake kissed him again, still eager. He fumbled with his own trousers, and Niall sucked in a breath as he felt the bare heat of Blake's cock jerk against his hip. "We're young. What will it take, fifteen minutes until we're ready to go again?"

"If that," Niall panted, throwing his arms around Blake as Blake jerked against him.

A grin teased Niall's lips as Blake kissed him distractedly, clearly more intent on coming than kissing. Niall helped the process along by sliding his hands down Blake's back and slipping his fingers into the cleft of his arse to finger his hole.

That was all it took. With a sharp gasp that turned into a loud groan, hot moisture spread across Niall's belly. Niall closed his eyes and smiled with his whole heart, overcome with the joy of what it all meant. Blake sagged heavily on top of him with a protracted sigh. Their bodies felt so perfect together, chests bared and damp, trousers caught around their thighs, adding an erotic feel to the moment. Niall couldn't stop touching and stroking Blake's arse and back and kissing the side of his face as it rested beside him on the arm of the sofa.

"That was incredible," he said when he could finally manage to form words.

Blake strained to prop himself above Niall by a few inches, gazing into his eyes with fire that was only dimmed, not extinguished. "I want more," he growled, leaning in to kiss Niall so hard it took his breath away. "I want everything you said you'd do in your letters."

"Then we'd better move to your bed," Niall said, one eyebrow arched mischievously.

They spilled off of the sofa, tumbling clumsily to the floor, giggling and giddy in their efforts to shuck their trousers and drawers and hurry into the bedroom. The room and the bed were small, but Niall discovered the sheets were soft and fine as he slipped between them. He reached for Blake, pulling him into his arms. Their legs tangled together and their arms circled each other as they settled on their sides. Niall wanted to touch Blake everywhere at once, and the feeling seemed to be mutual. Everything about the way their bodies fit together was perfection. They couldn't seem to stop kissing each other, as if kissing were a new discovery and they were determined to master it. They both moaned and hummed with abandon as they tasted and explored each other.

Exactly as Blake had predicted, they were both hard again in no time. It was almost a surprise to Niall how eager his cock was. They couldn't keep their hands off each other and laughed as their fingers bumped while trying to stroke and fondle the other. There was nothing organized or planned about the pleasure they gave each other, only the desperation to make each other feel everything they could.

"I want you to fuck me," Blake said at last, breaking away enough to gaze into Niall's eyes with wicked heat. "In the arse," he added, as though that were a necessary detail.

Niall laughed in spite of himself. "God, I want to," he sighed.

"Then do it." Blake wriggled away from him, flipping to his stomach and lifting his backside. "Do it now. I want you inside of me."

Niall laughed harder, stroking Blake's hip and side. "You really are a virgin, aren't you?"

Blake flushed, twisting to sit facing Niall. "In this way, yes."

Niall shook his head and leaned in to kiss him. "Well, my lovely virgin, you can't just go getting fucked in the arse without any sort of preparation." He paused. "I mean, I suppose you could, but it would be painful and awkward."

Blake's determined look of desire faltered. "It would?"

"Would you shove a large parsnip up your dry arsehole?" Niall asked with a sardonic look, one eyebrow raised.

"Maybe?" Blake grinned.

Niall laughed, hiding his face in the pillow for a moment. His heart swelled to the point where it felt like it would burst. He loved Blake, pure and simple.

"Wait here," he said, climbing over Blake and making sure their bodies touched in as many ways as possible before he got out of bed.

He dashed into the main room to fetch his satchel, taking out a jar of lubricant. When he brought it back into the bedroom, Blake gave him a curious look.

"Thank God this was planned," Niall said, sinking back into the bed and unscrewing the jar. "I brought this useful little salve."

"What's it for?" Blake asked, eyes glittering.

Niall sighed fondly. "God, it's going to be such a pleasure to teach you everything you need to know." His heart thumped faster and his balls ached as he added, "Roll over."

Blake did as he was told, then sucked in a hard breath as Niall spread a generous dollop of the salve over his hole. "Fuck," he hissed as Niall fingered him.

"If you really want this, you have to relax," Niall said, using his most authoritative director's voice. "You have to let go and accept it. Let me in, no matter how alarming it feels at first."

"God, you're making me want it even more," Blake panted. "That feels so good."

Niall had added a second finger to his teasing, giving Blake a taste of what was to come as he worked to help him loosen up. The entire process was enthralling and, perhaps paradoxically, filled him with a soul-deep tenderness. The level of trust Blake was showing him in baring himself so thoroughly was astounding. The way he lifted his hips and parted his legs farther on Niall's instructions, panting and making sounds of pleasure as Niall invaded him had Niall's throat tight with emotion.

"I'm close," Blake said plaintively after a few minutes. "So close. You'd better—"

Niall didn't let him finish his sentence. He was hard as iron himself, and after slicking his cock with the salve, he positioned himself behind Blake and pushed in fast, before Blake could change his mind.

They both groaned loudly as their bodies joined. Blake was so tight that it was almost impossible for Niall to go slowly instead of pounding into him until he found his own release, which wouldn't take long.

"Are you all right," he panted, arching over Blake's back to embrace him as much as he could.

"God, yes," Blake said, desperation and pleasure in his voice. "It feels...it feels...."

Niall started moving in earnest when Blake was at a loss for words. He finished the sentence for himself as his balls tightened and his body prepared to burst deep inside of Blake. It felt like paradise.

He picked up his pace, but it was only a few seconds

before Blake moaned, "Fuck, Niall," and came on the sheets.

Niall felt the contraction that racked Blake and made a sound of victory and pleasure. That sound continued as he rode on, reaching for the bliss that was within his reach, then exploding with it. He emptied himself inside of Blake, but quickly lost the strength to go on. He pulled away and collapsed to the side, which was fine, as far as he was concerned, because in that moment, all he wanted to do was hold Blake.

"God, I love you," Blake said breathlessly, twisting to his side and drawing Niall into his arms. "That was everything."

Niall's eyes went wide in spite of his overwrought senses as he embraced Blake in turn and met his kiss with surprise and passion. "I love you too," he managed between kisses, wondering how his life could have turned out so perfectly when so many odds were stacked against him.

"I want to do that again," Blake panted as the energy drained from both of them, leaving them unable to even kiss as they lay tangled in each other.

Niall laughed, touching his forehead to Blake's. "I love how eager you are," he said, stroking the side of Blake's face.

"This is all new to me," Blake whispered in return. "I want as much of it as possible. I want you as much as possible."

"And you'll have me," Niall smiled tenderly. His

tenderness shifted to teasing. "So much that we'll both walk around in a constant state of exhaustion, if we're not too sore to be capable of walking."

"It'll be the best kind of exhaustion and the best kind of soreness," Blake insisted, kissing him and rolling Niall to his back. "And it will last for the rest of our lives."

CHAPTER 8

What followed was the most blissful fortnight of Niall's life. Unashamed, unapologetic, he spent every night in Blake's bed. They had to make excuses, miss pressing engagements, and ignore previous commitments, but every night ended with them breathless and spent in each other's arms. Even when evening rehearsals for the play began as the performance date drew near, they found a way to end up naked and transported in each other's arms.

That didn't mean the letters stopped, though. Every afternoon, Niall penned a new love letter, detailing everything the two of them explored together in lurid detail, and every evening he'd receive an equally lurid reply. They started reading their letters aloud to each other once they were finally alone and in bed, late into the night, and acting out their wildest fantasies with each other.

By the day of the play's one and only performance, Niall knew they'd crossed into dangerous territory.

"We should practice our kiss," Blake said with a rakish, sideways look as they sat side by side in front of the mirrors that had been set up in the dressing room they shared backstage.

"I thought that's what we've been doing all week," Niall answered with a coquettish flicker of one eyebrow. "John and David think we're ridiculous."

"I don't care what your friends think. We haven't gotten kissing quite right yet." Blake grinned, pivoting to face him on his stool. He slid his hand along Niall's thigh, dipping to brush the spot where more than one bright red mark stood out against the pale skin near Niall's balls beneath the skirt he wore.

Niall failed to hide his giggle as he thanked heaven the heavy skirt of his costume did far more to hide his excited state than trousers ever could. He wasn't one to dress in drag, but he could suddenly see how it had its advantages. Blake's costume was far less concealing.

"We should probably run those lines one last time, just to be sure," Niall said in a playfully sensual voice.

Blake stood, extending a hand to help Niall to his feet. "Come, my darling. Let us celebrate our union instead of denying it. Let all the kingdom celebrate with us."

Niall sagged easily into Blake's arms, slanting his mouth over his and indulging in a kiss that was absolute madness, considering the dressing room door stood open behind them. He couldn't help but sigh as Blake's tongue danced with his. Blake's taste was so familiar to him now. He knew every contour of Blake's body, but still couldn't get enough. He circled a hand around Blake's waist and let it drop to his backside—a backside that was now very limber and used to intimate invasion.

"How much time do we have before places are called?" Blake whispered against his cheek as he moved to kiss Niall's neck, as he loved to do. He loved it so much that Niall had had to starch his collars and conceal the evidence with stage make-up in the last few weeks.

Blake's question was answered by the approach of heavy footsteps, and a moment later, Paul stuck his head into the room to ask, "Do you want to lead us through vocal warm-ups? Because Ian just told me that the lobby is already crowded with people eager to see the play."

"That's a good idea," Niall said breathlessly. He'd leapt out of Blake's arms well before Paul caught a glimpse of him, but he was overheated and knew he looked as guilty as sin all the same.

"I'll let the rest of the cast know," Paul said. He leaned away, then his face pinched slightly as he stepped forward again. "You may want to fix your lip rouge before you leave this room. It's a little obvious what you'd been up to."

"We aren't up to anything," Blake said, a little too quickly.

Paul merely laughed and stepped away, into the hall.

A moment later, they heard his voice call, "Vocal warm-ups on the stage, now."

Niall's heart beat in his throat, and it was all he could do to swallow it and gather his wits for the job ahead of him. It didn't help that when he turned back to Blake, Blake's lip rouge was smeared. He darted a look in the mirror to discover that his was just as messy.

"He's right," he sighed, reaching for a square of cloth to wipe his mouth, then started over with the make-up. "It is obvious."

Blake swore under his breath and leaned toward the mirror, hurriedly cleaning himself up and reapplying his own make-up.

Niall sighed as he touched a brush with a feminine shade of rogue to his lips. "We can't keep this a secret indefinitely, Blake. Too many people know the truth already."

"We have to keep it a secret," Blake said in a dangerously flat voice, staring straight ahead into the mirror.

"Secrets have a way of getting out, whether you want them to or not," Niall insisted.

"We'll just have to deny everything."

Niall put down his rogue brush so fast it clattered across the table. "You want to deny everything?" His voice was pitched too high and his chest squeezed in fear.

Blake sighed and lowered his head for a moment. "No," he said, finishing with his lips then tossing his brush aside. He straightened and faced Niall. "I don't *want* to deny anything," he said in a soft, strained voice.

He peeked past Niall to the open doorway. The sounds of warm-ups starting drifted down the hall. "I *want* to spend the rest of my life with you, but how are we going to do that?"

"We'll find a way," Niall said, resting a hand on Blake's cheek. He took a breath, steeling his courage, not for the performance that was about to happen, but for the impossible task that they'd have on their hands once that was over. "It's been done before, you know. Plenty of times. Men like us lead perfectly normal lives together. Quiet, unobtrusive lives."

"Do you really think either of us is destined to a lead quiet, unobtrusive life?" Blake asked with a grin.

"Niall! Blake! Are you coming?" Paul's voice boomed from the hall.

"As frequently as possible," Niall answered with a teasing flicker of his eyebrow before turning and heading out of the room.

Blake followed him. They were all smiles and excitement, joining the rest of the cast on the stage to warm up, but Niall felt an uncomfortable tension underneath their high spirits that hadn't been there before. The moment had come. The play was on. And as soon as it was over, he and Blake would have to face the thing they had spent the last month not talking about, not thinking about, and not considering. Decisions would have to be made.

As soon as their warm-up was finished, the house was opened and the buzz of dozens of people taking their seats slowly grew to a nerve-rattling crescendo.

"How many tickets did we sell to this show?" Ian asked as the cast paced restlessly across the stage, the full impact of what they were doing hitting Niall square in the chest.

"I heard that we sold out," Morton said with a huge smile. "It was all my doing, of course. Half the ladies of York wanted to come see the show once they heard I was the lead chorister."

A few of his friends laughed. Even Niall found it within him to laugh.

"I know my father and mother and Edward are here, and so are the Cannons," Ian said, sidling up to Niall's side as though they were the best of friends. "And your parents too, Stanley."

Niall whipped to face Blake, his eyes widening and his breath catching in his throat. "Your parents are here?" he asked in a strangled voice.

"They arrived in York the day before yesterday," Blake confessed, looking guilty.

"It's a shame that they had to stay with Lord and Lady Fairport instead of my parents," Ian said, chin tilted up in victory. "I'm certain your father would have loved to make Mr. Cannon's acquaintance."

"The Cannons were at Lord Fairport's most of yesterday," Blake said, fiddling anxiously with the cuff of his costume, then humming a few bars of his first solo.

Ian's face fell, but so did Niall's. "Your parents were taking tea with the Fairports and the Cannons yesterday?" he asked. While the two of them had been buggering each other senseless all afternoon.

Blake sent him a sheepish look. "We were busy studying, otherwise I would have mentioned something."

Niall met his eyes warily, anxiety pooling in his stomach.

"What were you studying for?" Ian asked. "Exams were finished yesterday morning."

"Places," the stage manager called, sending the roaming cast scattering to their places like mice with a cat thrown into the room. "Places, please."

Ian's question remained unanswered as he and Blake broke away from Niall to wait in the wings on the other side of the stage. As the orchestra finished tuning and launched into the opening notes of the overture, Paul stepped up behind Niall and thumped his shoulder.

"You are so fucked," he laughed. Coming from the only other member of the cast dressed as a woman, the comment had a bizarre feel to it.

"I don't know what you're talking about," Niall muttered, counting through the bars of the overture in his head and glancing across the stage to meet Blake's luminous eyes.

"He's going to be a duke, Niall," Paul said, not unkindly. "You're going to be a world-famous playwright."

Niall twisted to face him, choosing to focus on the least painful thing Paul said. "You really think I'm going to be world-famous?"

Paul laughed and shook his head, but there was far too much sympathy in his look for Niall's comfort. "You're good, Niall. You're great. You haven't let on to any of us, but I know for a fact you've invited at least a dozen theater managers and theatrical financiers from London to attend tonight's performance, and they're all here."

Niall's face went hot as the orchestra finished the overture and the curtains opened for the opening number, sung by Morton and his chorus.

"Tonight, the play," Paul whispered in his ear, just loud enough to be heard over the song. "Tomorrow, graduation. The day after that, London. You'll be leaving him as surely as he'll be leaving you, make no mistake."

"There's nothing between Blake and I," Niall hissed. "You're all just inventing things because we act so well together onstage."

"Right," Paul said, utterly unconvinced. "And I'm the King of Siam."

There wasn't time for anything else. The opening number ended, leading straight into Blake and Ian's entrance.

"What news, Reinhold?" Blake recited in his beautiful voice. "How did we fare in the wars?"

Niall swallowed hard and watched Blake, seeing nothing but the charm in his smile and the masculine lines of his body. He loved Blake with his whole heart, with his soul. Blake was everything to him. That had to be enough. Paul was wrong. This wasn't the end just because the show would be over soon. He would be in London, Paul was right, but future dukes spent time in London as well. Plenty of time. So what if they had to spend some time apart from each other? Nothing could keep them apart indefinitely. They would be able to make a life together, Niall was certain of it. Blake loved him and he loved Blake. That was all that mattered.

The play was a smashing success. Niall knew it from the moment he stepped on stage and delivered his first, sad soliloquy. He could feel the energy of the audience, knew that they were fully engaged in what they were seeing. They laughed whenever they were supposed to and applauded vigorously at the Act One finale. The chatter between acts was full of energy, and when the curtain rose on Act Two, the audience applauded in expectation of what they were going to see. It was everything he, as the author, could have asked for and more.

But the entire second act felt like a death march to the single moment of truth between him and Blake. By the time they reached the kiss, his heart was racing and sweat had broken out on his back.

"My heart rejoices to be the bride of such a valiant and noble prince," Niall said his line as he'd written it, clasping Blake's hands and looking into his eyes with what had been campy adoration up until that point. Before Blake could continue with his response, Niall rushed on with an ad lib. "My heart will always be yours, no matter how much time passes, no matter what distances come between us, and no matter how the fates conspire against us."

Blake's mouth hung open for a moment. Disbelief shone in his face, and if Niall wasn't mistaken, sadness glowed there also.

It all happened in the blink of an eye. It was going to end, and there was nothing Niall could do to stop it.

"Come, my darling," Blake grasped for his line, skipping several in the process. "Let us celebrate our union instead of denying it. Let all the kingdom celebrate with us."

Before Niall or anyone else could react, he grabbed Niall by his upper arms and crashed into him with a kiss that was a thousand times too bold for the audience they had. Niall made a sound deep in his throat that sounded very much like a whimper, but it was drowned out by the laughter of the audience. They thought the kiss was comedic, and a few people even applauded.

When Blake stepped away as the orchestra launched into the finale, Niall felt as though he were drowning. He shook his head and put on a wide smile, falling back into character. This couldn't be the end. He was simply being maudlin because so much was at stake for him with the play. Of course he and Blake would find a way to be together. Hadn't they spent the last several weeks telling each other how much they loved one another, how nothing could come between them? Hadn't they shared their bodies and their hearts in the most intimate way? Everything would be all right, he was certain of it.

The curtain closed to a flurry of applause and cheers. It opened again, allowing them to take their bows and receive a standing ovation. Blake received an extra round of applause, then pulled Niall forward as the entire cast applauded him. The cheers from the audience should have bolstered his spirits. That should have been the happiest moment of his life. He knew his career was made, knew it without having to talk to a single one of the London theater crowd who had come for the show.

"I don't think I've seen such a fantastic debut in all my days," the owner of one of London's most prominent theaters said, proving Niall right, once the performance was done and the cast had dispersed into the lobby to greet their guests and friends. Niall hadn't even changed out of his feminine costume, though he'd dispensed with the wig. John and David had joined him the moment he'd stepped into the hall and whisked him toward the men from London.

"It was a brilliant piece," another man, a critic, if Niall remembered correctly, agreed. "Do you have any thoughts of expanding it into a full-length play for next season?"

"Or of writing something else that I could stage?" a third man asked.

"I have several ideas in progress," Niall answered, flattered and beaming.

"This man is going to make you all wealthy," John said, slapping a hand on Niall's back.

Niall tried to smile at his friend's comment, but his

125

attention was shattered by a cry of delight from the group standing only a few feet from him—a group that contained Blake and his family, the Archibalds, and the Cannons. Niall's heart dropped to his feet when an older man, who bore a strong resemblance to Blake, shifted Blake to stand next to Annamarie Cannon. That group applauded. Blake smiled and nodded modestly, but then he sent a look of shock and horror to Niall.

"Excuse me," Niall said to his theatrical admirers, his voice so hoarse the words came out as a croak. "I have to see about something."

He stepped away from the London crowd. David's face fell in an instant, as though he could see what was coming, though John continued to chat with the theater people. Niall's hands shook as he moved closer to the circle forming around Blake and Miss Cannon. He had only a fraction of a second to notice that Ian looked livid before Mr. Archibald said, "I'm sure you'll want to tell your friend the happy news." He eyed Niall's gown with a smirk.

Niall swallowed hard, his throat going dry. "Happy news?"

"Yes," Mr. Archibald said, beaming at Blake and Miss Cannon.

Niall's head swam and his vision blurred at the edges as Blake glanced to him, looking as though he might scream.

"Congratulations are in order," Blake said, his voice rough and jagged. "I'm engaged to Miss Cannon."

CHAPTER 9

*N*iall waited, gaping. He stared hard at Blake, mouth dropping open slightly. Any moment now, Blake would laugh and lower his head bashfully, explaining that there had been some sort of mistake. He barely knew Annamarie Cannon and couldn't possibly be expected to marry her. Especially when his heart, soul, and body belonged to someone else.

Blake's smile remained in place, as brittle as it was. He met Niall's eyes with a shattering look of apology and pain. Niall continued to wait for Blake to deny the engagement and to step away from Miss Cannon, but she held his arm as though it were a trophy and beamed at him with an avaricious gleam in her eyes.

It was Ian who snapped, "This can't be possible. You're barely twenty. And you hardly know Annamarie."

Niall realized he was holding his breath when

everyone but Blake turned their attention to Ian. Blake didn't seem to be able to look away.

"Son, be a good sport," Mr. Archibald said in a low voice, stepping closer to Ian as if he would take his son aside for a private word.

"After everything we've shared?" Ian demanded on Miss Cannon.

Niall's eyes went wide and he glared at Blake as though asking the same question.

Miss Cannon lowered her head, blushing. She sent Ian an apologetic look, then shrugged slightly.

Niall tasted bile in his throat. Not only was Blake taking his sweet time to deny the engagement, he was stuck to a woman who most definitely didn't care a whit about him, only his title.

"The Cannons are only in England for a short while," Blake's father, Lord Selby, said, as regal as his title warranted. "Time was of the essence in securing the match. Which means, of course, that the wedding will be held before the end of the month."

Niall choked and started to cough. The end of the month was less than a fortnight, less than half the amount of time that he and Blake had known and loved each other.

"Are you well?" Lady Selby asked, frowning curiously at Niall. "It was a lovely show, by the way. It's such a shame that there was only one performance. You certainly brought out the best in my son."

"Excuse me," Niall croaked, turning away from the

group, unable to stand it for a moment longer. "Water," he said vaguely, then raised a hand to his mouth as he coughed again for show.

He headed for the auditorium door, breaking into a jog. John and David turned away from their conversation as he went. John tried to follow, but David grabbed his arm to stop him when Blake stepped away from his group.

"Niall," Blake called after him.

Niall heard Blake say something indistinct before the sound of his footsteps followed him into the auditorium. All but a handful of people had decamped to the hall, leaving the space feeling more empty than usual. The curtains had been opened on the medieval set, which a handful of students were already deconstructing to make way for commencement activities the next day. Niall ignored all of them, picking up the skirts of his ridiculous costume and hurrying down the aisle to the stairs.

"Niall, wait," Blake shouted, catching up to him quickly and grabbing his arm.

Niall stumbled as he reached the stairs leading to the stage. Blake grasped him with both hands to keep him from falling. Their eyes met, though Niall's stung with tears. Blake's eyes, too, were glassier than usual. For a moment, they stood there, nearly in each other's arms.

"This is a joke, right?" Niall asked at last, his voice hoarse. "Tell me this is all just some fancy of your father's and that you're going to march out there and set him straight."

"I—" Blake's mouth hung open for a moment after the single, strangled syllable, then he shut it and sighed.

"No," Niall said, spiraling into a sob. "No."

"I don't have a choice," Blake whispered, voice shaking.

"You always have a choice. We always have a choice."

"You don't under—"

"You utter swine," Ian growled, catching up to the two of them so fast that Niall felt as though his soul might leave his body.

Blake jumped away from Niall, whipping to face Ian. "What do you want?"

"I should challenge you to pistols at dawn." Ian charged down the aisle and right up to Blake until the two of them stood toe to toe. "Annamarie is mine."

"I had nothing to do with this," Blake said, holding up his hands in defense and blinking fast, the color leaving his face.

"You always have to be the best, don't you?" Ian went on, moving in on Blake and forcing him to step back until he nearly toppled over Niall.

Niall had to raise his arms and plant his hands on Blake's back to stop Ian from railroading them both. The touch was like fire, but he didn't want to let go. Ever.

"Believe me," Blake said with a wry, almost mad laugh. "Marrying Annamarie Cannon was not my idea."

"Of course it was," Ian snapped. "You had to upstage me and win the lead in this stupid musical, and you had to steal the woman I wanted."

"If I could give her to you, I would," Blake said, voice hollow. "Believe me."

"I don't believe you." Ian raised his voice. "You always have to come out on top, don't you? You have to be the most charming, the best at athletics, the darling of our professors."

"You have the wrong end of the stick," Blake insisted, growing more agitated. "This is *not* what I want." He glanced over his shoulder to Niall as he spoke, emotions intense in his eyes. "I don't want Miss Cannon."

"Horse shit," Ian shouted. Blake jerked back to stare at him, eyes wide. Even Niall was startled by the vehemence of Ian's curse. "If you didn't want her, then why did you fawn all over her and engage her in conversation so much these last few weeks?"

Niall pulled his hands away from Blake's back and retreated up two steps. Had he flirted with Miss Cannon?

Blake's mouth worked wordlessly for a moment and he glanced to Niall before looking back at Ian to answer, "I was being polite, gentlemanly."

"And was it gentlemanly of you to accompany Miss Cannon while she sang?" Ian demanded.

"I was asked to accompany her," Blake defended himself, twisting to meet Niall's eyes. "It wasn't my idea."

"You could have just played one or two songs for her." Ian took another step toward Blake, forcing him to back up again. Niall retreated to the top of the stairs.

"You didn't have to spend half an hour performing an entire concert with her."

"She wouldn't let me stop," Blake insisted. "No one else there that evening could play."

"*I* can play the piano," Ian shouted, poking his chest with a rigid finger. "I can do anything you can do."

"Then why didn't you do it?" Blake rounded on him with a sudden burst of anger. "Why didn't you step up and capture Miss Cannon's attention so that she wanted nothing to do with me?"

"Because you're going to be a bloody duke, you gilded piece of shit," Ian shouted. "How am I supposed to compete with that?"

A heavy silence fell as Ian glared at Blake, chest heaving with fury. Somewhere, underneath his own heartache, Niall felt sorry for Ian.

"I love her," Ian said, his energy draining. Misery pinched his face as anger left it. "How am I supposed to watch her marry someone else?"

A sob escaped from Niall before he could swallow it. Blake turned to him, a look of devastating guilt in his eyes. It was more than Niall could stand to see. He spun away, racing across the stage to the wings, highly conscious of the curious stares of the students breaking down the set. The world of the play that had been intact half an hour before was now disjointed and jumbled, with painted canvases of castles and gardens resting on their sides or already stacked for storage.

"Niall, wait." Blake shot after him again.

Niall clenched his jaw and squeezed his stinging eyes shut for a moment as he dodged discarded props and set pieces on his way to the hall leading to the dressing rooms. Some of the chorus members were loitering there, changed back into their ordinary clothes, their make-up removed. They laughed and drank bottles of beer, but Niall avoided them all when they tried to get him to join their merriment.

"Stop," Blake called after him, catching up once Niall dashed into the dressing room they'd shared. "Just stop and talk to me for a moment." Blake turned to shut and lock the door behind him.

"It appears as though there's nothing to talk about," Niall said, voice hoarse, barely able to get the words out. He crossed to the far end of the room, reaching behind him to tug at the fastenings of his costume.

"There is everything to talk about," Blake insisted, approaching him with arms outstretched, his heart clearly on his sleeve. "I love you."

Niall eyed him warily and turned his back as he shrugged out of his costume's bodice.

"I love you," Blake repeated, louder. "Don't you dare ever doubt that."

"It's rather hard not to doubt when I've just been asked to congratulate you on your upcoming nuptials." Niall's voice shook as he spoke.

"I don't want to marry Miss Cannon," Blake shouted in frustration, glancing plaintively at the ceiling before letting his arms and shoulders drop.

"Then don't marry her." Niall whipped around to face Blake, stepping out of his costume entirely and kicking it aside as he did. He was left in nothing but his drawers and socks, chest heaving painfully.

Blake had the audacity to rake him with a hungry look, but one that held as much hopelessness as desire. "I have to," he said, his voice cracking.

"You don't have to do anything you don't want to," Niall insisted, peeling his socks off and stepping right up to Blake. "You are your own man. Live your own life."

"I have a duty to my family." Blake twisted his head away, unable to look Niall in the eyes as he spoke. "I have a responsibility to the title."

"Miss Cannon doesn't love you. I do." Niall's voice dropped to a dangerous timbre.

"And I love you," Blake said weakly, dragging himself to meet Niall's eyes. The words were ringing hollower and hollower as defeat clouded Blake's expression.

"You are not some trinket to be bartered on the marriage market, Blake," Niall growled. "You are a man of strength and talent. You could have whatever life you wanted. The nobility isn't what it used to be. You could ignore your title and come to London to make a name for yourself on the stage, I know you could."

Blake shook his head with an agonized half-smile. He blinked, and tears spilled down his cheeks. "No, I can't. Nobility still means something to those stuck in it. I have no choice in the matter at all. The Cannons have money and our estate is failing. I'm going to be a duke." He shrugged. Niall had never seen him look or sound so lost. "What would people say if I abandoned everything I am destined for to run away with my male lover?"

"They'd say that you chose love over fortune." Niall gripped the sides of Blake's face. "They'd say you are a hero."

Blake shook and lowered his head, letting out a gasping breath. Tears fell on the doublet of his costume. "They'd say I was a pervert and a disgrace. They would throw me in jail, or worse."

"Do you really care so much what people say?" Niall asked in a whisper.

Blake peeked up and met his eyes with horrible sheepishness. It shot through Niall's heart like a poison arrow.

"I love you," Niall hissed.

He didn't wait for a reply. He jerked into Blake, grabbing a handful of hair at the back of Blake's head and slamming his mouth over his, kissing him with all the frustration and anger that boiled within him. He kissed Blake with the fire of love and desperation, forcing Blake's lips apart and thrusting his tongue as if he could claim what was his through action where words had failed.

Blake whimpered in surrender and threw his arms around Niall. "I'm sorry, I'm sorry," he panted, leaning his forehead against Niall's and gulping for breath.

"I don't accept it," Niall growled, ripping at the buttons of Blake's costume. "You don't want that woman.

You don't want anyone but me." And he intended to prove it.

He tore through Blake's buttons and shoved the doublet off his shoulders. He wore nothing underneath, so Niall was able to run his hands freely and possessively across Blake's chest and sides as soon as they were uncovered. He slammed into Blake with another kiss that pulled a moan of longing from Blake's lungs. Their affair had gone on long enough that Niall knew exactly where and how to kiss and touch him in a way that would drive him mad. He dug his nails into Blake's back, causing him to gasp, then drown that gasp with his mouth.

Passion and pain drove him on. He pushed Blake back toward the worn sofa against the wall. Blake moved as though under a spell, tear-reddened eyes half-lidded and mouth open as Niall reached for the fastenings of Blake's trousers. He made quick work of those, shoving them and Blake's drawers over his hips and thighs. A rush of victory and fury hit Niall as Blake's cock sprung to life, proving that even in the middle of a tragedy, he could still make Blake hard.

"I won't let you give this up," Niall hissed, pushing Blake onto the sofa when they reached it. He grabbed the fabric of Blake's trousers and pulled them off. Blake sagged against the sofa with an erotic combination of surrender and need. Niall tore off his drawers, freeing his aching erection, then climbed over Blake. "I won't let you cast aside everything between us."

"I can't—" Blake started.

Niall drowned his protest with a punishing kiss. Blake groaned into his mouth as Niall pressed their bodies together. He jerked his hips against Blake's, rubbing their hard pricks together. It felt powerful and perfect, and it made Niall's chest ache with misery.

He shifted his mouth to Blake's neck, kissing and biting him and doing everything he could to leave a mark. He didn't care how awkward it would be for Blake to explain to his precious family or his wealthy fiancée what the marks were or how he'd gotten them. If he could have, Niall would have marked Blake permanently as his. He would have marked him as a coward.

"I love you," he growled, shifting lower and teasing one of Blake's nipples with his tongue. He gripped Blake's hip hard with one hand while balancing himself with the other. "You can't tell me you don't want this, you don't want me."

"I want you," Blake groaned, then gasped as Niall reached between his spread legs to grip his balls possessively. The sound Blake made was half pain, half pleasure, but Niall couldn't bring himself to feel a shred of remorse for being too rough. He wanted Blake to feel him in a way he would never forget.

There was no way it could be entirely adequate, but Niall spit on his hand, slicking himself as best he could, then grabbed Blake's hips and tilted them up. He thrust into Blake's arse, wincing at the resistance and at the cry that ripped from Blake.

"You're mine," he hissed, panting with frustration

and pleasure as he fucked Blake hard and fast. "You will always be mine."

Blake answered with a sound of pleasure that was so erotic Niall nearly came right then and there. He forced himself not to and slowed down, intent on enjoying the bittersweet, painful moment for as long as he could. It was the last time he would ever feel Blake's skin against his, after all, the last time he would ever hear his lover's sensual cries as their bodies joined. In spite of everything, in spite of what Niall knew full well was cruelty on his part, Blake was clearly consumed with pleasure as they rocked together, tangled and twisted. His cock was hot in Niall's hand when he reached for it, in spite of the awkward angle of their joining. Blake's desperate sounds reached a higher and higher pitch until he erupted in Niall's hand, the jolt in his body throbbing through Niall.

Niall couldn't hold out any longer. With a guttural cry of his own, he came hard, deep inside of Blake. It was a victory that faded much too fast as the passion of the moment waned and he sagged over Blake. He wanted to stay inside of Blake forever, but it was too much, too awkward. He shifted so that he covered Blake's over-heated, sweating body with his own, and they lay in each other's arms, catching their breaths, until the hopeless-ness of the situation settled over them like a shroud.

"I love you," Niall panted, all energy leaving him. Tears stung his eyes. He nestled his forehead against the side of Blake's head.

"God, I love you," Blake echoed with a sob. His arms closed around Niall's damp back.

Niall lifted himself with the last of his energy to gaze down at Blake. "Then run away with me."

Blake's face twisted with guilt and grief, and he turned his head to the side. Tears squeezed out of his eyes when he closed them.

Niall pushed back farther. "You won't," he said, then sat up between Blake's spread legs. "You won't give up your so-called destiny for me."

"I can't," Blake wept. He covered his face with his hands for a moment as his shoulders shook. Then he took a deep, sharp breath and moved his hands away, staring up at Niall with a new spark of bitterness. "You don't understand what it's like. You've never had this kind of responsibility on your shoulders."

"You have a brother," Niall argued, though his heart wasn't in it anymore. "If it's the Cannon money you need, let Montague marry her."

"I can't abide what people would think of me, Niall. I'm not as strong as you are."

Blake's words left a bitter taste in Niall's mouth. He jerked away, swallowing hard. "I love you," he growled, as if it were a curse, and stood. Every part of him felt as though it were turning to cold stone as he stared down at Blake, splayed, naked and defenseless, slick with sweat and sex. "I will never love anyone other than you," he managed to choke out.

"Niall, I—"

"But I will never forgive you for this," Niall cut him off.

He turned away before Blake could say anything else, retreating to the far end of the room to dress in the ordinary clothes of his ordinary life. Nothing would ever feel extraordinary for him again.

CHAPTER 10

The deep, bitter gloom that settled over Niall as soon as he cleaned up, dressed, and fled the dressing room, leaving Blake behind without a word as he, too, cleaned up, stayed with him through the night. Once the heat of passion cooled and the sting of surprise faded, he was left with nothing but a gaping hole in his chest where Blake had been ripped out of his heart.

He was grateful that he'd managed to secure a single room in his dormitory. With the door locked tight, no one could see him weep his way through the night, curled into a ball on his bed, not even bothering to change out of his rumpled and messy clothes. The scent of Blake and sex lingered on him, and he was loath to let it go. He wanted to smell Blake on him always, to feel the heat of his body and taste the salt of his skin against his tongue for as long as he could. He wanted to hear the sound of

141

Blake's laughter and his singing in everything around him. He wanted his prick to throb with Blake's touch for the rest of his life, even if that meant he had to walk around in a state of arousal every day. He didn't think he could bear it if his sensual memories of Blake faded into hazy nostalgia, like he knew they were destined to.

By morning, after barely any sleep, his head pounding, his eyes sore, and his mouth dry, Niall was beginning to have second thoughts. The pain was too acute. The rage at having the most precious thing he'd ever known ripped away from him—and by Blake's own hands—was too much. He wanted nothing to do with a man who could toss aside love so cavalierly, without even trying to find an alternative way to be together. He wanted Blake erased from his memory forever.

He pushed himself out of bed, lurching toward his desk and throwing open the top drawer. The letters he'd received from Blake were all there, tied with a sentimental pink ribbon. He yanked the bundle out of the drawer and stumbled over to the fireplace. The fire had gone out during the night, so he poked at the embers, added kindling and coals to the heap, then went to work with a tinder box, relighting the flames.

The task took long enough that by the time he snatched up the bundle of Blake's letters again, he was having second thoughts. He stared at the bundle, his throat squeezing and tears threatening to fall all over again. For all he knew, the lurid scene in the dressing room the night before was the last time he would ever speak to Blake, ever see him, even. Did he really want to destroy every beautiful thing his lover had ever written to him, now that things had ended?

He sat there, glaring at the bundle of letters until he lost track of time. The fire heated the room to a sweltering degree, but the sweat that dripped down Niall's back seemed only fitting.

When a knock sounded at his door, Niall jumped.

"Cristofori, get up," John's voice sounded through the barrier. "You're going to be late for commencement."

Niall dragged himself to his feet when John knocked again instead just going away. With a deep scowl, he opened the door.

John didn't seem at all surprised to see him in a terrible state. His friend sighed sympathetically, pity in his eyes. "You owe me and David a favor," he said.

Niall's frown turned to confusion. "What? Why?" His words came out rough and weak.

"That little scene you played out with Blake in the dressing room last night." John lowered his voice and glanced up and down the hall to make sure they weren't being observed. "You were loud as fuck. Lord Selby came looking for his son, and it was everything David and I could do to get rid of him and keep the hall clear until the two of you had it out."

Niall's face burned hot and he glanced away, too embarrassed to meet John's eyes.

John surprised him by clapping a hand to his shoulder. "I'm sorry," he said. "I didn't realize you thought there could actually be something more. I thought you knew it was futile."

Niall swallowed hard and forced himself to meet John's eyes. "I was a fool," he croaked.

"Aren't we all?" John squeezed his shoulder, then reached into the inside pocket of his jacket. "If it makes you feel any better, he asked me to give you this."

Niall's chest squeezed as John handed him a letter addressed in Blake's neat hand. He took it, staring dumbly at it.

"Read it and hurry along," John said, backing away. "You really are going to be late for the commencement ceremony." He paused, sending Niall another deeply sympathetic look. "Go to the ceremony, get your degree, then get the hell out of here. London and greatness are waiting for you, me, and David. You don't need all this holding you back."

"No," Niall said, though whether in agreement or in protest, he couldn't tell.

He shut the door and leaned against it, staring at Blake's letter. Part of him wanted to throw it into the fire without reading it. It could only contain an apology, and Niall didn't want to hear it. His heart wasn't just broken, it was obliterated. He'd never thought he would love anyone the way he loved Blake, and he knew he would never love anyone like that again. What apology could possibly make up for that sort of devastation?

Time truly was wasting, though, and as he crossed to pour water from the pitcher on his wash table into a basin to bathe, he broke down and opened the letter.

It began without an introduction. "*I love you. I don't know what else I can say. I love you and I'm sorry. But mostly, I love you. I always will. Nothing and no one can change that. I love you.*"

A large, empty space took up the bottom half of the page, like a long, ponderous pause. Then, written at the very bottom of the page in a ragged hand, ink smeared, was, "*I love you.*"

Niall sobbed as he folded the letter and stuffed it back in its envelope. With shaking hands, he untied the bundle and rested Blake's final letter on top of the others before retying the ribbon. With that done, he dragged himself to his wardrobe and fetched his traveling bag from the top. He took the case to the bed and opened it, then tossed the bundle of letters inside. There would be time to pack for London later, but it felt achingly poignant and fitting to slam the case shut with the letters inside.

He shaved and dressed as quickly as he could, not caring what he looked like. If anyone noted how ragged he looked, he could blame it on a late night after the play. No one would question him. No one would possibly guess at the reason for his bloodshot eyes or the circles under them. He could say he'd been out carousing with the theater people from London. He could tell them he'd gone drinking and whoring with his cast mates. He could tell anyone anything, and they would likely believe him. Only he and Blake would ever know the truth.

The commencement ceremony was already underway by the time he made it to the auditorium. He was forced to slip in through the back door as the underclassmen serving as ushers glared at him. His graduating class sat to one side of the room, and there was no way for him not to draw attention to himself as he hurried down the aisle to take a seat with them. John and David craned their necks to watch him, nodding when their eyes met. As soon as he was settled, he hunched into his seat and prayed for the ceremony to be over. For once in his life, he was grateful that he wouldn't be called up on stage. It was bad enough when his name was called out as a graduate, along with the rest of his class.

When Blake's name was announced, agony seized him. Blake sat several rows in front of him and looked straight forward. The bastard smiled as jovially as he always did. He sat straight and wore his graduation gown as though it were royal vestments. Niall could just make out his profile. He knew every curve and every line of Blake's face. He knew the way Blake's jaw felt in his hand, knew the shape of his lips against his own. He knew the tiny lines that formed around Blake's eyes when he smiled from his heart and knew the way his nostrils flared when he was about to come. It was clear as day to him that, underneath the bright smile, Blake was miserable. But that only made Niall's heart break more.

"And now to announce the winners of this semester's academic competitions," the dean said from the podium on the stage. "We'll begin with the Classics exam. Professor Carroll." The dean turned to the row of faculty sitting behind him and gestured for Professor Carroll to come forward.

Niall had forgotten about the exam. It seemed like ages ago that he'd suffered his way through it, daydreaming and unable to concentrate.

A ripple of excitement ran through the graduating students as Professor Carroll reached the podium and cleared his throat. An underclassman brought him a long, flat case.

"Gentlemen, I was pleased with the marks you all earned on this exam," Professor Carroll began. "There were many valiant efforts in the essay portion especially, and it was difficult for me to choose from among the top scorers. But in the end, one student rose above the rest." He paused, and several of the graduating students leaned forward. "And that student is Blake Williamson, Lord Stanley."

The auditorium burst into applause. On the other side, a woman's cheer stood out above the others, and Annamarie Cannon leapt out of her chair enthusiastically as the audience, including Niall, rose to their feet for a standing ovation. Somewhere in front of him, Niall could have sworn he heard Ian cry, "No!" Blake rose and stepped forward as their classmates congratulated him and thumped him on the back. He was delayed in his progress toward the stage to accept his award as more of his friends stepped up to shake his hand.

"That man is blessed," the student sitting next to Niall laughed as Blake crossed the stage to Professor Carroll. Blake's face was pale and drawn, even though he smiled and nodded to the audience. When Niall turned to the man next to him, he went on with, "He scores the lead role in your play, graduates with top honors, wins the Classics prize, takes home the football trophy, and ends up engaged to an American millioniaress. And he's handsome and charming on top of all that. I've never known anyone whose life is so blessed."

Niall hummed in agreement and applauded distractedly as Professor Carroll took the medallion Ian had been so keen on out of its box and looped it around Blake's neck. Blake smiled modestly at the audience and bowed a few times, but Niall could tell he was in hell. He glanced to his father, acknowledging the man with a somber bow, but as far as Niall could tell, he avoided looking at his fiancée entirely.

As he turned to hurry off the stage and back to his seat, Blake's eyes met Niall's. Blake nearly stumbled over the hem of his robe. His smile vanished entirely for half a second before he plastered it back into place. Only then did Niall realize his own expression was as hard as iron. It matched the steely feeling in his chest. He glanced away, pretending to focus on taking his seat again, and kept his gaze averted until he was certain Blake was seated and not looking at him. Once the dean resumed his place at the podium to announce other awards, Niall peeked at the back of Blake's head.

He continued to stare at the back of Blake's head, eyes narrowed, through the rest of the interminable ceremony. Try as he did to hate Blake with everything he had in him, he couldn't. He loved Blake as passionately as ever. He felt every one of Blake's impassioned I love you's, scrawled messily on a crisp piece of paper, as intensely as he knew Blake felt them. But there was no point in it anymore. There was no use dreaming about what would never be either.

The second the ceremony was finished, Niall rose from his seat and bolted up the aisle, dodging fellow students, faculty, and the family of graduates as he went. It hadn't dawned on him to wonder whether his father had come to the ceremony, though it would have been a stretch for anyone in his family to make the trip. It seemed only fitting that he was alone in what should have been a moment of triumph.

It was his intention to break away from the auditorium and to leave the building before anyone he knew could stop him, but he was thwarted almost immediately, the second he stepped out into the spring sunshine.

"Cristofori," one of his English professors stopped him before he could bolt. "Congratulations on a truly excellent play last evening."

"Yes," one of the university's administrators stepped up to join the conversation. "I haven't seen anything so entertaining in years. You and Lord Stanley were absolutely spiffing playing opposite each other."

"Everyone involved enjoyed themselves," Niall said by rote. It was too late to run. He was trapped in what he knew would be an endless round of conversations and congratulations.

He chatted with everyone who came up to shake his hand and ask about his future plans as best he could. John and David joined him, silently offering their support and helping to deflect the conversations Niall didn't feel up to. But from the moment Lord Selby, Mr. Cannon, and the rest of Blake's family stepped out into the sunshine, Niall's attention flew mostly to them. He tried turning away when Blake walked out of the building, Miss Cannon latched to his arm like a barnacle, but a professor stepped up to the conversation he was having about the London stage in such a way that forced Niall to stand with Blake and his adoring fiancée directly in his line of sight.

Annamarie Cannon was the sort of wealthy, artless Dollar Princess who didn't care that she was stepping on every rule of social propriety Great Britain had. She simpered and fawned all over Blake, turning Niall's stomach. Worse still, Blake looked like an absolute block of wood as he stood there, letting her make a fool of him. His smile was tight and his shoulders tense, and even though Niall was yards away, he could tell that Blake's eyes were absolutely dead.

"Is it true that Joss Hanover from the Royal Swan Theater has offered you a contract to write three plays for him?" one of the men talking at Niall asked.

It took every inch of Niall's will to drag his gaze away from Blake so that he could answer the question. "Yes, it is," he said, unsure which of the four men staring expectantly at him had actually asked the question.

"You're going to take him up on that offer, I assume," another said.

"I would be a fool not to," Niall answered.

He was distracted again as Ian charged out of the theater, making a beeline toward Blake's group. Niall's gut squeezed in dread at the pure venom in Ian's expression.

"You cheated." Ian was loud enough for everyone on the lawn to hear him, let alone Niall. "I know you did. You cheated to win that medallion, just as you cheated to win everything else."

"Excuse me." Niall broke away from his conversation, sending a wary look to John, then marching toward the confrontation. He should have left well enough alone. He should have let Blake deal with what he had coming to him without help. But goddammit, he loved the man, and even though he'd been painfully rejected, he had to help.

"I beg your pardon," Blake said, blinking fast, face coloring. His eyes grew wide and he visibly sucked in a breath when he saw Niall approaching.

"That medallion should be mine," Ian growled. The Cannons and Blake's family looked alarmed at Ian's vehemence. "You weren't even going to sit that exam until I mentioned it to you."

"Ian, don't," Niall warned when he was close enough to join the group. "It isn't going to do any good."

"You know I should have won that prize." Ian turned to Niall as though appealing to him would change everything. "You know I love Miss Cannon a thousand times more than he does."

"Oh!" Miss Cannon gasped and clapped her hands to her mouth.

For one, glorious second, Niall thought he saw love in the young woman's eyes. His heart balanced on edge, praying that they could play out a drama of another sort and Miss Cannon would fly into Ian's arms, refusing to marry a man she clearly didn't love. He prayed she would let Blake go so that the two of them could work out the impossible after all.

"Young man, I'm sorry that you've been disappointed," Mr. Cannon said, stepping in and resting a hand on Ian's shoulder. "But my Mimi told me she wanted to be a duchess, so that's what she's going to be." He beamed at his daughter.

Miss Cannon glanced between Ian and Blake for a moment, looking as though she might burst into tears, then grabbed Blake's arm and sank into his side. "It's for the best," she told Ian.

Niall swallowed the bile that came to his throat. He

met Blake's eyes for a moment, but didn't know whether to be encouraged or revolted by the helplessness he saw there.

"Do you have anything to say about this?" he asked all the same. He had to give Blake one last chance to set things right. They could still have a future together. This didn't have to be the end.

"Of course, he has something to say about it," Lord Selby said, chuckling. He moved to Blake's side and clapped a hand on his shoulder. "He has to say that he's very happy with the way things have turned out."

Niall's gaze dropped away from Blake's, landing on the scarab medallion around his neck. It really was beautiful, all things considered. The scarab was onyx and its carvings were inlaid with gold. Perhaps Ian was right and it was worth more than Professor Carroll thought it was after all. Not that it mattered. Like everything else precious about Blake, it wasn't his to have an opinion about anymore.

"Congratulations," Niall said, head lowered, not meeting Blake's eyes. "If you'll excuse me."

He turned and walked away, too hollow even for tears. The only thing he carried away with him was an ache in his chest that he knew would never go away.

"Give me just a second to say goodbye to my friend," he heard Blake say behind him.

Niall thought about speeding up so that he could get away before Blake caught up to him, but it would only have drawn attention. All he could do was stop and wince, then turn to face Blake as he approached.

"Did you get my letter?" Blake asked, breathless and looking almost frightened as he faced Niall.

"I did." Niall swallowed hard.

"And?" Blake bristled with pent-up energy.

Niall shrugged. "What do you want me to do?"

"I want you to—"

"This isn't over," Ian said, barging into their painful moment, full of fury.

Niall huffed a breath and rolled his eyes before breaking into a bitter laugh. He and Blake would never have the chance to close the book on their affair with all these interruptions.

"I've had enough of this," Niall said, stepping away.

"So have I," Ian agreed. He glared at Blake. "I won't let you get away with ruining my life like this."

"Your life isn't the one that's been ruined," Blake said with acute feeling, voice shaking. The deadness in his eyes was too much for Niall to look at.

"I will win in the end," Ian said. "Just you wait."

"I'm done." Niall took another step back. "I can't be a part of this anymore. It's over. Goodbye, Blake." He turned and strode away as fast as he could.

"Niall," Blake called after him, but there was no way Niall was going to stop.

A few people tried to waylay Niall as he marched back to his dormitory, but he ignored them, rude as it was. He didn't want to speak to anyone, not to be congratulated and not to talk about his plans for the future. As far as he was concerned, the future was an endless stretch of bleak loneliness. He knew, deep within him, that it didn't matter how much success he had or how many accolades he received, the best part of his life was already over. He knew love meant more than riches or success. And he knew he would never have it.

He threw off his academic robe as soon as he reached his room and set to work packing his suitcase. If he hurried, he could catch a train out of York and be in London by nightfall. He threw everything he cared about into his case, intent on leaving the rest of it behind. He wanted to take as little with him as possible into the life that waited for him.

He only hesitated when he snatched up the bundle of stationary he'd bought to write his letters to Blake. There were still a few sheets of paper left. He stared at the blank pages in his hand, wondering what to do with them.

The answer came to him with a painful jolt. The only thing he could do with them was use them.

He sat at his desk and took out his pen, setting it to the page. Every tragedy needed a final act. Every story came to a conclusion eventually. He poured his heart out onto the page, saying everything he didn't want to, everything he dared. If he got it all out, maybe he could leave it behind him. He needed to purge his soul and leave his emotions behind if he ever hoped to start over.

As soon as the letter was written, he folded it and

stuffed it into an envelope. He scribbled Blake's address, then threw the pen down, determined to leave it behind as well. He leapt up from the desk, put on his coat and hat, and grabbed his suitcase in one hand and the letter in the other.

"You," he said to the first hall boy he saw once he reached the dormitory's ground floor. The boy had delivered several of Niall's letters in the past. "You know where to take this?"

"Yes, sir," the boy said.

Niall handed him the letter along with a large coin. "Then deliver it."

"Yes, sir." The boy gaped at the amount he'd been given.

At least one person would come out of the whole, sordid affair better off. He plunked his hat on his head, not looking back as he marched out of the dorm. His future was ahead of him, and it was a future without Blake.

THE CHAMELEON CLUB – 1890 – THE PRESENT

"SO THAT'S IT?" JOHN ASKED AS NIALL FINISHED HIS story and sagged back into his chair. The tea was long gone and only crumbs remained of the scones. "That's how you left things?"

Niall nodded somberly. "I didn't see Blake for ten years after that."

"But you saw him last month in Leeds," John said, as though organizing the details of the whole, sorry tale in his mind.

Again, Niall nodded. "Briefly. He fetched me, Jewel, and Wrexham from the train station and took us to our hotel. He wanted me to go with him to Selby Manor to meet his children." The words felt strange on his lips, bittersweet. He cleared his throat. "And to say hello to Annamarie."

John made a sound of sympathy. "I trust you said no."

"I would rather stick this fork in my eye," Niall muttered, toying with the silver fork at his place.

John hesitated a moment before asking, "Do you think he told Annamarie he'd invited you to visit?"

Niall heard a different question behind John's words. John was asking whether Annamarie knew about him and Blake. "She found out somehow," he sighed, rubbing his face. "I don't know whether it was a confession or if she stumbled across the truth. Whatever it was, she took the children and left."

"You have to go help him," Mr. Oberlin blurted. Niall had forgotten John's new assistant was sitting there, listening to the entire story. "You still love him. You have to help him."

"I think you should too," John said, slightly more circumspect. "To honor what you once had, if nothing else."

"What did we have?" Niall scoffed. "According to his letter, he's spent all these years thinking it was 'the folly of youth'." He couldn't keep the bitterness out of his voice.

"We all have to tell ourselves things to make it through each day," John argued, like the lawyer he was, though his voice and expression were full of tenderness. "Think of what he had to endure in his position. Think of his children, his son, the heir to his title."

"I don't give a flying fuck about his title," Niall seethed. It was the bloody title that had made things impossible for the two of them to begin with.

"But you care about him," John said, his voice as soft as ever. He rested a hand over Niall's as it splayed across the tablecloth. "I know you care about him. I knew it back then, and I know it now."

"He hurt me, John." Niall's voice shook with emotion. "You have no idea how badly he hurt me."

"No, I don't," John agreed with a nod. "Nor do I have any idea how much hurt Blake has endured as well."

Niall was silent, not knowing how to reply to that truth. All he could think about was how changed Blake had been when they'd seen each other briefly the month before. He could only see the heartache in Blake's eyes when he'd turned and walked away ten years ago. He could still feel the warmth of Blake's skin against his, still hear the sounds of his sighs and singing, still taste the musk of his cock. He still wanted Blake, in spite of everything.

And apparently, Annamarie didn't anymore.

"I don't know," he said, letting out a heavy breath and bowing his head. "I just don't know."

"Yes, you do," John said, giving his hand a squeeze. "And you know what you have to do now."

CHAPTER 11

"*My beloved, my heart. I am devastated. You have utterly destroyed me. I love you more than I love the air I breath. I love you more than the feel of sunshine on my face. I love you more than the food that nourishes me. I love you more than any word I have ever written.*

"*You are the air I breathe. You are the heat of the sun. You nourish me and give me life. You are the inspiration that fires me and makes every moment livable.*

"*And now you've ripped all that away from me.*

"*If I could forget the sensation of your body tangled with mine, hot and wet with love, I would. If I could forget the taste of your mouth and your skin and your cock, I would. If I could banish forever the sound of your laughter and your whispers, the sweet words we exchanged deep into the night and the promises we made to each other, they would be gone forever from my memory. If I could forget the way you made me feel that I was loved, that I was safe in your arms, that I was precious, as I felt in my soul of souls that you are precious, I would walk away from everything and be happy.*

"But I know I won't ever be able to forget. I won't be able to break my heart away from yours. I won't be able to remove you from every fiber of my being or see anything but your smile when I feel joy. If I'm ever able to feel joy again. Love like ours only comes once in a lifetime, but ours has been wrecked like a ship dashing against a rocky shore.

"It didn't have to be this way. We could have chosen another path.

"I love you with all my heart, but I will never be able to forgive you. N."

BLAKE LAY ON HIS BACK IN THE MIDDLE OF THE nursery floor, staring at the faded, dog-eared page in his shaking hands. His throat squeezed impossibly tight and his eyes burned, though after all of the unmanly tears he'd shed in the last few weeks, he didn't think he was capable of shedding any more. That didn't stop his eyes and his head from hurting.

He lowered his arms, letting Niall's final letter—the one that had been delivered to him after the graduation ceremony, after Niall had walked away and left him to his gloomy fate—fall to his chest. The rest of the letters Niall had sent in that glorious month they'd had covered him like a blanket of paper snow. In the back of his mind, Niall's sensible voice murmured, "You shouldn't keep reading them like this. Paper is fragile, and they're already falling apart."

It was true. He'd read Niall's letters over and over in the last ten years, so many times that he'd been forced to repair most of them with bits of linen and paste. They looked bandaged and broken now, the white paper long since faded to yellow. But they were all he had left of the only happy time in his life. Perhaps they didn't look like snow as they covered him. Perhaps with all the bits of linen they made him look like a mummy lying in a tomb. It seemed fitting. He'd been dead for at least ten years now.

"Stop being such a maudlin, indulgent prick," Niall's voice scolded in his head. "You're as bad as Alan throwing a tantrum."

He sat up, his back cracking as he did, and let out a heavy sigh. Niall's letters dropped around him. It felt as though it took a supreme effort of will to gather them up, one at a time, catching bits and pieces of Niall's words, and fold them. Once he had them neatly in a pile, he raised the pile to his nose and breathed in. If he concentrated hard enough, he could still make out Niall's scent on them.

He dragged himself to his feet, stretching his shoulders and wincing as he crossed the nursery to the piano. He accidentally kicked one of Alan's red, wooden blocks as he went, sending it flying to the corner of the room where the girls' mountain of stuffed animals stood. The faces of bears, elephants, rabbits, tigers, and monkeys looked as sad and expectant as he felt, missing them.

God, he missed his children! He sat heavily at the piano he'd insisted be brought into the nursery, in spite of Annamarie's protests, and set the pile of Niall's letters on its top. His fingers flew across the keys as he started in on one of Greta's favorite songs. It was happy and light, and he could hear the sound of her and Jessie's laughter as they danced. Some little girls demanded to be lulled to sleep at night with a story. His girls always wanted a dance.

A breathy sob escaped him as he switched from playing the dance tune to a lullaby. He squeezed his eyes shut, amazed at how much pain missing people could cause. His children had been gone for three weeks, four days, and twelve hours. Niall had been gone for ten years, five months, twelve days, and two hours. He'd sent his plea to Niall twenty days ago, and still he was alone.

"Papa, tell us the story of Siegfried and Greta again," his own Greta's voice sounded in his head.

"Greta was a princess," he said aloud, pivoting on the piano stool.

He ended up facing an empty room. Rows and rows of books stood on the shelves against the far wall. A miniature table and four tiny chairs sat in the center of the room, its child-sized, silver tea set laid out as though the girls would rush in from the adjoining bedroom at any moment. Jessie's favorite doll sat with her mild, painted-on smile in one of the chairs. Jessie would be beside herself to have left the doll behind. Annamarie should have known better and taken the doll.

Not that Annamarie had ever been interested in the children the way a mother should. She cared enough for Alan, considering he was the heir and her insurance that she would always have a place in society, but the way she ignored the girls was criminal. *He* was the one who loved them. *He* was the one who oversaw their lessons and taught them to sing. *He* was the one who kissed their fevered brows when they were sick, the one whose bedroom they ran to in the middle of the night when they'd had bad dreams. He was the one who took them to every theatrical performance that passed through Leeds and who had promised them that someday he would take them to London, to a real musical. He was the one who—

"Sir?"

Blake gasped and jerked straight, dizzy from failing to breathe as his thoughts ran wild. He blinked rapidly and glanced around, trying to remember where he was and what he'd been doing. Threads of panic wormed their way through him as the reality of his situation came back to him. He was alone. The girls were gone. Niall was gone. Everyone who loved him and whom he loved had been stolen away from him.

"Sir." Xavier, his valet, cleared his throat and took another step into the room. Deep concern cut lines in the young man's face.

"Yes. Sorry." Blake shook his head and stood. He

rubbed the heels of his hands against his burning eyes, then scrubbed a hand over his thick beard. Had he forgotten to shave for days again?

"Sir, you really shouldn't sit up here all alone like this." Xavier walked deeper into the room, hands clasped behind his back. He was the only one in the household who had leave to address Blake informally, since he was Blake's valet and closest friend, but even informality seemed formal coming from Xavier. In spite of his unremarkable birth and his employment, Xavier held himself like a king. The image was helped by his patrician good looks, though Blake hardly noticed things like that anymore.

"I came up here to...." Blake let his arms fall to his sides. He couldn't remember why he'd come to the nursery except that he'd finished his lunch, and coming up to the nursery to see what his children were up to was simply what he did with his afternoons. Or at least what he had done.

"You need to wash and dress." Xavier lowered his voice to a gentle tone as he crossed to stand by Blake's side. "It's been too long."

"It hasn't been—" Blake stopped. Truth be told, he couldn't remember the last time he'd had a proper bath. There didn't seem to be any point in it, considering the house was empty and Niall hadn't responded to his letter yet. Not even a letter of his own or a telegram. The horrible thought struck him that Niall hadn't been lying.

He really wouldn't ever forgive him. Blake had been abandoned completely and—

"Sir." Xavier rested a hand on Blake's arm, startling him out of the spiral of his thoughts. With a sympathetic wince, he said, "She will bring them back. She knows how much you love them. She isn't so cruel that she would keep them away from you forever. She's just having a bit of a pout is all."

Blake let out a breath and sent Xavier a thankful look. Even though the man was wrong. Xavier didn't know why Annamarie had left. And he most certainly didn't know about Niall.

"I'll have a bath," he said, sagging in defeat.

Xavier hesitated. "You'll have to be quick about it. There's a gentleman downstairs to see you, and I'm not sure if he's willing to wait for—"

Blake launched into motion before Xavier could finish, his heart in his throat. Niall. He'd come at last. He hadn't been abandoned after all. His heart was saved.

He raced downstairs, running right past his room and the hallway that led to the other wing of the house— where Annamarie had her rooms—to the stairs. He nearly tripped over himself as he flew down to the foyer, then shot on across the hall, looking into every parlor along the way to discover where his butler had put Niall.

"He's in your office, your grace," his butler, Dobson, said, cutting Blake off before he could run through the entire house, like the lunatic he was.

Heart in his throat, Blake tore across the hall and

burst into his office, sweaty and panting. Hope blossomed in his chest to the point where it was painful, then crashed spectacularly when the grey-haired man studying some of the books on the shelf in his office turned to stare curiously at him.

"Your grace, are you well?" Kinesin, his solicitor, asked, stepping away from the shelf.

Blake couldn't catch his breath. Disappointment rang through him, like the echoing vibrations of a gong that had been rung too hard. Desperation not to tip his hand and reveal his secrets slammed into him, and he straightened, tugging at the hem of his jacket.

"Forgive me," he said, forcing as much cheer and affability into his voice as he could. He strode purposefully across to his desk, praying he didn't look as bad as he thought he did. God, what had happened to the last few days? Had he really not changed clothes since yesterday morning? "I was all the way upstairs seeing to a few things." He made an excuse, slipping behind his desk and gesturing for Kinesin to have a seat opposite him.

Only when Kinesin reached the desk did Blake remember it was polite to shake the man's hand. He reached out, alarmed by how obvious it was that he hadn't bathed. Thank God there was a desk between them.

After Kinesin shook his hand, wariness at Blake's unkempt state registering briefly on his face, and sat, Blake sat as well. "What can I do for you this morning,

Mr. Kinesin?" he asked, sounding as pleased with life as a duke should.

"I've come about the sale of your brother's estate," Kinesin said, looking graver than ever.

"How are things progressing with the buyer?" Blake leaned back in his chair, hoping to put as much distance between him and Kinesin as he could so that he didn't overpower the man with his slovenliness.

Kinesin's frown deepened. "They're not, your grace."

"Oh?" A different sort of worry struck Blake. Since Montague's arrest for the horrific crime of masterminding a child kidnapping ring earlier in the summer, Blake had been acting on his behalf to do whatever it took to sell off everything Montague owned, including Castleford Estate. Whether Montague spent the rest of his days in prison or not had yet to be determined, but his brother had already made it known that if he ever was released, he planned to leave England for South America or Australia, or some other place so far away from the scene of his crimes that no one who knew him would ever see him again. Blake was more than happy to oblige. If he never saw his brother again it would be too soon.

But there was the problem of the estate.

"The buyers were appalled by the condition of the place," Kinesin went on. "The house itself sustained so much fire damage that it will need to be demolished and rebuilt."

"I thought the prospective buyers were aware of that and eager to do the work," Blake said.

"They were." Kinesin nodded. "But then they saw the cages."

Blake swallowed hard. The key reason he'd spent so little time at Montague's house was because of those ghastly cages. Montague had kept a menagerie on his property, but one look at the cages gave any outside observer the feeling that his brother had been keeping a park where he tortured helpless animals. And Blake had had enough of a feeling of being caged and tortured to last a lifetime.

"So no sale, eh?" He fought to present himself as the mild-mannered, unflappable, pleasant-to-be-around man that everyone thought he was.

"Not to those buyers," Kinesin said with a sigh. "I'll keep looking, though."

"Thank you, Kinesin. We need to get that estate off our hands as fast as possible."

"Agreed." Kinesin arched one eyebrow. "The taxes levied on the place are truly staggering, and your brother ran everything productive about the land into the ground. If you don't find someone to take it off your hands by the end of the year, you'll be bankrupt. What remains of your wife's money won't be enough to save you."

Blake's heart dropped to his acid-filled gut. Kinesin had the good sense to look sheepish at his mention of Annamarie. Everyone knew she was gone. Everyone knew she'd run off with a lover too.

"We wouldn't want that," Blake said hoarsely, standing. "Advertise for the place as far and wide as you can.

On the continent and in America too, if necessary. Perhaps some foreigner who hasn't heard Montague's story would be willing to take the place off my hands."

"Yes, your grace." Kinesin stood. He hesitated, then reached across the desk for Blake's hand. "Chin up, your grace," he added with a pitying smile. "Women are fickle creatures. Whatever tiff the two of you had, she'll come back. They always come back."

Blake smiled and hummed, but his heart felt blacker than ever. They did not always come back. Twenty days, and Niall hadn't answered him. He wasn't coming. Annamarie hadn't sent so much as a ransom note or a list of demands. She'd simply vanished and taken the children with her. For all he knew, they could have boarded a ship bound for America. If so, he'd never seen them again.

"Your grace?"

Blake sucked in a breath. He was gripping Kinesin's hand so tightly the man's skin had gone white.

"Sorry," he said, letting go. "I'm greatly distressed."

The look in Kinesin's eyes said he knew that was an understatement. "It'll work out, your grace." Kinesin nodded, then turned to head out of the room.

Blake followed him, which was only polite. Even though he wanted to sink into one of the leather sofas in his office, curl into a ball, and sleep until the terrible nightmare was over. With any luck, he'd wake up on graduation day ten years ago so that he could make the decision he should have made in the first place.

But no, if he'd thrown Annamarie over to run away with Niall he wouldn't have Greta, Jessie, and Alan.

"Why hasn't she sent a note?" he hissed aloud once he was in the hall.

He winced, realizing he was talking to himself again. Thank God Kinesin had moved on. Dobson was showing him out at the far end of the hall.

"Sir?" Xavier approached him from the other end of the hall. He had what appeared to be a clean set of clothes draped over one arm.

"Is something the matter?" Blake frowned.

"You have another guest in the conservatory."

Blake's heart swelled all over again, nearly making him sick. He couldn't breathe. His head swam. He pushed a hand through his hair. The stray thought that it had grown too long and was a curling mess flew at him from nowhere.

"I figured you wouldn't want to speak with her in your current state," Xavier went on. "So I brought these down for you to change into."

Once again, Blake's hopes crashed. Speak with *her*. It wasn't Niall.

"Yes, of course. Thank you, Xavier. I suppose you can help me change in here."

He stepped back into his office, Xavier following him. Xavier shut the door as Blake peeled out of his rumpled clothes. He sniffed himself in disgust, wishing Xavier had brought a washbasin down with him. There was nothing to be done, though. At least the clean clothes hid some of his stench. Xavier helped tie his tie and straighten his cuffs before sending him on his way to the conservatory.

A second wave of disappointment hit him as Lady Inglewood, one of his closest neighbors, turned away from his grand piano, where she was squinting at the hand-written sheet music he'd left there, and smiled benevolently at him.

"Lord Selby," she said, swishing across the room to greet him, her hands outstretched. "You poor thing."

Blake took her hands and smiled, playing the role he knew damn well he was expected to play. "Lady Inglewood. How lovely to see you." He was sunny, friendly, and above all, masculine. "What brings you to my humble abode this morning?"

"No one has seen you for days, your grace," she said, gripping his hands harder. "We are all so worried about you."

"I'm getting along as best I can," he sighed, but smiled as he did. "One must always make the best of things."

"Yes, yes, of course, dear man." The august lady went so far as to pat his cheek before taking a step back. "But you know how all of your friends and neighbors worry. Especially with you being all alone in this big house." There was a particular flash in her eyes as she studied him. She was fishing for information, that much certain. "You're still alone?" she asked, proving as much.

"Annamarie has not returned, no." He lowered his head slightly and clasped his hands behind his back.

"Do you suppose she will ever return?" Lady Inglewood asked, far too curious. "Americans can be so fickle, you know. So many of the so-called perfect matches I've heard of with those dollar princesses have ended in heartbreak and divorce." She put just enough emphasis on the last word that Blake knew what she was truly asking.

"I have to find her first," he said with a bit too much bitterness.

"Of course, of course." Lady Inglewood was back to being sympathetic in a heartbeat. "I'm sure you long for her return, and for the return of your children?" He lifted her brow just a bit.

"Yes, I miss my children terribly," he said, unable to hide his pain, even though it was clear Lady Inglewood was asking if Annamarie had taken the children as well. Blake hated the sorts of games Lady Inglewood and her friends played, but two could play at them. "You don't happen to know who Annamarie's lover is, do you, Lady Inglewood?" he asked bluntly.

"No, I'm afraid I don't, your grace," she sighed. The veil of propriety dropped for a moment, and she shrugged. "I've asked around, but no one knows. As far as everyone was aware, you and your duchess were a perfect match. Neither one of you has raised so much as a hint of suspicion when it comes to extramarital affairs. Everyone knows how loyal you have been."

Blake smiled and glanced away. Yes, he had a reputation for being steadfastly faithful. A reputation gained through having half a dozen women throw themselves at him over the years without so much as a kiss or a tickle. If only they knew. As for Annamarie, she'd carried out her affairs discreetly.

Lady Inglewood cleared her throat and stepped closer. "I've come to invite you to a small supper party tomorrow," she said, then rushed on to, "And I won't take no for an answer. You've been declining every invitation sent your way for the last several weeks, and we all know why. But you must know that you will be among friends with us. We genuinely are worried about you, dear. You need to be in company again." She touched his arm the way his mother might have.

Blake lowered his head and nodded. "You're right," he said. "I shouldn't hide myself simply because I'm...." He searched for the right word, settling on, "Embarrassed."

"Everyone knows it's not your fault, your grace," Lady Inglewood said. She leaned in. "Everyone also knows your father was the one who chose Lady Selby for you. You'll make a much better choice the second time around."

Blake's face burned. He should have known he'd be thrown back on the marriage market before his first marriage had truly ended. Lady Inglewood was right about one thing, though. He wouldn't make the same mistake twice. He already had an heir, so he was free from the torture of trying to get another.

"Thank you, my lady." He touched Lady Inglewood's hand on his arm. "I would be delighted to accept your invitation for tomorrow evening."

"Good." Lady Inglewood took a step back, beaming. "I will have my cook prepare roast lamb, since I know how much you enjoyed it last winter." She stepped toward the door, as though her mission were done and it was time to get on with preparations. "Until tomorrow evening, dear."

"Until then." Blake smiled and bowed slightly as she left.

The moment she disappeared into the hall, his smile dropped and his body sagged. His friends and neighbors meant well, truly they did. He'd worked his fingers to the bone for ten years to convince them all he was the happiest man alive and the life of every party he attended. They were all good people in their own ways and he did enjoy their company to a degree. But not one of them knew the man he truly was. Not one of them guessed at anything beneath the polished veneer he presented.

Heart aching over the prospect of adding a return to society to everything else gnawing at him, Blake moved to the piano. Playing was the only thing that gave him even a shred of peace anymore. He brushed his fingers over the keys for a moment, seeing Niall's smile in their brightness as he did. Then he began to play one of his own compositions. Not just any composition, but the one he'd been working on while rehearsing Niall's play. It was the song he'd begun when he saw Niall for the very first time, before they'd ever spoken. It started smooth and haunting, then built to an emotional crescendo. He'd penned that part after they'd met, after rehearsals had started, after they'd become lovers. It was rich and full of feeling, but that theme fell away into a faded replica of the original theme toward the end. He'd written that bit afterwards, after his heart had been shattered. It was almost too poignant to play, and as its final, hollow notes lingered in the air, he closed his eyes and bowed his head, consumed with grief.

"You finished it."

Blake snapped his head up, gasping so hard that this throat hurt, and whipped around to find Niall standing in the doorway.

"It's beautiful."

CHAPTER 12

*B*lake stood so fast, a strangled cry ripping from his lungs, that he knocked the piano stool over. When he turned to reach for it, he slammed his toe hard into the seat. Pain radiated up his foot and he yelped before grabbing the stool and setting it upright. When he jerked around to face Niall again, every part of him was in agony.

Niall stood framed in the doorway, looking tired and worn from traveling. They'd seen each other a month earlier, but that utilitarian reunion hadn't felt like a reunion at all. Niall had been busy with Everett Jewel and his friend's investigation. They'd spoken for maybe an hour then. Seeing Niall in his home now, shoulders bunched and expression wary, was the sort of reunion Blake had longed for these past ten years. Niall. In his home. In the flesh.

"You came," he breathed, stepping forward, then immediately falling into a limp as he crossed the room.

"I almost didn't," Niall confessed in a low, stiff voice.

The sting of that admission couldn't penetrate Blake's overwhelming joy at seeing Niall again. Niall's suit was finer than the sort of things he'd worn at university. He'd matured, grown more muscular. He combed his hair differently, but he still didn't wear a beard. His jaw seemed squarer than it had before, and his blue eyes were definitely more steel than sky. All the same, Blake ignored the palpable shield he felt around the only person he had, or ever could consider a lover, to stumble into his arms.

Niall was as rigid as a statue as Blake embraced him. Their bodies crushed together awkwardly, all elbows and edges, but Blake didn't care. He closed his eyes and buried his head against Niall's neck for a moment, breathing in the scent he'd only dreamed of for years.

Niall remained silent, and far too quickly, their embrace turned uncomfortable. Blake wasn't forgiven. He could feel it in the brittle way Niall held himself, in the gaping chasm between them, even as their bodies pressed together. He kept a bright smile firmly in place as he stepped back, though. The world thought he was a golden boy, blessed with title, wealth, and unending happiness. By God, if he could pretend for his neighbors, he could pretend for Niall too.

"You look well," he said, throwing everything he had

into keeping his voice light and welcoming. "London suits you."

Niall's jaw was clenched so hard Blake worried his teeth would shatter. "You grew your beard in," he said in a stilted voice.

Blake ran a hand over the bottom half of his face. "It tends to do that all on its own. Neglect does wonders for hair growth."

Niall blinked. His gaze seemed to shift almost imperceptibly from Blake's beard to his lips. The air between them crackled before Niall snapped his eyes up to meet Blake's. "When was the last time you bathed?"

Blake burst into a self-deprecating laugh. It would have been charming, he was sure, except that he couldn't stop. "I don't know," he said, certain he was smiling like a maniac. Why couldn't he stop laughing? "I can't remember the last time I slept either," he went on, growing more hysterical by the moment. He had to pull himself together, but instead, he shrugged and said, "May, eighteen-eighty?"

He felt his expression pinch, his eyes burn, his lungs squeeze. He could see the panic that must have washed through him in the sudden alarm in Niall's eyes. That only pushed him closer to the jagged edge. He couldn't draw breath. Or feel his hands and feet. His heart pounded. He was going mad. No, he'd been mad for a while now. It was just getting worse.

"Please, have a seat," he said, his usually rich tenor coming out brittle and high-pitched as he started toward a

pair of settees near the French doors. "Tell me all about
your journey. How is your play coming along? I've been
reading all about it. Everyone is saying this one will be
your greatest triumph yet. I only wish that I could make
the trip to London to see it. I've been meaning to take the
girls down to London for a theatrical holiday, but I can't...
I can't...."

He couldn't breathe in spite of the fact that air was
squeezing in and out of his lungs at an alarming rate. He
felt hot and cold all over, and his head throbbed and
swam. The corners of his vision started to go black, and
he tipped toward one of the settees.

"I've got you." Niall's voice was suddenly soft and
close. He slung an arm around Blake and helped him to
sit. "Breathe," he ordered. "Put your head between your
knees if you need to, but breathe."

Blake wasn't sure how he made it to a sitting position.
As soon as the dizziness passed, shame rushed in to take
its place. What kind of a man was he if the simple sight of
an old lover sent him into a spiral of panic?

No, Niall was so much more than that. He was
suffering from the shock of having his heart slammed
back into his body.

He did as Niall ordered him and focused on breathing. Breathing should not have been so hard. He gulped
down one breath after another, counting them at first, as
Xavier had once suggested he do, then letting the air flow
in and out more steadily. As soon as he was able to
breathe deeply and clear his head, he sat straighter,

resting his hands on his knees. As he expected, they were shaking, but with a little concentration, he was able to get that to stop.

Only then did he realize that Niall was rubbing his back. It felt so good that he thought he might cry. But he couldn't do that either. He had to push past his pathetic behavior and be a man.

"You came," he said hoarsely, starting the whole reunion over. Slowly, he dragged his gaze up to stare at Niall.

"You said you needed me." Niall's expression was hard and blank. He wasn't going to let Blake in, even though he'd come all the way from London.

"You must have so much to do for your play." Blake cleared his throat and shook his shoulders, pulling away from Niall and scooting to the other end of the settee. They were grown men with mountains of responsibilities. He needed to act like it and face Niall like a gentleman. "I should be congratulating you on all your successes."

"Success is its own punishment," Niall said, inching away. "The bigger you become, the more everyone wants you to fail. Everyone expects this new play to be the talk of the town, but it's been fraught with problems so far. As every production is. But if I don't deliver perfection, I'll be tossed aside, like yesterday's fish. But that's not what I came here to talk about, Blake." The steel in his eyes was so hard as he stared that Blake wanted to wither. "Tell me what happened."

Blake opened his mouth, but nothing came out. How could he even begin to describe what had happened? How could he condense the misery of the last ten years of his life into a simple explanation?

"Annamarie took off with the children," he said, barely above a whisper. He intended to be strong about it, but his spirit was shattered and his face crumpled as though he would sob.

He pulled himself together as soon as he felt himself slipping, though. Dobson appeared in the doorway, looking deeply concerned. Blake shot to his feet.

"Dobson, please have tea for Mr. Cristofori brought to...to the nursery," he ordered.

"The nursery, your grace?" Dobson looked thoroughly confused.

"Yes. I have something to show Mr. Cristofori there." Blake shot forward, glancing over his shoulder at Niall to indicate he should follow.

Dobson clearly thought Blake had gone insane, if the look he gave him as he passed was any indication. Niall rose and followed Blake with a frown, almost no emotion apparent in his look. Blake tried not to think about it, tried not to guess what Niall must think of him as he climbed up the main staircase, headed down the hall, then mounted a second set of stairs to the children's floor.

"I spend most of my time in here these days," Blake explained lamely as he showed Niall into the room.

Niall glanced around at the scattered blocks, at the pile of stuffed animals, the pegs that contained dozens of tiny costumes, the tiny tea set and Jessie's favorite doll, Alan's miniature set of tin armor, and the piano. Blake had no idea what Niall made of it all.

"She doesn't even particularly like the children," Blake said, feeling as though he had to be as honest with Niall as quickly as possible to keep from falling apart again. "She only took them to spite me."

"Why would she do that?" Niall asked, his frown deepening.

Blake swallowed and crossed to the piano. He took up the stack of Niall's letters and walked over to them, holding them out. "She found these."

Recognition dawned in Niall's eyes, and he took the letters gingerly. He opened the one on top, the last letter he'd sent on that horrible day. For the briefest of flashes, grief radiated from him and his eyes came alive with emotion.

"She found them years ago, actually," Blake said, heart pounding. It was only a matter of time before one of the maids came up to the room with their tea, so he had to say the important things quickly. "Thank God we only signed them with initials. Annamarie spent the first few years of our marriage demanding to know if they were written by a Nancy or a Nellie or a Nora." He laughed and shook his head. Niall closed the letter he'd been scanning and frowned at Blake. "Do you realize that not once did you write a single word that would betray those letters were written by a man?"

Niall glanced at the pile of letters again, but didn't open any. "I didn't realize."

"I reread them from Annamarie's point of view. Everything you described, no matter how sensual, could have been felt or performed by a woman. She spent years believing I was pining for a female lover my father made me cast aside to marry her."

Niall jerked his head up to stare at Blake again. "So she knew you had a lover?"

Blake nodded. "She knew I didn't want to marry her. She didn't particularly want to marry me either."

"Then why did she?" Niall asked, his jaw clenched.

"You mistake me," Blake said, pacing to the piano and running his fingers across the keys before glancing back to Niall. "She wanted to marry my title. She wanted to be a duchess. She wanted to make her father proud and lord it over her friends in New York. She wanted to strut around England, mistress of a grand estate and talk of the town." He paused, dusting off the resentment he'd felt for her during the first few years of their marriage and examining it, but not truly feeling it anymore. He shrugged. "The poor thing had to put up with me in order to have all that."

"But she knew you were in love with someone else?" Niall stepped closer to the piano, handing the letters back to him.

Blake took them, staring at them for a moment before resting them back on the piano. "Yes. And in case you were wondering, she didn't care. Mind you, she did what she thought she had to do to make me interested." He felt sick at the memories, hurrying away from the piano and Niall and toward the bookcase. "I thought it was a stroke of luck that she fell pregnant almost immediately after we were married. It was hard enough forcing myself to bed her after knowing what true passion—" He shook his head, pinching the bridge of his nose.

He leaned against the bookshelf and winced. "It was bittersweet when Greta was born."

"Greta?" Niall's question was louder than Blake expected. Niall stalked across the room to him. "You named your firstborn child *Greta*?"

Blake sent him a guilty look. "It's Margaret, actually," he confessed. "I thought Annamarie might figure things out if I insisted we name her simply Greta."

"Did you—" Niall flinched, his cheeks going red. "Did you name your firstborn child after me?" he asked in a rough whisper.

Blake could only answer with a miserable, sheepish look.

Niall stared at him, appearing more incredulous than flattered, so Blake pushed away from the bookcase, crossing the room to lean against the doorway into the girls' bedroom. Their beds were still unmade from when Annamarie had whisked them away in the middle of the night, while he'd been asleep downstairs. He'd refused to let the maids touch the room.

"A girl meant we had to try again for an heir, of course," he said, staring into the room so that he could avoid looking at Niall. "Jessie was born just over a year later." He turned back to Niall, who had taken a few steps toward him and stood with his arms crossed, a scowl on his face. "Jessica," he clarified. "After Shakespeare. There was a miscarriage after that, and for a while after, Annamarie didn't want me in her wing of the house, let alone her bed, thank God."

"You lived in separate parts of the house?" Niall asked, narrowing his eyes.

Blake nodded. "My room is downstairs, just below the nursery. Annamarie has the entire south wing to herself."

Niall's mouth dropped open and he shook his head, but he didn't say anything.

"Then Father died unexpectedly, and I was left a duke at age twenty-five. I think Annamarie knew at that point I had to have an heir. We finally succeeded in that. Alan just turned five in August." He paused, wincing, but knowing he had to spill it all. "Alan Siegfried Williamson, current Marquess of Stanley, future eighth Duke of Selby."

Niall jerked his head away, blinking as if fighting tears, his jaw so tense Blake was certain it ached. "And she still didn't suspect a thing?" he asked in a gravelly voice.

"No." Blake stepped cautiously closer to him. "She didn't seem to care that I didn't touch her once after Alan was conceived. Maybe she thought I had a mistress. She certainly had lovers after that."

Niall snapped to look at him again, eyes wide. "And you know that for certain?"

Blake nodded. "I caught one of them sneaking out of the house in the early morning once. I should have thanked the man instead of pretending I didn't see him."

"Thanked him?" Niall let his arms drop. "Blake, listen to yourself. You are not a carpet to be walked all over."

"Aren't I?" he asked, feeling himself shrink inwardly. "Don't I deserve to be stepped on after the way I—" He turned away, shaking his head, and marched across the room to the piano. Without sitting, he played a few bars of one of the girls' favorite dancing songs before losing the heart for it.

"And what about you?" Niall demanded, his voice darker as he walked toward the piano. "Did you take a lover?"

Blake's shoulders sagged and he let out a heavy breath. "Not really. There was a footman three or four years ago." He shrugged. "When my previous valet came down with influenza, he stepped in for a week. He figured things out right away. I...I had him suck me off a few times and I returned the favor once, but...." He shook his head, feeling dirty for doing it, much less telling Niall. "I couldn't have him in the house after that. Fortunately, he was a good man. I explained the truth of things to him, why I had to sack him. I paid him a generous stipend and helped him to get a position as a valet for a friend. He never said a thing." Blake forced himself to face Niall. "I was only tempted because he reminded me of you," he whispered.

Niall looked as though Blake had slapped him. It was horrible, a nightmare.

"Don't tell me you haven't had lovers since...." Blake swallowed hard, walking away from Niall and plucking Jessie's doll from her seat at the table.

"I have," Niall said without emotion. "Several."

Blake's heart shattered, though he had no right to be hurt. He nodded, hugging Jessie's doll.

"None of them were serious," Niall murmured. "None of them were you." His voice cracked.

Blake sucked in a breath, daring to hope, and pivoted to face Niall. He couldn't do a damned thing, though. The maid swept into the room with a full tea tray. She smiled and moved easily at first, but the second she saw the look on Blake's face, her smile dropped. She must have sensed the tension sizzling through the room. She set the tray on the girls' table, pushing their make-believe tea set aside, then stood and curtsied.

"Will you be needing anything else, your grace?" she asked, averting her eyes from both him and Niall.

"No, thank you, Bonnie. This is lovely." Blake smiled at her, letting her know she could flee as far and as fast as she wanted.

Bonnie curtsied again, then did just that. As soon as she was gone, Blake moved to the table, returned Jessie's doll to her chair, and sat in one of the ridiculously small chairs—one he'd had reinforced to hold his weight while he played with the girls—and set about pouring tea.

"When you came up here last month with Jewel and Wrexham," he said without looking at Niall as he poured, "I didn't know how long you'd be up north. I asked Annamarie if you could stay here for a while. I wanted you to meet the children." He glanced up at Niall, who frowned down at him, hands behind his back. "They're wonderful, Niall, all three of them. I didn't know it was possible to love someone so much until I had them in my life. It's a sort of love that I've never felt before. I'm their father, and they are mine. You can't know what that feels like until you have it. But that doesn't replace how I feel about you," he said before he could stop himself.

Pain laced Niall's expression for a moment before he could hide it. "I'm happy for you," he croaked.

Blake focused on the tea once more, fixing Niall's the way he remembered he liked it, then standing and taking the cup to him. "Annamarie didn't want to have company. She remembered you as nothing more than a low-born playwright. I argued that you were so much more than that. I insisted you be invited to stay, that you were dear to me." He turned back to the table to fetch his own tea. "That's when she made the connection with the letters."

"Niall, not Nancy or Nellie or Nora," Niall said, face red, sipping his tea.

Blake nodded. "She put the pieces together—why I only ever came to her bed after drinking, why I didn't

189

care about her lovers, why there was never so much as a whisper of a rumor of me with another woman. She figured it out after ten years, and she was appalled." He swallowed a gulp of tea that went down wrong, choking him.

"Did she leave because she was heartbroken?" Niall asked.

Blake lowered his teacup, flushing. "She left because she thought I would be a threat to the children, particularly Alan. Or so I assume, given the argument we had the evening before she left." Saying as much out loud lashed Blake with bone-deep grief and revulsion. "I love those children with everything I have," he managed to squeeze out, voice ragged. "It's disgusting that she would think I would harm them in any way, especially that way. What kind of a vile mind would assume that just because —" He snapped his mouth shut, shaking his head. He had to put his teacup down. There was no way he would be able to stomach any more of it.

"I share your disgust in the way we are portrayed where children are concerned," Niall said, a little too formally. "But from what I know, I didn't think Annamarie was that spiteful."

"I don't think she is," Blake said, forcing himself to breathe and face Niall again. "I think her mind was poisoned by whoever her current lover is."

"And who is he?"

Blake shrugged and shook his head. "I have no idea. It was Howard Vale for a while, but they broke things off about two years ago. I suspected there was someone else, but she's been better about hiding things for the last year or so."

Blake sank onto the piano stool. Now that he'd said everything he had to say, he didn't have an ounce of energy left.

"So Annamarie left you because she discovered what kind of man you are? She took the children because her current lover probably told her you'd be a danger to them?" Niall frowned. "It doesn't add up." He paused. "Have you heard anything from her since then?" Niall asked, walking to the piano and setting his teacup down on its top, next to the letters.

Blake shook his head. "Not a word. I don't know where they are, I don't know if she plans to bring them back, I don't know if she wants a ransom for them, and I don't know who her lover is." He laughed. "Oh, and on top of that, I have to sell my criminal brother's burnt-out estate before it becomes enough of a liability to bankrupt me, making Father's entire plan for me to marry Annamarie moot. And apparently, word has gotten around that I might be in the market for another duchess." He shook his head, burying his face in his hands. "I can't stand it anymore," he said, emotion thick in his voice that he couldn't have hidden if he'd wanted to. "I can't bear it anymore. I just...I just want my children back. I just want to be left alone to watch them grow. I just want to be happy again."

He didn't think he had a single tear left in him, but

when Niall rested a hand on his slumped shoulder, Blake sobbed. It was unmanly and messy, but it couldn't be helped. He was completely wrecked, but Niall was there.

"I'll help you find them," Niall said, his voice shaking with emotion, though his body was stiff beside Blake. "I'll help you track down Annamarie and her lover. And I'll help you find a buyer for the estate. I know people who know people."

"Thank you," Blake breathed. He tilted his head to lean his cheek against Niall's hand, even though it stretched his neck into an awkward bend. He would have buried himself against Niall and never let go if he thought he could get away with it.

"I'm staying at the Mandrake Hotel in Leeds," Niall went on, "and I can—"

"No, you have to stay here." Blake jerked clumsily to his feet, eyes wide with desperation.

Niall pursed his lips and stared at Blake. "I can't stay in your house, Blake."

"I can't be here alone for another night," Blake pleaded with him. "God, it's awful being here all by myself, everything so empty." He glanced around at the abandoned nursery.

"You have servants," Niall argued.

"Who treat me as though I'm some sort of golden statue," Blake said. "It's not the same."

Niall let out a heavy breath, rubbing his face. "All right, I'll stay here. But I'm not staying in your bed," he said with blistering firmness, meeting Blake's eyes.

"No," Blake whispered, shaking his head. He supposed that was too much to ask for anyhow. Though he would have given the moon and the stars to have Niall's mouth on his again, to hear the sounds of pleasure he made, and to feel him inside of him. As painful and frantic as their last time had been, Blake could still feel every last sensation Niall had caused. He hadn't stopped wanting Niall for a single day since then.

"I can have Xavier, my valet and my friend, fetch your things from the Mandrake," Blake said, crossing to the door. He didn't trust himself to stay so close to Niall, now that he knew Niall would be with him through the storm. "Everything will be all right now," he went on, mostly for himself. "Now that you're here, I'm certain we'll be able to sort everything out."

CHAPTER 13

*B*lake was a broken man. It was far more difficult for Niall to witness the fact than he'd anticipated. The way Blake seemed reluctant to leave his children's nursery—even after he'd sent his valet, Xavier, to fetch Niall's things from the Mandrake Hotel—was only one shattering bit of proof of that. Blake sat at the child's size table, inviting Niall to sit as well, and asked him more questions about London and the theater and Niall's current play than anyone ever had. But whether he was aware of it or not, Blake continually glanced into the pink and frilly bedroom off to one side of the nursery and the smaller bedroom, decorated with medieval scenes of knights and dragons, on the other, as if he expected his children to bound into the room at any moment.

There was something tragically fitting about the way Blake looked as he sipped his tea at a table miles too small

for him, like he didn't fit in the life he was forced to live.
And yet, he had clearly adapted. He knew exactly how to
position his knees so that they didn't bump the impossibly small table, and knew how to smile and look fascinated by everything Niall said. Though it was clear to
Niall that Blake had slipped into some safe, protected
part of his mind after spilling out his story, and what he
showed to Niall was a shell of who he truly was.

Eventually, Blake's butler announced that supper
would be served in the dining room in an hour, and
wouldn't his grace like to bathe beforehand? Blake
seemed to awake from his jovial stupor then, flushing
with embarrassment and making excuses as he leapt up to
leave. His last words as he dashed out of the nursery
were, "Make yourself at home. My house is yours."

Niall rose as soon as Blake was gone and exchanged a
wary look with Mr. Dobson. He had a feeling the grand
ducal house with all its riches and finery was no more of a
home to Blake than the flat he'd taken in York during
university. In fact, that flat was probably three times the
home Selby Manor was.

Supper was a stilted affair in which Blake did most of
the talking. Niall was too exhausted, body and soul, to do
more than nod and smile when appropriate at the tales
Blake related of taking his son, Alan, fishing for the first
time several weeks ago, the fancy Greta had taken to
Lord Milton's son, who was twice her age but had been
kind to her at a garden party that spring, and the way
Jessie had climbed to the top of the sheepfold on one of

their tenant's farms. More alarming was the fact that Blake ate as though he'd been skipping meals for a fort-night and kept running his fingers through the thick curls of his hair, as if he didn't understand why it was so long. That distracting gesture left Niall longing to bury his hands in Blake's hair in spite of the gnawing resentment that still hadn't dissipated in his gut. Apparently, lust didn't care how wounded his heart was.

"Would you like another dessert?" Blake asked at the end of the meal, as Niall's eyelids and spirits were begin-ning to droop. "I could have Mrs. French bake a cake for you."

Niall's eyes shot wide at the insane offer.

"Or we could adjourn to the conservatory and I could play for you," Blake suggested. "Composing has been one of my few joys these past few years, aside from the chil-dren." His overly bright expression faded fast at the mention of the children.

"Blake, I'm exhausted." Niall rubbed his temples, his heart squeezing painfully. "I just want to go to bed." When Blake drew in an expectant breath, Niall said, "To sleep." Though he'd be a fool to deny the pull he felt toward Blake, even after all the years and pain between them. He told himself it was a natural, nostalgic reaction to a man he'd felt such pleasure with, that it'd been months, nearly a year, since the last time he'd had sex, and that his need was only skin deep. He told himself that, but knew it was a lie. He still loved Blake, and he hated it.

He pushed is chair back and stood before those feelings could get the better of him. "If you don't mind, I'll have Mr. Dobson show me up to my room."

Blake leapt to his feet as well. "I had the maids prepare the guest room across the hall from my bedroom."

Niall fixed him with a flat stare and blew out a frustrated breath through his nose. "No."

"I didn't mean—" Blake tried to defend himself, but gave up with a sigh, shoulders drooping.

"Good night, Blake." Niall stepped away from the table. "We'll sit down and begin sorting things out tomorrow."

It felt wrong somehow to walk away from Blake in his own house, knowing how much distress his friend was in. He couldn't even, in good conscience, think of Blake as just his friend. He was more than that, and he was less. But Niall had reached the end of his rope and needed time alone to regroup.

He had no idea what he was going to do. He stripped off his clothes, ran a washcloth over himself to clean away the grime of travel, dressed in crisp, cotton pajamas, and climbed straight into the huge, soft bed Blake had given him. And immediately cursed at himself for going hard at the sound of Blake's footsteps in the hall. Those footsteps paused just outside of the door before the door across the hall opened and shut. Niall flopped to his back, hissing for the twist of disappointment that hit him.

He flat refused to relieve himself of the throbbing

tension being near Blake brought with it, but that meant he spent most of the night tossing and turning and aching instead of resting. No matter how many times he told himself he should be focusing his mental efforts on puzzling out where Annamarie had gone, whether Blake's children were safe, and how he could sell his brother's estate, Niall's mind was filled with memories of Blake's plaintive pants as he neared orgasm and the rich sound of his laughter as they'd dashed across campus on their way to his flat.

Not even a brisk morning stroll across the grounds of Blake's estate could diffuse the fiery tension that gripped Niall the next day. It was made worse by the sound of the piano echoing through the house when he returned. He deliberately avoided the conservatory, heading straight up to his room to change out of his walking clothes and into something more formal, then delayed going down-stairs for another hour. But the inevitable was exactly that, so at last he gave up and went in search of Blake.

"I trust you slept well," Blake greeted him when Niall located him in a room that looked every bit like the office of a duke should look. There was a map of the estate on one wall and shelves of books about agriculture, animal husbandry, and law. Blake stood over his desk rather than sitting as he rifled through papers and letters. He glanced at Niall for only a moment before focusing on his work again.

"Perfectly well," Niall lied.

Blake glanced up at him again. He knew Niall was

lying, but he didn't say anything about it. Oddly enough, Blake looked refreshed, as though he had slept well for the first time in a long time. He'd shaved as well, which did nothing to calm the raging need to take Blake's face in his hands and kiss it until they were both breathless.

"I've been reading through Annamarie's correspondence from this summer," Blake rushed to say as Niall slowly approached the desk. "Normally, I would never presume to intrude on something of hers that is so personal, but it dawned on me this morning that there might be a clue as to her and the children's whereabouts in her letters."

"Have you discovered anything?" Niall asked, impressed with the idea to read her correspondence.

"Not yet," Blake said, sounding paradoxically hopeful, sifting through the letters. "Although there are several letters from her mother and sister that seem to say she has been wanting to travel back to New York for some time. She went four years ago." He glanced up at Niall. "The children and I stayed home."

Niall nodded, unsurprised. From what Blake had told him the day before, and from what little he remembered of the woman from ten years ago, Annamarie was exactly the sort to go on holiday without her husband and children. "Anything about who her lover might be? Any letters from him?"

Blake shook his head. "There are a few old ones from past lovers. I wondered if she might have turned to any of them for help or advice. But it appears as though all of those doors have closed."

Niall reached the opposite side of the desk from Blake, studying him more than the array of letters and other documents. Something was different about Blake. He was calmer. Only by a fraction, but it was a start. Niall wondered if sleep had brought about the change or food. He wondered, but he knew it was his presence that had changed things.

"Do you think she would take the children to New York?" he asked, addressing the main problem head on.

Blake straightened and shoved a hand anxiously through his hair before meeting Niall's eyes. The deep worry there was different from the frantic way Blake had been the evening before, but it was somehow worse. "Very possibly," he said in a quiet voice. "And if she does, if she takes the children out of the country, I'm not sure whether I'll be able to get them back."

"Of course, you will," Niall reassured him on instinct, even though he had no idea of the laws of either the United States or Great Britain where custody of children was concerned. "I doubt it will come to that anyhow. Didn't you say that Annamarie wanted to be a duchess and lord it over English ladies? She can't do that in America."

Blake hummed in consideration. "I'm not sure that's what she truly wants now. Now that she knows...." His words faded and he glanced out the window nearest his desk.

"Somebody somewhere must have seen her." Niall took things in hand once more. "A duchess traveling with three children under the age of ten will be noticed. Even if she is traveling with a lover. Have you hired investigators? Notified the police?"

Blake glanced back to Niall with a guilty look. "The police haven't seen hide nor hair of her. I didn't think to hire an investigator, though."

"We could do that ." Niall nodded, taking charge. "I know of a few men who might be of help in London. We could telegraph them, and someone would be on the case by tomorrow at the latest."

"Good," Blake let out a breath of relief, more tension draining from his shoulders.

Niall felt a burst of pride at being able to put Blake's mind at ease, even though he rejected the sentimental notion. He hadn't come to renew things with the man who had callously left him; he'd only come to sort out his mess.

"We'll send a telegram to David Wirth as well, asking him if he knows anyone in The Brotherhood who might be looking to invest in a dilapidated country estate," Niall went on.

"The Brotherhood?" Blake blinked in puzzlement.

Niall was just as confused. "Don't tell me you've never heard of The Brotherhood."

Blake shrugged and shook his head. "Is that some sort of secret fraternity of estate buyers?"

Niall almost thought he was joking. "It's an organization of men like us," he explained, still incredulous that someone of Blake's position had never heard of them.

"Like us?" Blake stared at him.

"Homosexuals."

Blake flushed dark red, glancing to the doorway and windows, as if their conversation might be overheard. "How is that even possible?"

Niall's jaw dropped. Blake couldn't be that ignorant. "Possible for homosexual men to form an organization to promote their own interests and to look out for each other?"

"It can't be very popular." Blake flushed deeper, rolling his shoulders awkwardly.

"It has hundreds of members, Blake. Possibly thousands."

Blake's eyes went wide. "There are that many men who—" He snapped his mouth shut.

"God, you've been alone too long." Niall nearly laughed. Until the truth behind his casual statement hit him. He stared hard at Blake. "You're not alone, you know. Did you think you were?"

Blake's astounded look and the way he sat heavily in his chair was all the answer Niall needed.

"Oh, Blake." Niall walked around the desk and sat against it, close to Blake. "Don't tell me you've been isolating yourself all the way up here out of some sense that you're an anomaly."

Blake didn't answer. He merely glanced sheepishly

up at Niall. "I know I'm not an anomaly as such, but I thought...."

Niall waited for him to finish his thought, but he didn't. He stood and stepped back around the desk. "You need to spend more time in London. People are more open about things down there, and with a population of greater than five million, there is more than enough room to blend into the woodwork. But that's not what we need to focus on. We'll make a trip into town to send a telegram to David. He can help with both the estate and finding an investigator."

"Perhaps someone at the party tonight knows who Annamarie's lover is."

Niall froze at Blake's words, as though someone had poured ice water down his back. "Party?"

"Yes." Blake rose, the look of false cheer back on his face. "Lady Inglewood has invited me to supper tonight. You'll accompany me, of course."

Niall turned slowly to face Blake, clenching his jaw. He felt as though he'd stepped into a trap. "I have no interest in attending supper at the house of a Lady Inglewood, or anyone else."

"You have to go with me." Blake leapt forward, edging around the desk to grab Niall's arm. "I haven't been out in company since Annamarie left. All of my friends and neighbors know what happened. They're hungry for information, hungry for me, and I don't think I could face it all without you by my side."

Niall swallowed, his throat going dry. It wasn't that

he didn't know how to comport himself around the wealthy and titled. He'd had to woo more than a few investors for his plays over the years. He knew how to speak the language and play the game. And with the fame he'd garnered in the last few years, he knew how to hold his own. But if he showed up anywhere by Blake's side, considering what was happening in Blake's life, people would talk. And for the likes of them, talk was dangerous, even for a duke and a famous playwright.

At the same time, he knew he couldn't get out of it.

"All right," he said with a weary sigh, rubbing his eyes. "We'll go to Leeds first and send the telegrams, then we'll clean up and go to this supper."

The trip into Leeds was simple enough. Blake seemed to have worn himself out with talking the evening before and said surprisingly little as they ran their errands. He drove Niall to distraction by asking that they take a side trip to a few mundane businesses so that he could purchase shoe polish, hair tonic, and other sundries that his valet could have or should have fetched. Niall wondered if the errands were an excuse to spend more time with him, but that seemed ridiculous, considering they were staying under the same roof. When they returned to the house, Blake took him on a tour of the estate, pointing out all of the improvements his father had made. At no point did he mention any work he specifically had done. The tour only confirmed to Niall that Blake wasn't truly invested in his birthright.

After the tour, they parted ways in order to clean up

and dress for supper. Niall dreaded the event more and more as the minutes ticked by. His dread proved well-founded almost immediately as soon as they set foot in Lady Inglewood's parlor. The esteemed noblewoman had invited two dozen people or more, many of them young ladies with their mothers. Every eye in the room shot straight to Blake as soon as they entered. Worse still, Blake smiled at everyone and greeted his hostess and her friends as though they were chums.

"I cannot tell you how delighted I am that you invited me this evening, Lady Inglewood," he said, bowing over the hostess's hand like a cavalier. "Allow me to introduce you to a dear old friend from university, Mr. Niall Cristofori." He turned to Niall, all smiles and dead eyes.

"Niall Cristofori?" Lady Inglewood's expression lit with recognition. "The playwright?"

"At your service, my lady." Niall took the woman's hand and bent over it. If Blake could play the role of jovial party guest, he could as well. Though he would never play it half as well as Blake did.

"I saw your *Persephone* in the West End four years ago," Lady Inglewood went on. "I don't think I've ever enjoyed myself so much at the theater."

"Thank you, my lady."

"Lord Selby, why didn't you tell me you were friends with *the* Niall Cristofori?" Lady Inglewood scolded Blake lightly.

"You never asked," Blake joked. There was something brittle and false about the joke, and Niall cringed inwardly.

"Let me introduce you to my guests, sir." Lady Inglewood took Niall by the arm and pulled him into the room. "You have to help me," she whispered as soon as she'd pulled Niall far enough away from Blake. "We are all deeply disappointed by the way that horrid American has absconded with Lord Selby's children and heir. Of course, a divorce must be forthcoming, but we're all trying to temper the blow by finding a far more suitable duchess for your friend."

Niall bristled with rage at the bald admission, but kept his smile in place. "Are you certain that isn't a bit premature?" he asked.

"Not at all," Lady Inglewood dismissed the idea as they neared the far end of the room. "I'm sure you must see that your friend is desperate for love and affection. In fact, we've all thought so for years. It is no secret that the duchess has been stingy with her affections and that it was in no way a love match. But Lord Selby is so lovable, don't you think?" She turned to glance across the room to where they'd left Blake, forcing Niall to do the same.

Acid churned in Niall's gut at the sight of Blake surrounded by three young ladies with stars in their eyes as they chatted with him. The sharks had moved in before he'd even made it across the room. He found himself livid on Blake's behalf.

And if he were honest with himself, he was green with jealousy.

"You must help me convince his grace to play while the young ladies I've invited to dine with us sing after supper," Lady Inglewood went on in a whisper. "You are a man of the theater. Consider it an audition for the duchess's understudy."

Niall was offended on behalf of the entire theatrical profession for the comparison. "Wouldn't it be wiser to let Lord Selby determine his own fate in his own time?" he asked.

"Nonsense." Lady Inglewood laughed and cuffed his arm too familiarly. "Men should never be left to their own devices in matters of love."

A sick, twisted feeling hit the pit of Niall's stomach. No wonder Blake had been maneuvered into a marriage he didn't want with a woman he barely knew all those years ago. If the entire mindset of the upper class was that men were incapable of knowing their own mind in matters of love, then Blake hadn't stood a chance from day one.

Something he'd tried to explain to Niall ten years ago.

Guilt and a warm, pulsing compassion took over from anger in Niall's heart. Blake had tried to tell him. John had tried to tell him too, for that matter. Back then and mere days ago. He hadn't listened. Youth and love had blinded him to reality. Not that he had ever cared much for reality. His world was one of invention and story-telling. He created his own reality and gave it life on the stage. But now he was beginning to see that not everyone had that luxury. Blake might have grossly underestimated how many men like them existed in the world, but Niall had the uncomfortable feeling that he'd overestimated his ability to shape the world in the way he wanted it.

"Supper is served, my lady," Lady Inglewood's butler announced from the doorway.

"You must accompany me in, Mr. Cristofori." Lady Inglewood gripped Niall's arm tighter. "You might not rightfully belong at the head of the line in terms of title and precedent—your friend Lord Selby deserves that honor—but you are a celebrity, and how often can a humble countess like me say she has a celebrity at her table?"

"I am at your service, my lady." Niall nodded graciously, but inwardly he seethed. By what right were people shunted to the front or back of the line simply because of the honorific attached to their name? A title did not make someone a decent man or woman.

All the same, the rush and jumble that followed as men lined up and ladies scrambled to accompany them, all so that the group could claim the right seats at the long, gilded, dining room table, made Niall want to roll his eyes and scream. The only consolation he had as they were seated for supper was that he ended up directly across the table from Blake and that the food was exquisitely good.

"I don't care much for the theater myself," the dowager countess seated on one side of Niall said halfway through the meal. "There's always something profane about it. And theatrical sorts—" She shuddered.

Niall clenched his jaw and prayed for patience. "It is a colorful world," he said. He sent a glance across the table to Blake, who was ostensibly listening to something one of the candidates for future duchess was saying. Their eyes met, and by the flash of amusement Blake's look contained, Niall could tell exactly where his attention truly was.

"My nephew, Albert, was involved with an actress once," the dowager went on. "Vile creature."

Niall only just managed to keep a straight face as Blake's eyes sparkled with mirth. "Perhaps I know her," he said, deadpan.

Blake coughed and reached for his wine.

Niall's mouth twitched into a grin before he could school it to neutrality. What the devil was wrong with him? He was miserable in the current company, offended by everything around him, and in the midst of being insulted by a stodgy dowager. On top of that, he was wary about being around Blake again and unsettled by everything he'd felt and thought since arriving the day before. He should not be sparked into silliness by a single glance thrown across the table by a man who had shattered him.

"Cristofori," the dowager went on with a sniff. "What sort of name is that? Are you Italian, sir?"

"His great-great grandfather was Bartolomeo Cristofori," Blake interrupted, turning away from whatever silly thing the woman next to him was saying. "The inventor of the piano."

"Is that so?" The dowager glanced suspiciously to Niall.

"It is," Niall answered as something bumped his foot under the table.

The woman seated on Niall's other side—a woman who wasn't old, but who had the feel of having put herself firmly on the shelf—made a sound of interest.

"You play the piano beautifully, Lord Selby," the marriage bait on Blake's left said. "You must play for us later."

"You must accompany me singing," the young lady on his right said, attempting to snag back his attention.

"I do enjoy playing," Blake said with a smile for each lady that Niall found far too docile.

The thing that had bumped him tapped his ankle. Niall choked on the last bite of his dessert tart as he realized it was Blake's stockinged foot. He reached for his wine to wash the bite and the surprise down, noting that the table was perhaps the narrowest dining table he'd ever sat at. In fact, he wouldn't have been at all surprised if the thing had been purposefully designed for exactly what Blake was doing. Though how Blake had managed to remove his shoe without anyone noticing was a mystery.

"I never did trust the Italians," the dowager went on as Niall glared at Blake. Now was neither the time nor the place to play games, and Blake should have known it. Particularly given how strained things were between the two of them.

Blake shifted from smiling indulgently at the woman

on his right to look at the one on his left. As he did, he glanced across Niall's scolding glare. The only sign that he noted Niall's disapproval was a slight reddening of his cheeks and the way he jerked his foot aggressively up Niall's calf inside of the leg of his trousers. Niall nearly sputtered, mostly because the sudden show of mischief from Blake instantly had him aroused to an alarming degree. He could have strangled Blake then and there. He should have known better than to try something in public when he knew there was still a wall of unresolved tension between them.

"It was probably an Italian that Lady Selby ran off with."

The comment from the dowager snapped Niall to full attention. Judging by the way Blake's foot went slack against his ankle, Blake had heard her too, though his silly smile for the lady on his right was still in place.

"And do you know who Lady Selby ran off with?" Niall asked the dowager bluntly, in no mood for games—hers or Blake's.

"Heavens, no," the woman balked, reaching for her wine. "Whatever makes you think I would know the first thing about such a fast crowd?"

Niall scowled. He had the dowager pegged as the sort who had been as wicked as the devil in her younger years, but who pretended innocence in her dotage.

"Perhaps it is time to adjourn to the parlor for some light entertainment," Lady Inglewood announced from the end of the table. "I'm certain we will all enjoy Lord

Selby's playing. And perhaps, if we're lucky, his esteemed friend from London, Mr. Cristofori, will join him."

Blake's foot pulled away from Niall's leg as Niall protested, "I'm not one to perform in public."

"Nonsense," Blake scoffed. "You're as entertaining a performer as anyone else to grace the stage."

Niall sent him a wary look. At the rate he was going, Blake would get them into more trouble than either of them needed. The chairs were scraped back and the company began to chatter as they dispersed to the parlor. Niall was in no state to stand up from the table as things were. He glared at Blake as he stood, either oblivious to the less than perfect state of his trousers or pretending for all he was worth that he wasn't half aroused. Niall reached for one last gulp of wine before daring to attempt to stand.

"Mr. Cristofori, might I have a word with you?" the spinster on Niall's left asked.

Niall had never been so glad to be given an excuse to stay right where he was. "Yes, of course."

The spinster glanced around anxiously before leaning closer to him. "It's just that you mentioned Lady Selby's lover."

A burst of excitement filled Niall's gut, but before he could do more than open his mouth to ask the woman to go on, Blake was by his side, forcing him out of his chair.

"Come on," Blake said, eyes shining with excitement. "We've been called on to perform."

"I'm not interested," Niall growled, rising with an apologetic smile for the spinster, then shuffling Blake over to the side of the room so he could reiterate with more meaning, "I'm not *interested*."

"Of course, you are," Blake whispered back, pushing him toward the door. "You haven't changed *that* much. Stop fighting it."

Jaw clenched, Niall let Blake hurry him out of the dining room. He had a feeling nothing good could possibly come out of the rest of the evening.

CHAPTER 14

Ten years dropped away in the blink of an eye, and all because Niall was there. Blake hadn't felt so light or so young in a decade as he played his heart out, not caring who sang as he accompanied or what requests they made. It made no logical sense, but it was as though he were alive again, as though his blood had resumed flowing and his heart beating. He didn't even have to be speaking directly with Niall for the comfort and joy of his presence to buoy him. He just had to look at Niall's pinched, frustrated, vexed, beautiful face and the reluctant fire in his eyes to feel as though the door to his cage had been thrown open.

"Surely you will sing this one with me as a duet, Lord Selby," Miss Lloyd asked, batting her eyelashes as she took her place by the piano, where all of the young ladies attempting to catch his attention had stood while singing.

"I'd be delighted," Blake smiled back at her, heart

light. Any chance he had to sing his heart out, quite literally, was a welcome one, the way he was feeling that evening.

He played the opening strains of the love song Miss Lloyd had requested, then started into his part. He glanced carefully at Niall as he sang. His heart leapt in his chest and he had to sing through a broad smile at the sight of Niall sitting with his arms crossed and a flat look on his face. Having Niall cross with him for flirting in public was as luxurious as fine chocolate.

And why shouldn't he be happy? For the first time in a decade, his world felt right. Niall had finally come, swooping in with command. He'd come up with solid ideas to sell Montague's estate. He'd had the presence of mind to think of hiring an investigator to find Annamarie and the children. And he'd not only allowed Blake to purge the bitterness of the last ten years of his life by listening to his story, he'd casually informed him that, in fact, he wasn't a lone, perverted oddity in a world of upper class propriety and decorum.

He wasn't alone anymore. Niall was back in his life, and he would be damned if he would make the same mistake he'd made ten years ago and let him leave this time. The fact that Niall appeared to be furious with him was the very best sign he could have hoped for. There was a very fine line between anger and passion, and even with the chasm of time between them, Blake could feel how close Niall was to crossing that line, just as he had always been able to feel a shift in Niall's body just before he came.

"Bravo! Encore!" Lady Inglewood's guests applauded when the song was over. Blake grinned modestly at the approval, gesturing to Miss Lloyd, who curtsied and simpered at him as though she were the focus of attention.

"Just one more song," Blake said as the young women vying for his attention began arguing with each other about which of them would stand up with him next. "And this one is a solo. Written by my friend, Mr. Cristofori, as it happens."

"How very exciting," Lady Inglewood clasped her hands to her chest and glanced to Niall with an adoring look.

Blake shared that adoration, and a growing part of him wasn't willing to hide it anymore. He'd suffered enough, and Niall had come when he'd called. "This is a song from a musical that Mr. Cristofori wrote and that we performed in together at university," Blake explained as his fingers flew across the keys, remembering the opening notes. "It's always been one of my favorites."

He launched into the song, slowing the tempo and filling the flippant words with more meaning than Niall had ever intended when he'd composed the piece. He'd played it so many times over the years, altering the melody and harmonies slightly to give the ditty more depth, and he was proud of the final product. He sang it directly to Niall, in spite of the danger he knew it presented to both of them. He was well aware as he sang that his emotions were on his sleeve and that two dozen sets of eyes were watching, but he counted on the reputation he'd gained as everyone's friend and no one's lover but Annamarie's to hide the truth.

Niall kept his expression carefully blank through the song, but Blake could see the heat in his eyes. Heat of anger, yes, but more than just that. As he finished, smiling modestly for Lady Inglewood's guests, Niall clapped twice, then narrowed his eyes.

"What a delightful way to end the evening." Lady Inglewood met Blake as he stood and stepped away from the piano, toward Niall. Niall got up and moved gingerly toward him. "I'm surprised you didn't attempt a career on the stage yourself, your grace. You certainly could have managed it." Lady Inglewood laughed at her own joke. Blake knew as well as she did that a career on the stage would have been impossible for the likes of him. But as he glanced to Niall, his heart thrummed as though anything were possible now.

"I think I would have enjoyed a life on the stage," Blake said, his spirits high. "Don't you think that life would have suited me?" he asked Niall.

Niall hummed noncommittally, then said, "I think we should be getting back to Selby Manor."

"I quite agree," Blake said. Particularly since he had every intention of pushing his luck to the limit that night and attempting to get Niall in bed. He felt drunk with love and with daring.

Niall was on to him before they even left Lady Inglewood's parlor, though. "No," he said as they marched into the hall, where Lady Inglewood's butler and footmen had the guests' coats waiting. "Don't even think it, don't even imagine it. It's not going to happen. You're treading on thin ice as it is, and I've half a mind to head back to London if you keep grinning at me like that."

"Was it Shakespeare who said 'the lady doth protest too much, methinks'?" Blake whispered as they approached a small group of departing guests.

Niall merely scowled at him, jaw clenched, as he took his coat from one of the footmen.

"Mr. Cristofori." Blake and Niall both turned to see Miss Yates, who had been seated next to Niall at supper, heading down the hall toward him. "If I might have just a moment of your time."

They had nearly made it out the door and paused for Miss Yates, but another of Lady Inglewood's guests, Lord Rochester, stopped them. Miss Yates's shoulders dropped in disappointment, and she fell back, deferring to Lord Rochester.

"I remember that musical," Rochester said, narrowing his eyes and glancing between Blake and Niall. "I remember a lot of things about that spring."

"You were in the class below us," Blake said, remembering himself.

"You were a stagehand for the production," Niall added in a strained voice.

"For the *entire* production." Lord Rochester grinned

knowingly. "It was the most fun I had that term. I've been telling people for years that I once worked with the great Niall Cristofori." His grin widened as they all put their coats on and headed out into the cool, autumn evening. "Suddenly, quite a few things make sense."

"I can't imagine what you're talking about," Blake said, sobering. Rochester knew. Niall had been right about him getting the two of them in trouble. Then again, Blake highly doubted Rochester would whisper a word to anyone.

"Is that your carriage?" Niall asked, marching straight toward where Blake's driver had pulled up in front of the house.

They climbed into the carriage without another word. Blake's high spirits were only slightly dented, but he could sense Niall's annoyance as though it were a strong perfume in the air.

"Rochester doesn't really know what he thinks he knows," Blake said as soon as the carriage was in motion and there was no danger of their conversation being overheard.

"Of all the irresponsible, incendiary, block-headed things you could have done," Niall started, shouting in spite of how close they sat.

"No one suspected a thing," Blake argued, just as loudly, laughing in spite of himself. "All anyone cared about was throwing their eligible daughters at me. Lady Inglewood's crowd isn't the sort to entertain that sort of suspicion anyhow."

Niall gaped at him in the near darkness of the carriage. "How can you say that when Rochester more or less accused us of buggery on the front steps?"

"It was a harmless bit of fun," Blake argued. The first harmless bit of fun he'd had in as long as he could remember. At least, fun that hadn't involved his children.

Thoughts of them dampened his spirit a bit. He shouldn't even consider having fun when he still didn't know where his children were. But Goddammit, he felt like a man who had dragged himself through a desert and sighted an oasis. He hadn't known a single moment of grown-up happiness since the day Niall left him. It didn't matter that his life had effectively fallen apart, all he saw in front of him was one chance for happiness, even if it was fleeting, and by God, he was going to grab it.

He brushed his foot against Niall's leg the way he had under the table at supper.

"Don't you start," Niall barked, flinching away from him.

"Why?" Blake demanded. "Are you scared?"

"What?" Niall's voice rose an octave. "No! Of course not."

He was terrified, and Blake knew why. It was for the same reason that his heart was spinning wildly out of control. Once they started, they wouldn't be able to stop. And even though he was well aware that the prospect filled Niall with dread, it made Blake want to run and sing and rejoice at his resurrection.

His estate was only a handful of miles from Lady

Inglewood's, and the carriage rolled up to the front door before Niall could do more than pout sullenly for a few minutes.

"Come on," Blake teased him as they climbed down from the carriage and marched into the house. "Surely you must see the humorous side to this whole thing."

"Humorous side?" Niall whipped back to face him after Dobson took their coats. Niall eyed Blake's butler warily, cleared his throat, then marched into the parlor Dobson must have prepared for them in anticipation of their arrival. It held a tray with various sparkling decanters of liquor and some of the biscuits Blake liked. "Humorous side?" Niall hissed more quietly once they were alone in the room. He paced toward the fireplace. "You clearly need to spend more time in London to see what our sort are up against if you think flirting so outrageously that an old schoolmate remembers things is humorous."

"You just told me that London is swimming with our sort and that it is safer and I'm not alone," Blake said with an impatient laugh as he followed Niall in his pacing. "You've no idea how much it lifted my spirits to find out that I'm not one in a million."

"Oh, you're one in a million, all right." Niall sent him a wary look, but one that was brimming with life and fire.

"Niall, you have no idea how happy I've been these last twenty-four hours." Blake pursued him across the room. "You can't imagine what having you back in my life means to me."

"Am I back in your life?" Niall stopped abruptly near the table laid out with their snack.

"Don't you dare tell me you're just passing through." Blake grew serious as he marched up to him. "I let you leave once and it wrecked me. I'm not letting you leave again."

"I only came here because your letter was pathetic," Niall argued, pouring himself a whiskey.

"No, you didn't." Blake rested his hands on his hips and stared at him. "You came here because I asked you to."

"That's what I just said." Niall took a long swig of his drink and looked away.

"They're not the same thing and you know it."

"Don't go making more out of things than they deserve," Niall said in a hoarse voice, then finished the rest of what he'd poured for himself. He set the tumbler down, but looked like he might pour a second drink.

"Don't go brushing the best thing that ever happened to either of us under the carpet because you're still angry with me," Blake countered.

Niall snapped his eyes up to glare at him. "Is this what getting enough sleep and a decent meal or two does to you? Turns you into a deluded fool?"

"You turn me into a deluded fool," Blake insisted, grabbing Niall's arms. "You always have and you always will."

He leaned into Niall, slanting his mouth over his and kissing him hard before Niall could react. One kiss wasn't enough, so he wrapped his arm around Niall's waist, tugging their bodies flush against each other, and kissed him again, thrusting his tongue into Niall's mouth. He tasted of whiskey and passion and everything Blake had only dreamed about for years. It was so good that he groaned with abandon into Niall's mouth, pressing his growing erection against Niall's hip.

Niall made a helpless sound as tension coursed through his body. He swayed away slightly, but as soon as their mouths parted and he gasped for breath, a bereft look flashed to his eyes. He grabbed the sides of Blake's face and slammed into him, kissing Blake so hard that he stumbled backward.

Niall moved with him, devouring his mouth with desperate pants. "We. Can. Not. Do. This," he gasped even as Blake tore at his jacket and fumbled to pull Niall's shirt out of the waist of his trousers.

Blake moaned with pleasure as he stroked his hands along Niall's bare sides, feeling his flesh for the first time in what felt like a lifetime. "I want you," he sighed, trying to feel all of Niall at once. "I never stopped wanting you, not for a moment. I've dreamed of you every night. I've ached for you. I—"

His words were cut short as they slammed into one of the sofas in the room and nearly tumbled across it. The shock was enough to knock them apart for a moment, and as it turned out, that was exactly the right moment.

"Your grace." Dobson cleared his throat in the parlor's doorway.

Blake swore under his breath, turning to face Dobson. He couldn't catch his breath and had to hide his mouth with the back of his hand, knowing how swollen and red his lips probably were from Niall's punishing kisses. Whether or not Dobson had ever suspected things about him, there was no doubt at all that the man knew now. Judging by the way he stood, he'd seen the way he and Niall had gone at each other.

"What is it, Dobson?" Blake stood straight and forced himself to face Dobson like a man. He tugged at the hem of his jacket in the hopes that it would hide the bulge in his trousers.

Dobson cleared his throat again, not looking directly at Blake as he said, "A Miss Yates is here to speak with you and Mr. Cristofori." Dobson spared a millisecond's glance for Niall—who had walked to the corner and was busy stuffing his shirt back into his trousers, back to Blake—before assuming his carefully unfocused look again. "Should I send her away, your grace?"

Blake was about to answer that yes, he most certainly should, when Niall pivoted to say, "She had something to say about Annamarie's lover, I think," with a startled look, as though he'd only just remembered it. Then again, he'd had plenty to distract him just moments before.

Dobson checked with Blake, who nodded. "Send her in."

As soon as Dobson moved out of the doorway, Blake twisted and nearly leapt across the room toward Niall.

"This isn't over," he whispered, veering to the side to pour himself a quick drink. "This has barely just begun."

Niall didn't answer him. His face was bright red and his blue eyes glowed with ardor and anxiety. He, too, hastily poured another glass of whiskey and downed half of it as Dobson showed Miss Yates into the room.

"Miss Yates, your grace," Dobson announced her.

Blake summoned every bit of acting ability he possessed to smile and greet Miss Yates, pretending that nothing at all was out of the ordinary and he hadn't been about to throw the only man he'd ever loved, the man he still loved with every fiber of his body, over the back of the sofa so he could have his sinful way with him. "Miss Yates, this is a surprise."

"I'm so sorry to bother you at such a late hour, your grace," Miss Yates said, hesitating in the doorway, as though she knew she shouldn't be there.

"Not at all," Blake smiled like the perfect host, gesturing for her to come deeper into the room. "Mr. Cristofori and I were just having a drink and reliving old times."

Niall sent him a look as though he'd lost his mind and had dragged him along for the ride.

"What can we do for you this evening?" Blake asked, tempted to offer the woman a drink, though that would have been wildly inappropriate.

"I won't take up much of your time, your grace," Miss Yates said. "It's just that I was seated next to Mr. Cristofori at supper, and something he said struck me."

It took a supreme act of patience for Blake to keep his smile in place. The woman had interrupted what had been about to turn into the sort of passion he'd waited ten years for because Niall had said something interesting at supper?

Niall seemed far more interested. "This is about the question I asked that dowager, isn't it?" he asked, striding across the room to Miss Yates. "When I asked her if she knew who Annamarie's lover is?"

"It is, sir," Miss Yates admitted reluctantly. She fidgeted with the lace on the front of her supper gown and looked warily at Blake. "You see, I believe I know who he is."

Someone could have fired a cannon in the room and Blake wouldn't have heard it. His knees suddenly went weak, and he had to grip the back of the sofa to keep from falling over. The worst part of it was that his shock was not joy at finding Annamarie out at last, it was dread that they might actually locate her and that she might want to come home and resume the horrific life they'd been living.

"Tell us what you know," Niall said with surprising gentleness, gesturing for her to have a seat.

Miss Yates held up a hand as she refused. "I will just say what I have to and be gone, if it's all the same to you. My mother will be beside herself as it is over the way I ran out of Lady Inglewood's party in pursuit of you."

"Understandable," Niall said.

"You know who Annamarie's lover is?" Blake asked, feeling about five steps behind.

Miss Yates blushed deeply. "I believe I do. In fact, I believe I know where she and her lover and your children are."

Blake's knees gave out in earnest. He sat heavily on the arm of the sofa. "Please tell me," he said, suddenly overwhelmed by longing for his children and guilt that he'd taken his eyes off of that prize for even a second.

"You see, I'm good friends with a Miss Mary Archibald. We were in school together, but she has since moved with her parents to Blackpool. She wrote to me just yesterday to tell me the odd story of her brother arriving in Blackpool with a duchess and three children. She refused to say who the duchess was, as she'd promised her brother she wouldn't tell, but she is aware of the events of your marriage." Miss Yates swallowed and pressed a hand to her stomach. "I believe the woman and children Mary was talking about are your wife and your children. And the man I am almost certain is her lover is Mary's brother, Ian Archibald."

iall felt the news of Annamarie's whereabouts and her connection to Ian like a punch in the gut. Somehow, it didn't surprise him at all that their old school chum would be involved in the sordid mess of the present. Ian had claimed to love Annamarie ten years ago, but whether he did or not, he had certainly vowed revenge on Blake for all the frivolous and imagined insults of youth.

That wasn't what Niall cared about, though. What made his insides twist with anger and had his heart racing was the way all color had drained from Blake's face during Miss Yates's explanation and how he gripped the sofa until his knuckles went white. Niall could feel the pain and the rage he saw in Blake's expression as though they were his own feelings.

"My children," Blake said, voice wavering. "Are they

well? Are they safe?" He rose shakily, but seemed to gain strength with every passing second.

"As far as I know, your grace." Miss Yates took a frightened step back, seeming to shrink in on herself. "Mary didn't say except that her mother found that caring for three restless children was an imposition, and she planned to demand Ian take his guests elsewhere."

"Elsewhere?" Blake's voice rose in tone and volume as he stepped toward Miss Yates.

Niall lunged forward to put a hand on Blake's arm, holding him back from harming the messenger. "Do you know if they have plans to depart for America?" he asked the question he was certain Blake would ask, were he in a better frame of mind.

"I don't know," Miss Yates said, growing more upset by the moment. "I've told you all that I do know, really. Mary's letter reached me yesterday, so she must have written it only a few days ago. They're all probably still in Blackpool."

"Then we must go to Blackpool as well," Niall said, speaking as the voice of reason. He tightened his grip on Blake's arm until Blake dragged his eyes away from Miss Yates to stare at him.

Blake's chest rose and fell in short gasps, hinting to Niall that he was falling into a state of distress of the sort he'd been in when Niall had first arrived the day before. Niall's heart went out to him. He'd known people who had fits like that before, and they were never easy for those who suffered. All he could do was to keep his hand firmly on Blake's arm and take charge of the situation.

"Thank you, Miss Yates. You may go," he said.

Miss Yates curtsied and turned to flee the room as though the fireplace were about to explode. Niall could only imagine what sort of courage it took for a woman who didn't appear to be naturally outgoing to come all the way to Selby Manor to share what she knew.

"Mr. Dobson," Niall called next, pulling Blake toward the doorway. The concerned butler appeared in an instant, as though he had been listening to the entire exchange. He glanced uneasily at Niall, reminding Niall of what else the man had overheard in the parlor, but Niall ignored it. "Have one of Lord Selby's carriages prepared to take us to the train station in Leeds."

"Yes, sir." Dobson nodded, then marched down the hall.

"Where is your valet at this time of night?" Niall asked Blake.

"I'll have him fetched as well, your grace," Dobson called over his shoulder.

A wry grin tugged at the corner of Niall's mouth. "I suppose having a whole team of servants at your beck and call is useful after all."

"I'd give them all up in a moment if it meant I could have my children back," Blake said, sounding as though he'd spent the time Niall used to order his servants around to calm his overworked nerves. "And if I could have you."

The anxiety and affection in Blake's eyes as he looked to Niall, shifting his arm so that he clasped Niall's hand, sent spirals of bitter-sweetness careening through Niall's heart. More than just Blake's appearance had changed in ten years. At university, Blake was the golden boy, destined to be a duke, who won at every game and scored top marks, while Niall was a country boy who was handy with a pen. After a decade, Niall was a celebrated theatrical genius with even more promise ahead of him, while Blake was a shell of a man who had been so beaten down by the circumstances of his life that Niall had a feeling it would take years to build him back up again. And yet, the urge to be the one to put Blake back together pulsed through him like the blood in his veins, an integral part of him that he couldn't separate himself from. Blake needed him, and if he were honest with himself, he needed Blake to be whole.

But none of it was going to be easy or quick.

"I hope you learned your lesson in there," he said, letting go of Blake's hand and crossing the hall to the stairs so that they could retreat to their rooms to pack their things. "Dobson will likely hand in his notice tomorrow."

"He's a good man," Blake said, following Niall. "I'm sure if I just explain things to him—"

"Like you explained things to that footman years ago?" Niall arched a critical eyebrow at Blake when he reached his side. Blake had enough sense to look sheepish. "You're too trusting, Blake. Even after everything everyone has done to you, you believe too much in the good nature and circumspection of others."

"Don't you?" Blake asked, genuinely surprised.

Niall breathed out heavily as he reached the door to his room. "I've learned never to believe what someone says unless I see it in writing. I've learned that even someone who professes to love you with their whole being can hurt you in ways that cannot be healed."

He could see at once that his words were as pointed as a dagger in Blake's heart by the bereft look that came to Blake's face.

"Go pack your things," he went on, lashed by guilt that he figured he deserved to feel. "I'll meet you downstairs."

It didn't take long for Niall to repack the things he'd only just unpacked that morning. His suitcase still rested on one of the guest room chairs, and most of his things hadn't been unfolded or pressed yet. He packed everything, not particularly wanting to return to Blake's estate once their mission was completed, no matter what the outcome. The kiss they'd shared in the parlor still burned on his lips. He could still feel Blake's hands on his flesh as if he'd been scorched. His heart ached as though the wound of their love being ripped apart were new, and he was certain that if Dobson and Miss Yates hadn't stopped them, he would be in Blake's bed that very second, fucking as though his life depended on it. And it probably did.

But he couldn't bear to put himself back in a position

where he would be hurt all over again. If the supper party at Lady Inglewood's had proven anything, it had proven that even if Annamarie divorced him, Blake would be expected to marry again. And after the way Blake had behaved, the bastard would go along with everyone else's plans, smiling and being affable and dying on the inside. Niall wasn't going to stick around to see it. He would help Blake get his children back, then he, too, would return to his life.

The journey to Blackpool proved far more arduous than Niall had the patience for. They only just managed to catch a train heading west at the late hour once they reached Leeds, but it was far from being a direct route. After switching trains twice, they arrived in Liverpool by midmorning, then were forced to wait for hours, drinking copious amounts of coffee to keep from passing out with exhaustion, until they could take a train to Blackpool. Niall managed a few minutes of restless sleep on that leg of the journey, but was no more refreshed when they reached the seaside town than if he'd stayed awake the whole time.

"I've always thought Blackpool was a holiday town," Blake commented when they departed the station and stared dumbly up and down the street, no idea where to go or what to do next to find Annamarie, Ian, and the children. "It doesn't look like much."

Niall sent him a flat, sideways look. "It's October," he said. "No one goes to the beach in October."

Blake made a small sound as if conceding the point. "So where are they?"

Niall turned to stare at him fully. "They aren't going to meet us at the train station with the children dressed in their Sunday best, ribbons in their hair."

Blake's eyes flared with indignation as he dragged his gaze away from the traffic and met Niall's eyes. "I wasn't expecting a welcoming committee."

"With a question like that, you could have fooled me," Niall snapped in return. He spotted several signs for hotels near the train station and started forward.

"I'd forgotten how pissy you can be sometimes," Blake said, trailing after him.

"Me?" Niall skittered to a stop, waiting for Blake to catch up so that they could walk on side by side. "*I'm* the pissy one? I'm not the one who's spent the last twelve hours complaining about uncomfortable train seats, cold coffee, and biscuits without chocolate."

"I'm worried," Blake snapped in return. "Who knows what Annamarie and Ian plan to do? If they take the children out of the country, I might never see them again. So forgive me for not being my usual, jolly self."

"Is that who you were being at Lady Inglewood's party?" Niall snorted as he picked the hotel that looked the most discreet from the selection down the street in front of him and headed toward it. "Your usual, jolly self?"

"They expect things from me," Blake complained. "I oblige. And what's so wrong with that anyhow?"

"It's not who you really are," Niall said distractedly as he paused at a street corner and watched traffic for an opportunity to cross.

"No one would accept who I really am," Blake said sullenly.

"Did you ever even try?" Niall muttered, seeing his opportunity and crossing.

Blake kept up with him, frowning and looking half his age. "I was never given a chance."

"Well, you have a chance now." Niall stepped up onto the far curb and turned to face Blake. "Who are you going to be?"

Blake blinked and stumbled back as though Niall had elbowed him. A lost look came over him. "I don't know," he said at last with a shrug, shaking his head.

"That's your problem." Niall moved on, stepping up to his hotel of choice's front door. "Once you're ready to stop being who they tell you to be and to make a decision about who you really are, let me know."

Blake opened his mouth as though he'd've liked to say something else, but he didn't have a chance. The hotel's small lobby wasn't crowded, but there were just enough people lingering to make free conversation impossible. Niall stepped up to the desk and asked the concierge for a room.

As initial payment was made and a key was handed over, Blake stepped up with his friendliest smile and asked, "You wouldn't happen to know where the Archibald family lives, would you?"

Niall gaped at Blake as though he'd grown another head. "How many Archibald families do you think live in Blackpool?" he asked incredulously.

"Do you mean Sir Richard Archibald?" the concierge asked.

Niall's brow shot up as he turned back to the concierge.

"Yes," Blake said, a note of surprise in his voice. "I believe that's Ian's father's name."

"Right." The concierge added. "Sir Richard's son showed up a fortnight ago with a family no one knew he had. They live down near the pier, somewhere around Banks Street, I believe."

"Thank you so much." Blake beamed at the concierge, then turned to Niall with a self-satisfied smirk. "Haven't you heard that you catch more flies with honey?" His entire mood had been bolstered in the space of the brief conversation.

"Unbelievable." Niall shook his head, checking their room key and heading for the stairs. Truth be told, his mood had been bolstered by the snappy, prickly conversation as well. Bickering with Blake was a thousand times better than watching him fall apart under the strain of having his life turned upside down. In fact, their irritated banter had Niall heating in ways that were best not to think about.

They did little more than toss their suitcases on the two, narrow beds in the cramped hotel room before rushing downstairs again and out into Blackpool. The town had the distinct tang of the ocean in the air, and sea birds cried and circled above them as they asked directions, then headed to the pier. Niall had the feeling that the town would be the scene of all sorts of fun and merriment during the summer months. It had the worn out look of a chorus girl who had danced her feet off during the main show and was now catching her breath, getting ready to do the whole thing over again soon.

"What do you plan to do when we find the Archibald's house?" Niall asked as they turned onto a street that ran parallel to the beach. "You can't just charge in like the cavalry and demand to have the children back."

"Why not?" Blake's whole countenance had taken on a militant feeling. "They're my children. She can't legally keep them from me." His expression dampened as he added, "Unless she takes them to America."

"She took them for a reason," Niall spoke his thoughts aloud. "If she thinks they're a bargaining chip of some sort, she won't just hand them over, even if she stays here."

"I have no idea what she wants," Blake said with a frown, scanning the buildings they passed. "All I know is that she left because she found out about you."

Niall huffed an ironic laugh. "She's going to be thrilled to see me with you, then."

They reached Banks Street and asked the first person who passed them which was the Archibald's house. As soon as it was pointed out to them, Niall felt an odd tightness in his chest as Blake took the lead in approaching it. Blake could get what he was after with just a knock on a door. So where would that leave him?

He would go back to his life in London, as he'd intended to all along. At least, that was the easy answer. But as Blake squared his shoulders, scowled, and knocked on the Archibald's door, he wasn't sure that was what he wanted after all.

"Yes?" a young man asked as he opened the door.

"I demand to speak with Ian Archibald at once," Blake said.

The young man—a footman, or perhaps a butler in training—tried to shut the door, but Blake wedged his foot into it. A moment later, the lad disappeared and a stately, grey-haired woman took his place.

"What do you want?" she asked.

"Are you Lady Archibald?" Blake asked, still trying to be personable in what could have been the confrontation of his life.

"I am."

The woman's eyes were already growing round with recognition before Blake said, "I'm Lord Selby, and I want my children back."

"They're not here, your grace," Lady Archibald said, trying to shut the door on Blake.

Blake jammed his hand and foot against the door. "Then where are they? Your son has absconded with them and my wife. I demand to know where they are immediately."

"They are not here," Lady Archibald said with more feeling. "I found out who the lady was and what Ian was up to last week and I told them they had to go."

"Where did they go?" Niall asked, stepping in. "Are they still in Blackpool?"

"Yes," Lady Archibald answered. Blake's shoulders sagged with relief, but only for a moment. "At least, I think they are," Lady Archibald added.

"You think?" Blake stared incredulously at her.

Lady Archibald wrung her hands and shifted restlessly. She glanced over her shoulder, then stepped into the street, shutting the door behind her. "They argued. That woman, Lady Selby, wanted to take a ship to America as fast as possible. Said her father could help them. Ian refused to go."

"Refused to go?" Niall shrugged and shook his head. "Why would he refuse to do exactly the thing that would protect him the most and enrich him in the process."

"He said his business here wasn't finished, but once it was, they would take the first ship sailing," Lady Archibald reported.

"What is his business?" Niall asked.

"I don't know," Lady Archibald said with more feeling, stepping back toward the door. "I want nothing to do with it. Please leave me alone."

Blake lunged after her, grabbing her wrist. "Please," he pleaded with her. "I just want my children back. Ian can have whatever it is he wants. He can have Annamarie. She never loved me anyhow. I'll grant her a

239

divorce on favorable terms if she will just return my children."

"I...." Lady Archibald stammered, staring at Blake in alarm.

"Are you in contact with them?" Blake rushed on. "Can you tell her that? Tell her that." He stood straighter, letting go of the woman. "Tell her that I'll give her anything and everything, except the children. The children are all I want."

"Tell her we're staying at the Graydon Hotel," Niall added. "She can meet us there, or we'll go wherever she wants to meet."

"And who are you?" Lady Archibald narrowed her eyes at Niall suspiciously.

"My friend," Blake answered. "Please, just get the message to her."

"I cannot promise you anything, your grace," Lady Archibald said, opening her door and hurrying inside. "I'll...I'll see what I can do."

"Thank you." Blake managed to turn on his charm, in spite of the circumstances, in a way that had Niall shaking his head. As soon as Lady Archibald slammed the door on them, his smile dropped. "Do you think she'll contact Annamarie?" he asked, his powerful stance slackening as he and Niall stepped back into the street.

Niall let out a breath and rubbed a hand over his face. "If she truly knows where they are."

"We should hang back and see if someone leaves the house," Blake said, backpedaling down the street and studying the buildings on either side of the Archibald home. They were in a relatively prosperous neighborhood filled with stately houses, most of which had attractive gardens.

"That's not a half bad idea," Niall agreed.

They pretended to walk away, heading toward the beach, but paused at the street corner and took up a position to watch the house.

Except that after an hour, not a soul had come or gone from the Archibald house. A few maids dashed between houses, as though they were running errands, but none of them went near the Archibald's house. What had started out as a good idea filled Niall with increasing irritation as each second ticked past. His back still ached from traveling, his stomach growled, and even with the cold sea breeze blowing off the water, his eyes were drooping. He and Blake had leaned against the stone wall of the building on the corner. Their shoulders were jammed together, as if they were propping each other up.

"Either she's not leaving the house to contact them or she doesn't actually know where they are," Niall said at last, as the sun dipped into a bank of clouds near the horizon.

"Or she was lying to us and they are all inside that house somewhere," Blake grumbled. His voice was thick with exhaustion.

A jolt of anger flickered through Niall. "That's a possibility too. But what do we do? Stand here all night? Go back and demand to search the house?"

"That's what I'd choose to do," Blake grumbled.

"I'm not sure it would do any good," Niall sighed. He pushed away from the building. "Honestly, Blake, I think the only thing we can do is go back to the hotel and wait for Annamarie to contact us."

"There has to be some other action we can take," Blake hissed, straightening as well. "I hate this feeling of helplessness. I hate that we're so close and still so far apart." His eyes flickered to Niall as surprise entered his expression.

Niall's chest squeezed. "I know." He rested a hand on Blake's arm, well aware of the double meaning of his words. "But there really isn't a damn thing we can do about it."

Blake nodded reluctantly, starting forward when Niall tugged him into motion. Niall hated it as much as Blake did, but sometimes there was nothing at all to be done when one's life hung in the balance but wait.

CHAPTER 16

By the time they returned to the hotel, Blake was so weary with defeat that he could only nod gratefully when Niall thought to purchase pasties and bottled beer to take up to their room, then sit on the end of one of the beds and eat the simple supper without conversation, barely tasting anything. It frustrated him beyond belief to think that his Greta, Jessie, and Alan were so near after they'd been apart for so long, but that he wasn't any closer to having them back in his arms than he had been at Lady Inglewood's party.

The frustration of being so close and so far went double when it came to Niall.

"There's no telling when or if Annamarie will send us word of where she is or when she wants to meet," Niall sighed as he removed his coat and jacket, then sat on the end of the room's other bed to eat his supper. "We should be ready to hear from her at any moment, or not to hear from her at all."

Blake huffed a wry laugh and swallowed the last bite of his pasty, washing it down with beer. "If she doesn't return the children to me tomorrow, I'm going to the police."

"I'm surprised you didn't suggest going to the police the moment we got here," Niall admitted, his mouth full.

Blake sent him a tired look. "I trust people too much, remember? I am trying to trust Annamarie to do the right thing in this situation. Frightening her could hurt my cause in the end."

Niall narrowed his eyes slightly. "You always refer to her as Annamarie. I don't think I've heard you refer to her as your wife until you said as much to Lady Archibald."

Blake crumpled the paper his pasty had come in and stood to remove his coat, something he hadn't done when they entered the room. "I don't think of her that way," he said, turning away from Niall to drape his coat over one of the room's chairs and toss the pasty wrapper into the bin.

"No," Niall said, sarcasm in his voice. "I suppose I'm the one you think of that way."

Blake glanced over his shoulder at Niall as he unbuttoned his jacket. Niall had been a bastard since they reached Liverpool that morning, but it was only because he was tired. And distraught. Blake might have been the one in the greatest amount of distress, but that didn't exempt Niall from feeling it as well. He'd been the same way in the week leading up to the performance of the play at university. In a paradoxical way, Niall in a rotten mood was even more endearing than cheerful Niall.

Blake shrugged out of his jacket and hung that on the back of the chair, then peeled off his waistcoat as well. There was no point in being modest in front of Niall. The man had already seen everything there was to see and then some. And at the moment, all Blake wanted to do was put on his pajamas and go to bed, hoping that tomorrow brought everything he'd been wishing for since Annamarie left.

"You're not wife material," he said at last, slipping off his shoes, leaving them in the middle of the floor, and opening his suitcase to retrieve his pajamas.

Niall laughed tiredly. "No, if either of us were to claim that role, it would be you." He stood and carried his pasty wrapper and empty bottle to the bin, glancing at Blake with one eyebrow raised.

"Me?" Blake's mouth twitched into a half grin as he shut the lid of his suitcase and tugged his shirt out of his trousers. "What makes you say that?"

For a brief moment, Niall stared at him, heat in his eyes. Blake's insides shivered in expectation as he pulled his shirt off over his head, daring Niall to look longer. By the time he tossed it aside, Niall had stepped away to open his own suitcase.

"You're much better as a hostess than I am," he said, his back to Blake as he fished for his pajamas. "At least,

I'm assuming you are. Isn't that what they teach aristo-
crats to do? Entertain?"

"It's part of the job," Blake admitted, unbuttoning his
trousers. The prospect of being naked in the same room
as Niall had him half hard within seconds, but he was
well aware there was no point in being aroused at the
moment. His prick didn't seem to agree, though. "Aristo-
crats have to do something, considering we're not
supposed to be employed in any way. Except for sitting in
the House of Lords."

"And why haven't you done that yet?" Niall asked,
his back still turned as he shrugged out of his clothes.

"Not interested," Blake said with a shrug, stepping
out of his trousers and drawers and reaching for his
pajama bottoms. "I've had no interest in traveling to
London."

"Are you avoiding me?" Niall asked.

When Blake twisted to peek at him, he found Niall
staring at his naked backside. Staring with craving in his
eyes. Blake caught his breath, a shiver passing through
him. He could still feel the burn in his arse from that
last time with Niall, and going by the look in Niall's
eyes, he wanted to relive those memories and then
some.

"Yes," Blake answered, meeting Niall's gaze and
holding it. He meant it both in terms of avoiding Niall
and inviting him to do whatever he wanted to him.

Niall snapped away, resuming his evening toilet.
"You'd also make the better wife because you're far more

domestic than I am." Blake could tell he was trying to speak casually, but a new tension had entered his voice.

"I won't deny that," Blake admitted, putting his pajamas on. "I am unashamed to say that I love my home and I love my children. My father used to chastise the hell out of me for doting on Greta and Jessie when they were babies. He said I was no sort of man at all for cooing and cuddling what he called mewling, disgusting infants."

"He said that?" Niall turned back to him, an offended frown creasing his brow.

It wasn't the frown that caught Blake's attention, though. Niall wore only his pajama bottoms. His torso was exposed, and the sight of it made Blake's mouth go dry. At some point in the past ten years, Niall had developed an extraordinarily masculine form. His broad chest was well-muscled with just a bit of tawny hair. His belly was flat and firm, and his waist was trim. Blake's half-erection hardened to a full-blown cockstand, and he had to slip quickly into bed to stop his arousal from being obvious to Niall.

"Father was a traditionalist," he said, hoping discussions of his father would settle his body. "Men were to enjoy shooting, riding, sporting, and whoring. They weren't to care two bits about feelings, children, art, or especially music."

"I bet he loathed your piano playing then." Niall continued to pretend he hadn't noticed how turned on Blake was, though Blake was completely certain he was not only aware, he was aroused as well. He guessed as much by the way Niall dashed under his covers as quickly as Blake had.

"He detested it," Blake laughed, squirming until he found a comfortable position on his side that prevented the bedclothes from tenting above him. "The only thing that stopped him from demanding I cease playing was how convenient it was as a way to entertain his friends. Well, that and death."

"There's always death," Niall quipped.

They both laughed uneasily.

"To tell you the truth," Blake sighed, "I was relieved when that fever took him. And to this day I feel like the worst sort of son for thinking as much. I did love him, but his death meant I could be free. I didn't have to live under his shadow, toeing his line, anymore."

"Had Alan been born by then?" Niall asked, shifting to his side to watch Blake.

"No, Father's death precipitated the need to conceive an heir," Blake said. "One of the first things I remember thinking after Father passed was that, once I got that job done, I would never have to sleep with her again."

"I'm sorry." Niall was all sympathy.

Blake grinned. His swell of emotion could best be described as bizarre, but of all people, Niall would understand how comforting sympathy was where that particular subject was concerned.

He shifted slightly to stare out the window past Niall's bed. "After Alan was born, I used to imagine what life would be like if Annamarie left me and went back to America."

"You did?"

Blake nodded, smiling at his old daydreams. "I imagined that the children and I would live a quiet life together in the country, maybe traveling to London on special occasions to see your shows in the West End. We'd travel abroad every summer, tour Italy, Germany, maybe so far as the Orient." He sighed. "We could go away and not ever have to come back."

"You just said you stayed away from London to avoid me, and now you're saying you daydreamed of bringing your children to see my shows?"

Blake pulled his gaze away from the window to study Niall. He looked utterly perfect and handsome, lying on his side in bed, his head propped on his arm, which rested on his pillow. Even the wary confusion in his eyes couldn't dent the blossom of tender feelings stirring in Blake's soul.

"It's a paradox, I know," he said. "In my fantasies, Annamarie was gone. In reality, she wasn't." He shrugged.

"But now she is," Niall said. Blake couldn't interpret the emotion behind his words. It couldn't be hope, could it?

"She's gone," Blake sighed, shifting anxiously to his back before remembering why he was trying to avoid that position. He was still as hard as iron, and the friction of his movements did nothing to help his state. "So are the children," he added, hoping that would be the antidote to the desire he couldn't shake.

"You'll get them back," Niall said, sounding confident, though when Blake twisted his head to look at him, he was troubled by Niall's frown.

A strange and prickly thought hit him. "Niall, are you jealous of my children?"

The flush that splashed across Niall's face was a dead-giveaway that he was, even though Niall answered, "No. Why would you say that?" He, too, rolled to his back and stared up at the ceiling. Blake could tell by the contour of the bedclothes over Niall's body that he too was hard.

The combination of jealousy and arousal had Blake grinning as if Niall had cracked a joke. "I'm flattered," he said, letting a laugh escape before he could stop it.

"About what?" Niall asked in a flat voice that only betrayed his feelings more.

"You don't have anything to be jealous of where the children are concerned," he said, grinning wider. "I love them with an entirely separate kind of love from how I love you."

His heart skipped a beat as he realized his admission, but as soon as it was out, he relaxed into it. He did love Niall. He'd always loved Niall. He hadn't stopped loving him for a single second in ten years. And for the first time in those ten years, he felt perfectly comfortable with the emotion, even if everything else in his world was a wreck.

After a long, heavy silence, Niall said, "I should hope

250

you don't love us the same way." He was trying to be cavalier about the comment, but Blake sensed so much more.

"Do you know what would be perfectly lovely?" Blake asked, his smile growing along with his confidence.

"What?" Niall asked. The frisson in the air between them was palpable.

"If Annamarie willingly gives the children back, we should all move to London." The beautiful daydream was suddenly so real that it stopped the air in Blake's lungs. "We'll divorce, of course, Annamarie and I, and she'll be free to return to New York and take Ian with her. They'll be happy together, and we'll be happy in London."

"We?" Niall's single syllable was quiet and rife with emotion.

"You and me and the children." Blake stretched his arms and folded them contentedly behind his head. He smiled up at the ceiling as he went on. "My family owns a massive house in Mayfair, but I rather fancy a smaller place, somewhere simple. Maybe near the theaters. We'll live there in perfect bliss, scandalizing everyone we meet. The duke and the playwright and their family. How dare they be so happy when the life they are living is so abnormal? But we will dare." He let out a happy breath, closing his eyes and reveling in his imagined future. "We'll dare because we'll be happy. And no one will be there to stop us, not my Father, not Annamarie, not the meddling dowagers trying to play matchmaker. It will just be us."

Blake let out a breath, then sucked it in hard, as Niall

shifted out of his bed. Blake only had time to turn his head, eyes going wide as Niall stepped out of his pajama bottoms. A moment later, Niall slipped into Blake's bed, settling on top of Blake and nudging his knees apart in order to bring them into blazingly intimate contact.

"You know why else you would make the perfect wife?" Niall asked, his voice rich with desire as he brought his mouth to within an inch of Blake's. "Because you are a sentimental fool. And, if memory serves, you strongly prefer to be on the receiving end of things."

Blake let out a vocal sigh, sliding his hands along Niall's naked sides and digging his fingertips into his flesh before saying, "God, do I ever."

He arched up to kiss Niall, but the movement proved superfluous as Niall bore down on him, kissing the air right out of his lungs. He was commanding and passionate, and within seconds, Blake felt like putty in Niall's hands. Their tongues explored each other, and Blake raked his hands through Niall's hair. He'd waited so long for that moment that it came as a surprise that he'd finally reached it.

"I tried so hard to stop loving you," Niall confessed between kisses, fumbling with the buttons of Blake's pajamas until he could push the front aside to stroke his chest and stomach. His hands dipped lower, shoving his pajama bottoms down and reaching to cup his balls and tease his prick with a touch that was far too light for what Blake wanted. "I couldn't do it," Niall went on, kissing Blake's lips, his neck, and his shoulder. "As much as I wanted to, I couldn't get you out of my heart."

"Neither could I," Blake panted, wriggling under Niall in an attempt to get his pajama bottoms off. He throbbed with need, wanting to feel every inch of Niall's body with every inch of his. An impassioned groan escaped from him when Niall licked, then sucked one of his nipples. Only a slight bump from the room on the other side of the wall stopped him from crying out even louder when Niall closed his hand over his cock to stroke him.

Niall froze at the bump, holding his breath for a moment. They panted, bodies taut with lust and touching in so many places, listening for clues as to whether whoever was in the next room suspected what the two of them were doing. Chances were whoever it was didn't have the first clue who was in the room next to them, but caution was warranted all the same.

"Stay quiet," Niall whispered as he resumed stroking Blake's prick.

Blake laughed aloud in response. "You expect me not to make a sound as you have your way with me?"

Niall paused, lifting himself up enough to grin saucily down at Blake. "You never were any good at keeping quiet."

Blake brushed Niall's sides, circling his hands around to grab Niall's backside and tug him down until their erections rubbed against each other. "If I had it my way, I'd scream."

A tremor shot through Niall's body. With a hungry grunt, he bent down to kiss Blake again, ravishing his mouth as though it were a prize in battle. Blake groaned as loud as he dared in response, digging his fingertips into Niall's arse and spreading him. When Niall made a sound of appreciation, Blake slipped a finger along his cleft, fingering his hole.

Niall swallowed a cry and pushed himself above Blake again. "Do you want this to be over before we've truly gotten started?" he demanded, pretending to be angry, though Blake could see the heat in his eyes.

"No." Blake shook his head, laughing. "I want it to last all night. I don't care how tired we are. I've waited ten years for you to fuck me again."

Niall arched an eyebrow. "Sorry to disappoint you, but I'm not ripping into your arse the way I did that last time again."

Blake couldn't stop smiling or laughing, even though it must have had him looking like a lunatic. "Lucky for you, I came prepared." He nodded to his suitcase.

Niall's eyes flared with surprise and lust. "You didn't," he hissed, climbing off of Blake and out of bed. He threw open Blake's suitcase.

"In the top compartment," Blake said. "And you should probably blow out the lanterns while you're up."

"Absolutely not," Niall said, breathless when he found the small jar of lubricant Blake had cheekily packed for the trip. Niall turned back to him. "I want a good look at your face when I make you come while balls deep in your arse."

Blake laughed harder, wriggling in anticipation and spreading his legs wide as Niall unscrewed the jar and helped himself to the contents. He almost begged Niall to let him watch as he spread the lubricant over his outstanding cock, but even the brief glimpse that he got sent him dangerously close to the edge.

"I shouldn't show you a lick of mercy," Niall teased him as he climbed back into bed, spreading what remained of the lubricant over Blake's arsehole and testing him with his fingers. Blake gasped and clamped his jaw down over the moan that wanted to escape from him. "You're as tight after ten years as you were that first time," Niall said, his voice shaking with need.

"Fuck me like you did then," Blake gasped, lifting his hips as Niall shifted against him to find the best position. "I've wanted you for so long."

He didn't have a chance to say anything else. With perfect command and precision, Niall found exactly the angle he wanted and shoved into him. Blake couldn't stop himself from calling out at the once familiar stretch and burn of Niall's cock splitting him. He didn't care who heard, it felt so good to have Niall inside of him again that tears seeped out the corners of his closed eyes.

"Ssh," Niall warned him, leaning closer for a moment as he moved slowly in and out. He paused while lodged tightly within Blake to lean down and kiss him as if to prove the point of the necessity of silence. The angle was too awkward for effective movement, but Blake didn't mind at all as Niall leaned back, lifting his hips higher so that he could thrust into him with strength and abandon.

It took a massive effort for Blake not to give voice to how absolutely right and perfect it felt to have Niall fuck him. It had been far, far too long. The sensation of being possessed by the man he loved more than life itself was so beautiful that it felt wrong not to express it with sound. He was splayed in the most awkward and submissive position possible, but he hadn't been happier in ten years.

He knew he wouldn't last more than a minute, but it was still a shock when his whole body throbbed and jerked with orgasm, sending cum spilling across his belly. Niall made a strangled sound of victory as he watched Blake come, and within a few hard thrusts of that, his face contorted beautifully as he, too, came. Blake watched in fascination as Niall's passion erupted, then melted away, leaving him dazed and satisfied.

Niall pulled out, then collapsed between Blake's still spread legs, their sweaty bodies falling together as every last bit of strength left both of them. Blake closed his arms and legs around Niall, overjoyed at entwining with him.

"I'll admit it," Niall panted, wriggling to find a way for the two of them to rest comfortably together. "That was amazing."

"It was meant to be," Blake gasped, fighting to catch his own breath. "*We* were meant to be. And if you argue that point with me, I'll fight you."

Niall laughed in exhaustion and snuggled against

Blake. "I'm too tired to argue tonight," he said, nuzzling the side of Blake's head. "I'll argue tomorrow."

"No, you won't," Blake told him, smiling in utter contentment as he stroked Niall's side. He closed his eyes and let out the breath it felt like he'd been holding for ten years. At last, he was back where he was supposed to be.

CHAPTER 17

*N*iall slept like the dead, in spite of the fact that he considered crawling into Blake's bed to put an end to the wildly impractical lust that had him at his wit's end a personal failure. Blake had hurt him once. Who was to say he wouldn't do it again? He'd been so determined to keep his distance, to help Blake with practical matters, but not to relinquish control of his heart. Everything about making love with Blake was a disastrous idea.

Except that as morning dawned and Niall drifted awake to the sensation of Blake snuggled against him, his breath hot on his shoulder as Blake's head rested on the pillow next to his, Blake's arm and leg thrown over him as he lay on his back, Niall couldn't help but smile with contentment. All the betrayal and heartache in the world couldn't change the fact that Blake belonged exactly where he was, tangled up with him.

Niall drew in a careful breath, twisting to his side and trying not to wake Blake. Blake stretched and adjusted without fully awaking until the two of them lay facing in each other's arms. The light of morning filtered through the curtains, illuminating Blake's stubbly face just enough for Niall to memorize how beautiful he was in sleep. He stroked his fingers along the side of Blake's face, feeling the roughness of his day's growth of beard. Blake's beard grew in faster than anyone's Niall had ever known, but why that made him want to laugh with joy was beyond him. He continued studying Blake's face with his fingertips, touching the sensual line of his lips and remembering how perfect they were for kissing.

"I'm afraid to open my eyes," Blake murmured at last, proving he was awake after all. "If this is a dream, I don't want to wake up."

"Neither do I," Niall said softly. He moved his hand to Blake's side, tracing lazy lines across his back and arse. They were already both half-erect, and for once Niall didn't mind his growing arousal. The cat was already out of the bag. Might as well enjoy it. He shifted closer to Blake, kissing him tenderly as he brushed his hand over Blake's hip to stroke his cock.

"I'm definitely dreaming," Blake said with a hitch in his breath, reaching for Niall's prick as well. "I wouldn't be this happy if this weren't a dream."

Niall smiled as he kissed Blake, his heart lighter than it'd been in ages. The world seemed so quiet, for a change, without any of the usual noise or pressures of who they were or who they were supposed to be beating down on them. They took their time, touching, kissing, stroking, and pleasuring each other as if they hadn't a care in the world. There was no desperation, only bone-deep pleasure when they each came, and when the post-orgasmic contentment settled over them, they drifted off into a half-sleep, hands entwined between them.

The subtle swish of something being pushed under the door startled Niall into full wakefulness an unknown amount of time later. He sat abruptly, knocking his elbow into Blake's chest as he did, heart racing. His fear of being caught in a position that could get both him and Blake arrested and fill the scandal section of every newspaper in England left him after one terrifying moment when he spotted a small envelope on the floor by the door. Depending on what the envelope contained, they still weren't out of the woods.

"What is that?" Blake asked exactly what Niall was thinking as Niall crawled over him to climb out of bed.

Niall snatched the envelope from the floor and tore into it, not caring what he looked like, standing there naked in the morning light and in desperate need of a bath. He unfolded the letter and scanned through it, pulse pounding, then read it aloud for Blake, "'*I know that you're here and I know what you're looking for. Meet me at Shell Cottage at ten o'clock this morning and we'll talk.*' It's signed '*Annamarie*', and there's an address included," Niall added.

Blake threw aside the bedcovers, leaping to his feet and crossing to take the letter from Niall. He scanned it, then glanced anxiously around the room. "What time is it?"

Niall strode to the pile of his things from the night before and searched for his pocket watch. He hadn't wound it before going to bed, but it was still ticking away. "Almost nine," he said with a frown, hoping the watch was running fast.

"We need to hurry," Blake said in a grave voice, heading to the room's washbasin.

Niall tried not to be irritated that the hotel hadn't updated its facilities to include indoor plumbing, but it was remote, after all. The best he and Blake could do with the time they had was to trade off at the wash table with the sponge and soap the hotel provided and to remove the evidence of everything they'd shared that morning and the night before. Blake didn't seem to care, but Niall still felt like he needed a good, long soak in a porcelain tub, possibly with Blake, as they dressed and headed out of the hotel without so much as stopping for breakfast.

The address Annamarie had given them was easy enough to find and required minimal stops to ask for direction. Shell Cottage turned out to be exactly what its name implied—a small cottage decorated with shells that sat right on the beach just beyond the area Niall figured was densely populated with holiday-makers in the summer months. It looked downright quaint in the morning sunlight. The tide was in and the gentle lap of the sparkling water would have made the scene idyllic, if not for their reason for being there.

"Greta!" The cry that burst from Blake's lungs as they reached the garden gate and spotted the children playing in the yard that faced the beach was powerful enough to make Niall's heart bleed. "Jessie! Alan!"

Before Niall could think to stop him, Blake tore through the gate and around the side of the house.

"Papa!" Three sets of small voices screamed with joy. All three of the children dropped what they were doing to run to Blake, arms outstretched.

An odd but potent burst of jealousy raced through Niall, making it difficult for him to breath. He'd known from the start that they weren't at university anymore and that he would forevermore have to share Blake's affections with his children—if their dalliance was anything more than a jolt of nostalgia to begin with—but seeing the undiluted joy on Blake's face as he dropped to his knees and accepted the embrace of three tiny souls who bore a strong resemblance to him was far more difficult than Niall anticipated. On top of that, he felt like an absolute monster for begrudging Blake anyone's love but his own.

"My darlings," Blake gasped, burying his face in his older daughter's hair for a moment. "I've missed you so much. You have no idea."

"We missed you too, Papa," Greta said, weeping. All three of the children were weeping.

"I want to go home," Alan wailed, setting the children off even more.

"We didn't want to go away with Mama at all," Jessie added. "She made us go."

"I don't like it here, Papa," Greta went on, Jessie and Alan expressing similar sentiments at the same time. "Please, take us home."

"We want to go home," Jessie agreed.

"Children! Get back at once!" Annamarie's sharp voice sounded from the far corner of the house.

Niall straightened, swallowing the lump of pity that had formed in his throat. Annamarie wasn't alone. A sour-faced maid was with her. The maid rushed forward to pull the girls away from Blake so fast Blake didn't have time to react. Annamarie wrenched Alan clumsily off his feet and marched him away herself. In the middle of their actions, Ian rushed around the house as though he'd run from wherever he'd been.

"Give them back," Blake demanded, face contorted in distress, pushing to his feet. "I don't care about anything else, just give my children back."

Ian scowled at Blake as though the devil himself had just crawled out of the ground. Then he spotted Niall at the edges of the scene. "You," he growled, expression twisting to disgust.

Niall's jealousy evaporated into razor-sharp purpose. "Ian." He stepped forward, taking his place at Blake's side. "You've changed."

Indeed, he had. The charm of youth had vanished

from Ian's face and form. His hair was receding, and he'd grown stout in a way that didn't suit his frame. He hadn't shaved that morning, which gave him even more of the appearance of a rogue.

"So have you," Ian said with a sneer. He glanced between Niall and Blake. "I should have known," he went on. "All those years ago, I should have known that the two of you were wicked and perverted."

"Don't say those things about my papa," Greta shouted behind Ian.

The nursemaid jerked hard on Greta's arm, causing Greta to yelp.

"Get your hands off of her," Blake growled, looking as though he would strangle the nursemaid as he tried to step forward.

Ian stopped him by grabbing his lapels and wrestling him in place. "Get the children inside," he snapped.

The nursemaid rushed to do as she was ordered, even though Blake shouted, "Leave them where they are. Give them back to me."

"Children shouldn't be around your kind of wicked- ness," Annamarie said, though to Niall, she didn't sound convinced. She swayed on her spot, wringing her hands and glancing between Ian and Blake. She bit her lip as well, looking as though she would rather be anywhere else but where she was.

"Why did you leave him if not because you don't want anything to do with the life he gave you anymore?"

Niall asked, moving closer to her. Instinct told him that the key to getting Blake everything he wanted was to appeal to Annamarie directly.

He worried in an instant that his instincts were wrong when Annamarie tensed and made a disgusted face at him. "Stay away from me, you...you abomination. It's your fault he never loved me."

Niall froze in the middle of walking to her, blinking at the odd way she phrased things. "I wasn't aware you cared whether he loved you or not."

"I want to be adored," Annamarie shouted with a sudden vehemence that Niall would have found comical under any other circumstance. "He was supposed to worship me and give me everything I wanted."

Niall's esteem for the woman dropped lower than it already was.

"I gave you a home, a title, a position in society," Blake said, more hurt than angry, though Niall thought he had every right to be furious. "I gave you beautiful children. They're all I want, Annamarie. You can have everything else, all of it."

"Do you see?" Annamarie flung one arm at Blake but glared at Niall as she did. "He doesn't even care enough to try to win me back. And it's because you've turned him into a perverted beast who would rather commit sodomy than love me."

Niall pressed his lips tightly shut and clenched his jaw. There was no point whatsoever in arguing matters of the heart and of nature with a woman like Annamarie. Instead, he put his mind to work searching for the right thing to say to convince her to give up the children.

"Isn't it as I told you?" Ian stepped away from Blake—who continued to stare beyond the corner of the house where his children had been taken away—to Annamarie's side. He rested a hand on Annamarie's back. "I told you they were beyond redemption."

"The children want to come home," Blake said, striding forward as if he would go after them.

Niall leapt toward him, grabbing his arm to hold him back. "We'll get them," he assured Blake. "But we need to deal with this first."

Annamarie snorted. "Do you think I would even consider handing innocent children over to evil men like the two of you now?"

"They are my children." Blake's expression darkened as he stared at Annamarie. "You never loved them."

Niall was convinced the bluntness of Blake's statement would only enrage Annamarie more, but instead, she lowered her head guiltily and twisted her hands together. "I will admit that I am not the most maternal of women," she said, face flushing.

"Precisely," Blake said. He drew in a steadying breath and rolled his shoulders before going on. "I know you, Annamarie. I might not love you the way you want me to. I'm not capable of loving you that way. But I have always done my best to care for you and respect you. Even you must admit to that."

Annamarie lowered her head farther, her face flushing deeper as she winced. Niall's heart sped up. Blake had the truth of things and knew the right way to tackle the situation after all. He could see that Annamarie would break in a matter of minutes.

"She will admit to nothing," Ian spat, ruining the groundwork Blake had laid. "It's bad enough that you're a perversion of what God intended a man to be, but to disappoint a woman as beautiful and charming as Annamarie is a crime." He simpered over Annamarie with an affection that was blatantly false to Niall's eyes.

Unfortunately, Annamarie seemed to lap up the sycophantic praise. "Oh, Ian. You always did care for me."

"Yes," Blake said suddenly. "He always did care for you. And you should have been allowed to marry him from the start."

"He wasn't a duke," Annamarie said in an undertone.

Niall scowled in disgust, but Blake seemed to ignore the comment and went on with, "Don't you want the chance to right that wrong? Allow me to grant you a divorce—one in which I will claim that you are the wronged party, even—and to bestow a generous settlement on you. You'll be free to marry Ian at last. I'll even support that life with a generous annual stipend. Just give me the children back."

Annamarie glanced up at him as though considering the offer. To Niall's mind, her eyes flashed with avarice.

But Ian railroaded the offer with, "That is nowhere good enough."

Blake let out a frustrated breath and rubbed a hand over his face. "You know what I want," he said, shrugging and letting his arms fall to his sides. "It's time you tell me what you want, what your involvement in this entire situation is. Name your price, Ian."

A deep wariness swirled through Niall's gut. Asking Ian what he wanted and giving the man the impression he would get it was a terrible idea, as far as Niall was concerned.

Ian seemed to confirm it by grinning slyly. "I want everything," he said. "I want everything you stole from me back then. I want your pride to suffer along with your wallet."

"So it's money you want?" Niall asked, wishing there was a way he could save Blake from everything he dreaded might happen next.

"Of course." Ian barked a laugh. "But more than that. I want the medallion, for one."

Niall blinked and shook his head. Blake looked equally as flummoxed. "What medallion?" he asked.

"The prize you won," Ian said. "Professor Carroll's medallion."

Blake's mouth dropped open. Judging by the confusion that still hung over him, he had forgotten about the prize entirely. "I have no idea where it is," he said.

"I don't care," Ian went on. "I want it. And I want half a million pounds."

Niall nearly choked at the demand, but Blake said, "It's yours," without so much as blinking.

Ian broke into a grin that was as surprised as it was pleased. "You'll bring me a bank draught for the amount when you bring me the medallion."

"Fine." Blake nodded. "Give me the children and I'll go in search of the medallion right away."

Annamarie turned as though she would call to the nursemaid, wherever she'd gone, but Ian stopped her with. "Not a chance. You bring me the medallion and a bank draught for the money first and I'll hand over the children."

"No." Blake's hands formed into fists at his sides. "I'm not leaving here today without my children."

"Are they safe?" Niall asked, resting a hand on Blake's arm to stop him from throwing himself at Ian.

"Of course, they're safe," Annamarie said, pressing a hand to her chest in offense. "What kind of a mother do you think I am if I don't at least keep my children safe?"

"Do you promise that you won't move them from this house until we return with the medallion?" Niall asked on, ignoring her protest.

"I can agree to that," Annamarie said. She looked as shifty as a thief swearing she wouldn't steal the jewels sitting in front of her.

Niall didn't trust her for a moment, but there didn't seem to be much else they could do. "Then we'll find the medallion and bring it to you," he said.

Blake turned to glare at him. "I'm not leaving without my children."

"You're not leaving with them until you get me what I want," Ian said. He crossed his arms and looked so smug that Niall wanted to punch him. Clearly, Ian thought he'd won.

"Think this through logically, Blake," Niall said, turning Blake to the side and lowering his voice. "It's the two of us against Annamarie and Ian, the nursemaid, and whoever else is in that house. Don't forget that Ian's family is nearby, and they're likely known in Blackpool. Think this through. What would happen if we took the children by force? We wouldn't get as far as the train station before the police caught up to us, accusing us of God only knows what crimes."

"Niall always was the more practical of you two," Ian said.

Both Niall and Blake turned to glare at him. Whether it was the truth of what Niall said or the absolute certainty of victory in Ian's stance, Blake's shoulders sagged. He rubbed a hand over his face and let out a heavy breath. "I don't trust them," he said as quietly as he could, meeting Niall's eyes. "I can't help but feel that if we don't take the children now, I will never get them back."

"Do you trust Annamarie?" Niall asked, gripping Blake's upper arms. "Do you truly believe the mother of your children would harm them or allow them to be harmed?"

Blake sent a mournful look past Niall to Annamarie. Annamarie stood hugging herself and looking miserable.

"You know I wouldn't hurt them," she said. It was the first genuine thing she'd said in the entire confrontation.

Blake nodded slowly. He cleared his throat and rolled his shoulders. "All right. We'll find the medallion and return it to you. I'll bring a bank draught, and when you hand over the children, make sure it is honored."

"Excellent." Ian clapped his hands together and rubbed them. "I trust three days is enough time for you to accomplish all of that?"

Blake looked like he would argue, but Niall answered, "Yes," for both of them.

"Good." Ian said. Niall gestured for Blake to leave with him, but before they could so much as turn around, Ian said, "Oh, there is one other thing I want from you as part of this deal."

Dread pooled in Niall's stomach. He should have known. "What?" he snapped, turning back to Ian.

"I want the two of you to make your affair public."

Niall's chest constricted. He glanced to Blake, who looked equally gob-smacked. "We'll be arrested," he said, seething.

Ian grinned as though that were his point. "*You* might be," he said. "Blake is a duke. I'm sure he can figure out a way for his title to protect him."

"I won't put Niall in danger that way," Blake growled.

Ian shrugged. "Then Annamarie and I will just have

to pack up our things and sail on the next ship headed for New York."

All color left Blake's face. Niall boiled with rage. Somehow, Ian had them up against a wall. He knew Ian detested Blake, but he hadn't thought Ian hated *him* that much. Then again, if his intent was to wreak revenge on Blake, ensuring that he would forever be kept apart from his lover while also exposing him to the worst sort of scandal would be an effective way of doing that.

The one glimmer of hope was that Ian had no idea how many options for protection men like him and Blake actually had.

"Fine," Niall answered on both his and Blake's behalf. "We'll do whatever it takes as long as you stick to your end of the agreement and return Blake's children to him in three days' time."

"I'll uphold my end of the bargain as long as I have proof you'll uphold yours," Ian said.

Niall nodded to him, then grabbed Blake's hand and marched away.

"What are you doing?" Blake hissed, trying to yank his hand out of Niall's. "This whole thing is madness. He's going to try to trick us."

"Of course, he is," Niall said, gripping Blake's hand more firmly. "Hold my hand so that he thinks it's a sign we're willing to expose ourselves."

"But we can't. I won't put you in that sort of danger," Blake insisted.

Niall laughed grimly. "First of all, I'm far smarter

than Ian ever was, and so are you," he said. "Secondly, there's nothing that says we can't trick him the same way he's trying to trick us."

Blake paused to glance anxiously at him as they reached the garden gate.

"Trust me, Blake," Niall said. "We will win in the end. I promise."

CHAPTER 18

*B*lake was numb for the entire journey back to Leeds from Blackpool. His heart told him that he was a horrible father for leaving his children without trying harder to extract them. But his head argued that Annamarie would remain true to her word and keep them safe, so he wasn't an utter failure after all. His head also argued that Ian couldn't be trusted and that Annamarie was blind when it came to anyone who flattered her the way she wanted to be flattered. And on top of that argument, his heart told him to trust Niall with his life, that Niall would ensure that everything worked out in the end.

"Are you quite all right?" Niall asked them when they finally stepped down from the carriage they'd hired in Leeds to bring him home to Selby Manor. "You've been uncharacteristically withdrawn since we left Shell Cottage."

Blake sent him a wry, exhausted look. "I suppose I've run out of things to say at this point."

"You? Running out of things to say?" Niall ribbed him as they mounted the stairs and entered the house.

Blake noted that Charles, his first footman, held the door for them, not Dobson. He responded to Niall's teasing with a weak laugh, then asked Charles, "Did Dobson hand in his notice?"

Charles looked both startled and anxious, "Um, yes, your grace."

Blake nodded and pursed his lips, both disappointed and wary. "Did he say why?"

"No, your grace, he just left." Charles shrugged and shook his head, gesturing for one of the younger footmen who loitered in the hall to hurry out to the carriage to fetch Blake's and Niall's bags. "Unless he told Mrs. Crocker, that is."

"Thanks. Tell Mrs. Crocker I'll speak to her in my office as soon as I've cleaned up a bit," Blake said, walking on.

"Yes, your grace."

Blake glanced over his shoulder to make sure Niall was following him. "I suppose this is where you tell me you were right, I told you so, and that I'm too trusting of people."

Niall made a noncommittal sound. "If Dobson values his career as a butler, he'll keep your secrets to himself. No one wants to hire staff who spills their secrets at the slightest provocation."

"True."

Blake continued on, hoping it *was* true. Then again, if Dobson blabbed about what he'd seen in the parlor several evenings before, Ian would be one step closer to having his demands filled.

"I'm going to have Xavier ask a maid to draw me a quick bath," he said as they reached his wing of the house, surprised at how clear his mind felt for a change and how easily he could make a list of everything he needed to do, now that he'd seen his children were safe. "Do you want me to have one brought up for you as well?"

A grin tugged at the corners of Niall's mouth that had all of Blake's thoughts scattering in an instant. "I'm half tempted to share your bath," he said in a quiet voice as they approached the doors to their rooms. "But it's late, I'm exhausted, you have a housekeeper to speak with, and we have a blasted medallion to find."

Blake shared Niall's wicked grin for a moment, enjoying the casual arousal that pulsed through him. It was so good to feel that way as a matter of course, even if there was nothing he could reasonably do about it at the moment. In spite of the mountain of catastrophes falling down around him and the fact that his children still hadn't been returned—and that the conditions for their return were so outlandish—Blake felt whole in a way he hadn't for too long.

"I still can't figure out why on earth Ian would care so much about a musty old school prize," he said as he reached his door and grasped the handle. He paused to think about it and glanced at Niall, who stood similarly paused by the door to his room. "I know he was expecting to score top marks on that exam, but it was just an exam."

"It was his pride," Niall said, ever the voice of reason. "But I also seem to recall that he kept harping on about the monetary value of the medallion itself."

Blake shook his head and shrugged. "Why bother with a medallion, no matter how valuable, and ask for half a million pounds at the same time?"

"Again," Niall said, frowning in thought, "pride. Or else the medallion is worth more than half a million pounds."

"I doubt it," Blake huffed a laugh. "More likely Ian thinks I'll renege on my deal to give him the money."

"Is that what you plan to do?" Niall's brow lifted. "Maybe hand him a fake bank draught?"

He hadn't thought so at the time he'd made the deal, but eight hours of traveling across the north of England by Niall's side and the satisfaction of making love to his heart's one true desire had filled him with a steadiness and confidence he thought he'd lost.

"We'll see," he said with a saucy wink, opening the door to his room.

An uncanny feeling of optimism stayed with him as he bathed and changed into clean clothes. In spite of the frustration of the encounter at Shell Cottage and Ian's bullish and nonsensical demands, Blake felt as though he could see the light at the end of the tunnel. Washing and changing felt symbolically like sloughing off the misery of recent years in favor of purpose and love. As paradoxical as it felt, a large part of him was grateful to Ian for swooping in when he did and removing the thorny problem of Annamarie from his life. Obstacles or no, Ian had unlocked the cage Blake had been living in for years and enabled him to be set free.

And how bad could it be, really, if his unconventional relationship with Niall was exposed? He smiled over that question as he made his way down to his office to speak with Mrs. Crocker about Dobson. At least he had a relationship with the man he loved again. And he fully intended to grab hold of his feelings for Niall with both hands and never to let go again. Damn the consequences. He'd let Niall go once and it had ruined him in every way that counted. What did he care about being ruined in ways that didn't matter as long as he could have Niall in his life and in his bed for the rest of their days?

"I've mitigated the damage as much as I can with the rest of the staff, your grace," Mrs. Crocker reported to him half an hour later, her face stony and her back stiff. "Mr. Dobson said very little about his departure, but he did advise the rest of the staff that their morals may be in jeopardy if they stay."

Disappointment pressed down on Blake. "And did he tell you why he left?" he asked, dreading the answer.

"Yes, your grace." Mrs. Crocker admitted with a reluctant sigh.

"And?" Blake glanced expectantly at her.

"I've known you since you were in short pants, your grace," she said. She paused, her face pinching harder, and went on as though it pained her to say what she needed to. "I've never seen you happier than in the last week, since Mr. Cristofori's arrival. And I don't mean that flippantly. He brings you joy like nothing else. And honestly, it's a lesser sin than what your brother is guilty of."

Blake nodded, but couldn't think of anything more to say.

"That being said, your grace, if you will allow me," she went on just as Blake was about to dismiss her. He nodded to her. She took a deep breath and continued. "If you intend to continue to pursue your happiness, might I advise you to take up residence in the family's London house for a while? As I understand it, such things are overlooked in London. But not here in the country." She paused again, more compassion coming to her expression. "No one would be the wiser, your grace. If, indeed, Lady Selby is not returning, and in light of your brother's sins, they would find it perfectly understandable that you wouldn't want to stay here."

"Do you know, Mrs. Crocker," Blake said, rising from his desk. "I completely agree."

It was somehow cheering to know his housekeeper had come to the same conclusions about where his future lay that he had. By the time he'd dismissed Mrs. Crocker and headed back upstairs to find Niall, he'd all but made up his mind that once he had the children back, the whole lot of them would waste no time in packing everything up and moving to London, just like the dream he'd shared with Niall the night before.

"You wouldn't mind, would you?" he asked Niall after explaining his conversation with Mrs. Crocker. "If we moved there immediately, without full planning? Just up and left? We could...." He stopped, biting his lip and glancing to Niall as though he were about to step off a ledge. "You could move into Selby House with us."

Niall's brow shot up so fast Blake thought he'd pull a muscle in his face. A moment later, Niall's expression settled. "Let's concentrate on finding the medallion first," he said. "We need that to get the children, and we need the children before we can think about the future."

It wasn't the answer Blake wanted. In fact, Niall's answer raised a storm of worry within him. Perhaps Niall didn't think what they had was forever after all. Perhaps it was all just a bit of fun for him. Ten years had changed him, so who was to say it hadn't changed Niall as well? Niall had mentioned he'd had other lovers since university. Perhaps he intended to—

"Blake," Niall spoke pointedly, snapping Blake out of his thoughts. "That wasn't a no. That was a 'let's deal with what's in front of us first'." Niall stepped forward, slipping a hand around to the back of Blake's neck, then leaned in to kiss him fast and hard. The buss settled Blake's nerves and brought him back into himself, particularly when Niall leaned back and grinned at him. "Stop looking as though you've seen a ghost and tell me where you last saw the medallion."

Blake smiled, warmth infusing him. How had he managed to survive for ten years without Niall to guide and steady him?

"To tell you the truth, I have no idea," he shrugged. "Everything from graduation day is a blur in my memory."

"You were wearing the blasted thing when we parted ways," Niall said, starting out of his bedroom, where Blake had found him, and making his way down the hall to the stairs.

"Was I?" Blake followed him.

Niall paused at the top of the stairs and turned to him with a humorless laugh. "Every last detail of the way you looked that day is burned in my memory forever, what you were wearing, the medallion, the shock and the grief in your eyes...everything." He lowered his voice at the end of his sentence before moving forward again.

Blake grabbed his hand, tugging him back. When Niall met his eyes with surprise, Blake blurted, "I'm sorry." Every bitter emotion he'd felt that day rushed back in on him, but for a change, those emotions felt distant and completed instead of fresh. "I did what I thought I had to do at the time. I didn't see any choice back then. But I'd never loved anyone the way I loved you then," he hesitated slightly before finishing with, "and the way I love you now. I never stopped loving you for an instant."

A softness filled Niall's eyes that made it look as

though the years dropped away from him. In spite of the fact that they were standing at the top of a wide staircase in the center of Blake's house, in full view of whoever might choose that moment to walk past, Niall stepped into him, taking Blake's face in his hands and kissing him passionately. It was a kiss that seemed to reach into Blake's soul, righting all the wrongs of the past.

"First we're going to find that medallion," Niall said, his voice hoarse with desire. "Then we're going to go to bed and make love loud enough to have your father rolling over in his grave."

A jolt of heat and excitement struck Blake like lightning.

"And after that," Niall went on, "we're going to march back to Blackpool and rescue your children, no matter what nastiness Ian attempts to throw at us. And when that's done, like Greta and Siegfried, we are going to build our castle just the way we want it, and we are going to live happily ever after."

Niall kissed him again, then broke away and charged down the stairs, leaving Blake reeling with joy and wanting to giggle like one of his girls.

"There wasn't any castle in the play," he said, following Niall down the stairs.

"I rewrote it," Niall called over his shoulder as he reached the ground floor. Blake pointed toward the library, which was as good as any a place to start their search. When Blake caught up to him, Niall caught his hand and said, "I'll rewrite it again and again, if that's what it takes to get the story right."

Blake had never been so happy to spend an evening poring through every parlor, office, and closet in his house. He had no idea how massive the house was until he had to check every crevice and nook in search of the medallion. Neither the speed nor the efficiency of the search was helped at all by the way he and Niall kept finding themselves in deliciously close proximity as they pulled trinkets out of cabinets and checked dusty corners behind large pieces of furniture.

"It's not in this vase," Niall said, leaning across Blake and pressing his whole body against Blake's in the process as he peered into an ugly old vase behind a settee in the library. The gesture bent Blake backwards over the settee, and Niall took advantage of the position to stroke his hands along Blake's side and nibble at his earlobe. "It's not behind the cushions of this thing either," he added breathlessly, grinding his hips against Blake's. They were both desperately aroused and growing more so by the second.

"It might be in the Egyptian parlor," Blake panted, wanting nothing more than to twist in Niall's embrace so that he bent forward over the back of the settee and to have Niall remove his trousers and bugger him into next Tuesday.

Niall pulled back, a comically puzzled look in his blue eyes to match his pink and swollen lips. "You have an Egyptian parlor?"

"It was Annamarie's idea." Blake struggled to stand straight, sliding his hands under Niall's jacket to grip his sides and leaning closer to his mouth. "She likes Egyptian things."

"Then why didn't we check there first?" Niall pulled away from him just as Blake was about to seal their mouths together in a kiss.

Blake groaned and laughed as Niall sped away from him, sending a flirtatious look over his shoulder. They couldn't find the medallion fast enough, as far as he was concerned. If they didn't locate the blasted thing soon so that they could go to bed and satisfy each other in every way possible, Blake wasn't sure he would be responsible for his actions.

His humor about the situation was dented slightly when their search of Annamarie's Egyptian parlor turned up nothing.

"Do you remember what the medallion looked like?" Niall asked, sifting through the curiosities in a glass-fronted cabinet in the corner of the room while Blake watched the way his arse stretched the fabric of his trousers instead of checking the artifacts above the fireplace.

"You're the one who claims to remember every detail of what I was wearing that day," Blake said, giving up his ostensible search to approach Niall from behind. "Don't you remember what it looks like?"

He pressed himself against Niall's back, cupping his backside and applying extra pressure to the cleft of his arse. Niall let out a shaky breath and turned into Blake's arms.

"I remember what you looked like, naked and splayed like you were gagging for it, two nights before," he said breathlessly, eyes zeroing in on Blake's lips.

Blake hummed deep in his throat and grabbed Niall's backside, jerking the two of them together. Niall sighed in acceptance, sliding his arms over Blake's shoulders and indulging in a deep kiss that had their tongues tangled in no time.

"No. Wait," he said a moment later, pulling away. "We have to find the medallion. Everything depends on it. It has to be here."

"Maybe it's in my bedroom," Blake said, desire outweighing guilt as he watched Niall skitter across the room to get away from him, trousers tented. He should focus everything he had on fulfilling Ian's conditions to return the children. But hadn't one of those conditions been to expose himself and Niall? What better way to do that than to risk being caught by the servants again? "I bet we could find it between the sheets."

"I bet we'd find something there." Niall glanced over his shoulder as he reached the bookcase lined with fake papyruses at the other end of the room. "Two obelisks is my guess."

Blake chuckled and started across the room to him. "I have a few ideas about where we could put—"

"What a magnificent room. I don't think I've ever been in here before."

Blake's heart nearly stopped in his chest at the utterly ludicrous arrival of Lady Inglewood in the room. He snapped a curse before he could stop himself. The one saving grace of the nerve-splitting moment was that a high-backed chair stood between him and Lady Inglewood, saving him from the embarrassment of the woman seeing him with an erection big enough to hang a lantern on.

"Lady Inglewood," he gasped. "What in God's name —er, that is, what brings you to Selby Manor so late at night?"

"Is it late, your grace?" Lady Inglewood blinked obliviously, hiccupped, then laughed. "I suppose I lost track of time. Lady Fairport is hosting a ball this evening, and she dared to suggest to me that I could not coax you out of your self-imposed confinement. I told her she was off her nut, of course, and that you'd been to my house just last week for supper. She had the gall to call me a liar, can you believe it?" As almost an afterthought, she added, "Oh, hello, Mr. Cristofori. Are you still here?"

Niall had jumped behind a table piled with books about Egypt, which rested at a convenient height to hide him from the waist down. "I'm still here," he said, face red.

"Sensational," Lady Inglewood said, slurring the word.

Blake gaped at her. The woman was drunk. Drunk enough that he wasn't sure she knew where she was or what she was seeing. That made it easier for him to step out from behind the chair, regardless of his state. "Lady Inglewood, who brought you here this evening, and can they take you home? I'm afraid you need a good, long rest, and perhaps some aspirin in the morning."

"Your handsome, young butler showed me in," Lady Inglewood said, pink-faced and grinning as Blake reached her side and rested a hand on her back to escort her into the hall. "Though I'm not sure the man knows what he's doing. He said he was going to fetch you." She happened to glance down at Blake's trousers and made a sound of surprise and delight. "Ooh! Lord Selby! Cheeky!" She snorted into laughter.

Blake glanced to Niall, barely able to contain his giddiness over the surreal situation as he escorted Lady Inglewood back to the front hall. "Charles," he called out for his first footman.

The hapless lad rounded the corner and let out a curse that had Lady Inglewood giggling and Blake ready to believe he'd passed through the looking glass. "I'm so sorry, your grace," he said. "She got away from me."

"Indeed," Blake said, sending the man as stern a look as he could manage, under the circumstances.

"Lady Fairport will be so disappointed," Lady Inglewood said, turning to grab Blake's lapels. She sagged hard against him, her eyes hazy. "And here she's convinced you're in deep mourning, now that your sweet wife has returned to America."

"America?" Blake laughed, suddenly anxious, prying her hands off of his jacket. "No, Annamarie isn't in

America." He stopped short of saying she was in Blackpool, though.

"She will be soon. At least, that's what I heard." Lady Inglewood patted his chest, then allowed Charles to show her to the door. "But rest assured, we'll find a better duchess for you."

"I'm so sorry, your grace," Charles said as he pushed Lady Inglewood out the door.

"Make sure she doesn't come back," Blake said, bristling with awkwardness over the whole situation. He turned back to Niall, who had waited by the stairs as the whole, bizarre incident played out. "That wasn't even remotely what I expected to ha—"

Niall grabbed his hand, yanking him toward the stairs before he could finish.

"Come on," Niall snapped. "Before we're interrupted again. I've decided we have to skip step one and move directly to step two."

CHAPTER 19

*N*iall didn't think he could have written the situation he and Blake found themselves in more dramatically if he'd tried.

"Kidnapped children," he muttered as he tugged Blake up the stairs, then hurried him down the hall to his room. "Ridiculous demands. Missing medallions. And now, drunken countesses interrupting everything."

"And searing desire," Blake added breathlessly as he leapt ahead, throwing open the door to his room and dragging Niall into the room behind him. "You forgot searing desire."

"Love, I could never forget searing desire," Niall said, slamming the door shut behind him with his foot and reaching for the lapels of Blake's jacket. "No matter how hard I tried. And believe me, I tried. I did everything I could possibly think of to wipe you from my mind like—"

Blake didn't let him finish. He grabbed the sides of

Niall's face and surged into him for a kiss that not only shut Niall up, it made him forget every thought he'd had for the last ten years. He let out a sound of acceptance and need as Blake thrust his tongue into his mouth and kissed him savagely. It was all he could do to scramble to push Blake's jacket off his shoulders and fumble with the buttons of his waistcoat.

"I knew things weren't over for us," Blake gasped between powerful kisses, fumbling with Niall's clothes the way Niall was attempting to peel off his. "I didn't care how bleak things looked at graduation, I knew it wasn't the end for us."

"You had more faith than I did," Niall confessed between ragged pants and kisses as he backed Blake toward the bed. "The world is cruel to men like us."

"The world is beautiful," Blake contradicted him, leaning back to stare into Niall's eyes. The intensity of the fire and the affection in Blake's hazel eyes was enough to drive the breath right out of Niall's lungs. "You are beautiful," Blake continued.

He leaned in for another kiss, but rather than being frantic and lusty, it was tender, and he slipped his arms around Niall's sides, embracing him with a sudden gentleness that conveyed love a thousand times more than lust. It was enough to melt Niall's heart and fire his desire to an even hotter intensity.

"I love you," he said, sliding his hands over Blake's shoulders and running his fingers through the silken mass of his hair. "I shouldn't. I should protect myself. I made this mistake once before."

"I will never hurt you again," Blake said on a sigh, pulling Niall's shirt out of his trousers so that he could dig his fingertips into Niall's back. "I will never betray you again, and I will never leave you for the rest of our lives, if that's what you want."

He pulled back with sudden anxiety in his eyes, his lips swollen from kisses, looking years younger, like his old self.

"God help me," Niall said, the tension of a decade leaving him, "of course, that's what I want. It's what I've always wanted. I never stopped."

He tugged Blake closer, closing his mouth over his and kissing him as possessively as he could. All the tenderness in the world wouldn't be enough to show Blake how deeply they were a part of each other. They were always meant to be. Class and duty and jealousy couldn't change that.

Blake responded to Niall's renewed passion with intensity. He pulled Niall's shirt all the way out of his trousers, then made quick work of his trousers' fastenings. Niall maneuvered them toward the bed as they did, and as the back of Blake's legs hit his mattress, he pushed Niall's trousers and drawers down his hips and reached for his prick. Niall groaned into Blake's mouth as they kissed and Blake stroked. Every fiber of his being responded with pleasure that seemed heightened to dizzying degrees by the love they'd just confessed. Niall tried as best he could to pull off Blake's clothes, but Blake was too intent on what he was doing to stop long enough to help him. Instead, Niall leaned back enough so he could rip his own shirt off over his head.

"You really are beautiful," Blake panted, spreading his hands over Niall's chest as soon as it was exposed, then sitting on the bed so that he would be at the right level to flicker his tongue over one of Niall's nipples and suckle it. The sensation was so electric that Niall gasped as he buried his fingers in Blake's hair. "You always were gorgeous," Blake went on, pushing Niall's trousers farther down his legs, "but your body is so perfect now."

Niall opened his mouth, but didn't know what to say to a compliment like that. He didn't have a chance to say anything as Blake stood suddenly and pivoted with Niall, switching their positions and shoving Niall gently to sit on the edge of the bed. Blake dropped to his knees to remove Niall's shoes, kicking off his own in the process and unfastening his own trousers as though the tightness was too much, then yanking Niall's trousers off from the cuff.

"I've missed this so much," Blake sighed, pushing Niall's knees apart and stroking his hands up Niall's thighs.

He followed that by toying with Niall's balls for the briefest of moments, then grasping the base of his cock and holding it how he wanted it. Niall let out a gasp that was far too loud as Blake bore down on him, taking him surprisingly deep before moving back to lick and caress the head of his prick with his tongue and lips.

"Dear God, I've missed this too," Niall laughed, though his breathless laughter turned into sighs of pleasure as Blake continued to tease and suck him.

Ten years hadn't lessened Blake's skill one bit. He'd been a fast learner at university, and he was quick to recall everything Niall liked. He remembered just the way Niall liked the stroke of his tongue and the friction of movement as he took him deeper and deeper. It was so good, in fact, that Niall felt himself spinning out of control far too soon.

"Stop," he gasped, pushing Blake away. "We're not students anymore. We're not going to bounce back and be ready for more if we spend what we have too soon."

"Speak for yourself," Blake said, glancing up at Niall from between his spread legs with a grin so cheeky it could have been enough to make Niall come. "I feel like I could go all night."

Niall's heart throbbed along with his prick. He hadn't forgotten how much he loved Blake, but he was remembering every last one of his reasons for loving him and then some. "You always were insatiable," he said, eager to explore that aspect of their relationship to the fullest. "Get out of those useless clothes and get your arse into bed where I can do what I want with it."

Blake flushed deeper, and wanton excitement lit his eyes. "Yes, sir," he said, rocking back and standing.

Blake tore off his clothes as Niall threw back the

bedcovers, then followed his instincts to check the drawer of the table beside Blake's bed. He was rewarded by finding a jar of ointment. As Blake kicked off his trousers, Niall unscrewed the lid so it would be ready when they needed it. By the time he was done, Blake lunged into bed with him, nearly tackling him in his eagerness to get on with things.

Niall laughed. "Are you in some sort of hurry?" he asked as Blake pushed his shoulders, forcing him to his back in the center of the bed.

"I'm making up for lost time," he panted, then rained kisses across Niall's cheeks, lips, and neck. "I miss this neck so much," he groaned, nipping and sucking at it.

"Hopefully you're more careful about leaving marks than you were ten years ago," Niall gasped, arching into every touch, every kiss. He couldn't get enough of the feel of Blake's back in his hands, even though Blake kept moving and making it impossible to grab hold.

"I think leaving a mark would be what Ian wants," Blake said, then moved to kissing Niall's chest.

"I don't want to think about him right now," Niall said. "I don't want to think about anything but—" His sentence ended in a long, vocal sigh as Blake reached between his legs to finger him. It was sweet and sensual, and Niall could feel just how close they both were. Neither was going to make it much longer. "If you want to fuck me, I have absolutely no objections to that," he panted.

"No." Blake shifted to the side, reaching for the jar

and handing it to Niall. "I mean, yes, sometime soon I most definitely want to fuck you until we're both raw."

Niall gasped with giddiness at the idea.

"But tonight, I need you in me," Blake said, a sudden, serious look coming into his eyes. "I need you in me hard."

A swoop of gravity passed through Niall's insides as Blake shifted to his stomach, holding his backside up. "This is not some sort of punishment for the way things happened," he said, lifting to his knees and scooping a generous dollop of the lubricant onto his fingers. "I'm never going to hurt you again the way I did after the show." He coated his throbbing prick all the same before setting the jar aside.

Blake let out a deep gasp of pleasure as Niall teased his hole with the rest of the lubricant on his fingers.

"Blake," Niall said, leaning over him, his cock pressed against Blake's backside without thrusting in. He waited until Blake glanced over his shoulder at him. "Love is not a punishment. We were both wrong back then. But we can make things right now."

The tension in Blake's shoulders shifted. "I love you so much." He arched back against Niall, urging him on.

The moment was so paradoxically sweet that Niall gave in to every instinct he had to merge with the man he loved. He gripped Blake's hips and worked himself slowly and deeply inside of him. They both groaned at the pleasure of their joining, but rather than fucking Blake hard, like he's asked for, Niall started tenderly, moving in concert with him as their bodies adjusted to each other.

He ratcheted things up as soon as he felt Blake grow restless, giving them both more of what they wanted. It was glorious to be so much a part of each other that way, and in no time at all, Niall was thrusting with all the intensity Blake could have asked for and more. It was so good that he reached around to hold Blake's hard cock, letting the motion of his thrusts move his hand until Blake was practically sobbing with pleasure.

The sudden tightening of Blake's muscles and the warm burst that spilled into Niall's hand as Blake came with a cry were too much for Niall to resist. He jerked into orgasm seconds later, spilling himself deep inside of Blake. The moment was so perfect and so beautiful that he groaned, then curled around Blake's back, all tension leaving him. He bit Blake's shoulder lightly before pulling out and collapsing to his side.

Blake lay limp and smiling with him. "How could I have gone for so long without that?" he asked, struggling to catch his breath. "My arse feels so perfectly used right now."

Niall turned his head to Blake, grinning, then burst into laughter at the look of utter transportation in Blake's eyes. "You always did look like a dream right after being fucked."

"It's because I enjoy it so much," Blake said with feeling. "But only when you're the one doing the fucking."

Niall laughed, every muscle in his body feeling warm

and liquid as he splayed on his back. There was no point in denying that, in that moment, he was blissfully happy. Even more so when Blake shifted to cuddle against him. Blake was all heart, and he wore that heart on his sleeve, especially where Niall was concerned. It came as a shock to Niall how much he had missed being showered with that sort of affection. He'd spent ten years hardening his heart so that he wouldn't be hurt again, but that had been a terrible thing to do. He should have known that, in spite of his best efforts and insisting he wouldn't fall into Blake's arms again, he was meant to be right where he was, by Blake's side, sweaty and satisfied.

"I suppose all of your theatrical lovers have been much better than me," Blake said, eyes glittering and mouth swollen as he grinned. "They must have more experience."

"Stop," Niall warned him, twisting to his side and gathering Blake into his arms so that their overheated bodies plastered together in a dozen places. "I haven't had *that* many theatrical lovers. Or any other kind of lovers either."

"But you have had some," Blake went on, playing with a damp piece of Niall's hair.

"None that mattered," Niall said, wishing parts of his past could be erased.

"Theater people are notoriously immoral," Blake said, imitating the dowager from Lady Inglewood's dinner party and resting his head on the pillow as he continued to gaze into Niall's eyes and touch his face.

"But I always loved theater people. One theater person in particular."

Niall grinned, nestling closer against Blake and wedging his knee between Blake's legs. "The theater is a wonderful world, really."

"I would like to have some part in it," Blake sighed. "It hasn't seemed possible before now, but with you here, anything could happen."

"Anything?" Niall arched one eyebrow.

"It's not like I've put theater behind me entirely," Blake went on. "Our play has lived forever in my heart. And a few years back, when a call went out from a theatrical troupe passing through Leeds, I donated several—"

He stopped short, his whole body tensing.

"What is it?" Niall lifted himself on one arm to look down at Blake.

Blake sat so fast that he nearly tossed Niall aside. His eyes went round. "I gave it away," he said.

"Gave what away?" Suspicion grew in Niall's gut.

Blake turned to him with a forlorn look. "The medallion. I remember now. I gave it away to the theater in Leeds. They were doing a production of *Anthony and Cleopatra*, and they needed Egyptian props, costumes, and set pieces. I let them come to the house to see what we had and take whatever they needed." The dread in his eyes grew. "Niall, the medallion Ian wants is gone. It's been gone for years."

Niall sat up as well, hissing a curse. "What do we

do?" he asked. "Do we go to Leeds to find it?"

"I...." Blake shoved a hand through his hair, shifting restlessly. "It was a traveling company. They formed in Leeds, but they had plans to travel all over England, Scotland, and Wales."

"So the medallion could be anywhere," Niall said, gut clenching.

"There is no possible way we'll be able to give Ian what he wants." Blake reached the same conclusion Niall had reached.

"He'll have to hand over the children anyhow," Niall insisted, resting a hand on Blake's arm when he saw the signs of one of Blake's anxiety spells coming over him. That didn't seem to be enough to ward the attack off, so he drew Blake into his arms, wrapping his arms and legs around him. "We'll think of something," he insisted. "It's been ten years. Ian probably doesn't even remember what the medallion looks like. You have an entire room of Egyptian artifacts downstairs. I'm certain we can find something or fashion something that Ian will believe is the medallion he's after."

"I doubt it will work. Ian is too determined to ruin me," Blake said, resting his head against the side of Niall's for a moment.

"We'll try anyhow," Niall said. "We can...we can put the medallion in a box and say it's for safekeeping. That could buy us the minutes we need to get the children away from him. Or we could find a way to send him and Annamarie a telegraph, asking for more time."

Blake stiffened in Niall's arms, wrenching back to stare at Niall, eyes wide. "There is no time," he said, panic overtaking him again. "My God, why didn't I put two and two together earlier?" He shoved a hand through his hair, then struggled away from Niall, climbing out of bed. "Lady Inglewood might have been drunk, but she tried to give us vital information, and we missed it."

"Are you certain you're not just flying into a panic over every little thing?" Niall climbed carefully out of the bed and shadowed Blake as he moved frantically toward his wardrobe as if he would dress again.

Blake shook his head. "Lady Fairport was under the impression that Annamarie had left for America."

"Yes? So?" Niall frowned.

"So she was close with Annamarie," Blake said, facing Niall with a grim look as he chose a clean suit from his wardrobe. "I would be willing to bet anything and everything I have that there's a ship sailing from Liverpool to New York in three days or less, and that Ian has purchased tickets for himself, Annamarie, and the children. If they get on that ship—"

Niall stopped him by grabbing both his arms and staring hard into Blake's eyes. "This is all speculation. You don't know that any of this is true. All we know for certain is that Ian wants that damn medallion for some reason, that he wants Annamarie, but is willing to hand the children back over to you, and that he wants to destroy both of our reputations. Anything else is just speculation."

"But can we truly risk assuming that?" Blake asked. "Can we assume Ian will be honest with us, that he'll wait three days before taking off with Annamarie and the children, or that he hasn't already formed plans to cheat us?"

Niall pressed his lips together and clenched his jaw. "No, we can't," he admitted. "But we can't go flying off in the middle of the night either," he said. "Come back to bed, try to sleep, and we'll leave for Blackpool again first thing in the morning."

"We can't wait that long," Blake said, desperation in his eyes. "They could be gone by then."

"Remember what happened when we tried this before." Niall rested a hand on the side of Blake's face. "We had to take whatever trains we could find, and it took us longer to get there than if we had waited until morning. Come back to bed, think of something we can pass off as the medallion Ian is looking for, and we'll return to Blackpool tomorrow. That's still more than a day before Ian will be expecting us."

Blake looked uncertain, but some of the fear drained from his eyes. "I just want them back," he admitted at last. "I want us to be able to build a life together, as a family."

The sentiment was as outlandish as it was adorable. Niall smiled in spite of himself, his heart warming at the utterly impossible idea. Blake was all but suggesting he transform into a second father to Blake's children overnight. The idea that two men—one of them a famous playwright and the other a bloody duke—could raise three children in domestic bliss, without anyone lifting an eyebrow or the police being called in, was ludicrous.

And yet, he'd seen stranger things happen. Max Hillsboro, the son of a duke and a lord in his own right, had thrown his lot in with Stephen Siddel, and the two of them lived together, operating an orphanage for girls in Darlington Gardens, the new square in Earl's Court that was almost entirely populated by members of The Brotherhood. Alistair Bevan was a viscount, and it was no secret in certain circles that he and his valet, Joe Logan, lived more or less openly as lovers. As long as they were excruciatingly careful, perhaps there was a way that he and Blake could form a happy family with Blake's children. And Niall did like children. He'd just never in a hundred years imagined himself having any.

"I want that too," he said at last, pulling Blake close and kissing him affectionately. "But there's nothing we can do about it right this moment. Tomorrow." He kissed Blake again. "Come back to bed. I'll even let you fuck me silly, if that makes you feel better."

Blake let out a weak laugh, smiling as the tension drained from him. "As much as that tempts me, I don't think I could again tonight."

"And neither could I," Niall admitted, steering Blake back to bed. "We'll just sleep. We're going to need our strength tomorrow anyhow. We're going after Ian, and he won't know what's coming for him."

CHAPTER 20

*N*iall was a genius, and Blake didn't know how he'd managed to stay afloat without him for so long. Or perhaps it was the simple fact that Blake could finally let go of the mountain of responsibility and fear and anxiety that he was naturally inclined to carry around with him and share that burden with his soulmate. Whatever it was, he miraculously managed to sleep for a few hours before waking in Niall's arms.

Xavier helped them pack while Blake wrote out a bank draught for as much money as he could, sealing it in an envelope with instructions on how to contact his solicitor for the transfer of the rest of the money Ian had asked for. If Ian reneged on his end of the deal, they would contact Blake's solicitor immediately, telling him to instruct the bank not to honor the draught. While he did that, Niall sifted through the Egyptian parlor until he found a necklace that was close enough to what he remembered the medallion looking like to pass and a box to put it in. Then Charles saw them to the train station in Leeds before most of the rest of the household staff had made it above-stairs. Exactly as Niall had figured, they were able to purchase tickets for a train heading on a more direct route to Blackpool, although it did pass through Liverpool first.

"There's a ship leaving for New York tomorrow," Blake noted gravely as they searched for food in the station while waiting for the train to Blackpool. Several of the passenger lines departing out of Liverpool had their departure dates and times posted on boards that were decorated with enticing advertisements. The White Star line had a ship departing the next day, just after the time Ian had set for the exchange of the children for the medallion.

"Maybe Lady Fairport was right after all," Niall said with a sigh as the two of them stood shoulder to shoulder, staring up at the board. "It's a good thing we didn't wait the full three days."

Knowing Ian might very well have planned to steal away to America the moment the handoff was supposed to take place made Blake extraordinarily anxious as they traveled the final leg of the journey to Blackpool. Once they reached the seaside town, they took a room in a different hotel than they'd stayed in days before, just to be safe, dropped their things, then headed for Shell Cottage.

The moment they neared the cottage, Blake's high

hopes crashed. He could see at once they were too late, in spite of their best efforts.

"It's abandoned," he said, pausing just inside the garden gate as his heart raced and his knees threatened to give out.

Indeed, the curtains were pulled shut in every window of the cottage that they could see, even though it was a rainy day and keeping them open would let in much-needed light. They walked around the side of the house and on to the back, where the garden met the beach, but everything was desperately quiet. The steady roar of the waves combined with the patter of rain on the cottage's roof and the cry of sea birds only added to Blake's sense of hopelessness.

"We're too late," he said, as they rounded the cottage to the front again.

"Maybe not," Niall said with a frown, marching up to the door. He banged on it, then stood back, waiting for someone to open up.

No one came. Not when Niall knocked again, and not when they went to peer into as many windows as they could reach. The house was empty.

"I knew we shouldn't have left the children the other day," Blake hissed, cursing himself. He sucked in a breath that turned into a sob. "It's all my fault."

"It is not your fault." Niall raised his voice slightly, glaring at Blake, but Blake could tell it was Ian he was angry with, not him. Niall paused for a moment before charging out to the road. "We'll go back to the

Archibalds' house. Ian's mother was there before, and even if she isn't there now, one of the servants might know where Ian and Annamarie have gone."

"What if they're in Liverpool already?" Blake asked, heart pounding, as they strode along the main road that skirted the beach on their way to the Archibalds' house.

"Then we'll go back to Liverpool," Niall said, bursting with determination. "We'll plant ourselves on the dock where that ship is departing, if we have to. The one thing we won't do is let Ian and Annamarie board a ship with your children."

The situation was beyond desperate, but Blake found himself smiling and his heart warming all the same. His title and the expectations it brought with it be damned, he would follow Niall to the ends of the earth—or at the very least, London—just to stay by his side. Plans for relocating his life already filled his head, calming and pushing aside his panic and instilling him with a confidence that might not have been founded, but was certainly encompassing.

Niall marched straight up to the Archibalds' house and pounded on their door once they were there as though he were a king and not just a playwright. "Lady Archibald," he demanded. "We must speak with you at once."

Footsteps sounded behind the door almost immediately, and within seconds, a frightened-looking maid opened the door.

"We're here to speak with Lady Archibald," Blake

said, stepping up in an effort to show he was as strong and powerful as Niall. "Better yet, we'd like to speak to Ian Archibald or Lady Selby, if they're here."

Eyes wide, without saying a word, the maid pulled back into the house. She wasn't fast enough to slam the door on them. Blake stuck his foot in to stop her, and when she ran off into the house, he and Niall marched into the front hallway.

"How dare you barge into my home like this?" an older man that must have been Sir Richard Archibald—though he'd aged considerably since the one time Blake had laid eyes on him, at graduation—demanded from a chair in the parlor just off the front hallway. "Essie, what is the meaning of this?"

Before Blake could turn to address the man, Lady Archibald came charging up the hallway from a room in the back. "They aren't here," she said, looking both angry and afraid of what Blake and Niall might do.

"Where are they?" Blake demanded. "Where are my children?"

"I want no more part of this," Lady Archibald replied with startling force. "Ian is my son, but this is going too far."

"Is he here?" Niall asked, standing close by Blake's side.

"No, he is not," Lady Archibald said, glaring at him.

"Then where is he?" Niall asked on.

Lady Archibald pursed her lips and balled her hands into fists at her sides. "I will not tell you where he is, but it is not far. I've no doubt you would do him harm if you were able to reach him, and I would like the first go at wringing his neck."

"Please. All I want is my children back," Blake pleaded with her. "Do you know if they're safe?"

"They are," Lady Archibald said. Before Blake could go on, she said, "I will send him a message immediately, demanding that he contact you wherever you are staying."

"We are at the King's Arms," Niall said.

"Then I will tell him to go to you there to finish this sordid business." Blake opened his mouth, but Lady Archibald continued over him with, "Now leave at once, before I change my mind."

Blake looked to Niall to make the decision. Niall stared hard at Lady Archibald for a moment before letting out a heavy breath and nodding to Blake.

As soon as they were outside and had made it to the street corner, Niall paused, hunching his shoulders against the rain and turning back to watch the house.

"Do we wait here?" Blake asked. "Like last time?"

Niall's face pinched. "They must have another way of leaving the house so as not to be observed," he said. "That could be how they avoided being discovered last time."

"Then we've no choice but to wait at the hotel." Blake scrubbed a hand over his face, letting out a growl of frustration. He hadn't bothered to shave that morning in his haste to leave Selby Manor, and a thick growth of stubble covered the lower half of his face.

Niall heaved a sigh and nodded, and the two of them started back to the hotel.

They barely had time to bathe and change into dry clothes when a note was pushed under their door. Blake lunged for it, tearing it open, while Niall leapt out into the hall.

"Who gave you that letter?" Blake heard him ask someone in the hall while he pulled a short letter out of the envelope.

"A maid, sir," the young voice of one of the hotel's porters answered. "I don't know who she were."

Blake didn't hear whether Niall and the lad had any further exchange. He scanned the letter, his heart in his throat. *"You know what I want and I know what you want. Bring the medallion and a bank draught to Shell Cottage immediately, and the children will be returned to you."*

Niall walked up behind him to read the letter over Blake's shoulder. "He must have thought we would send the police to Shell Cottage to get the children back. That's why they weren't there."

"They're there now," Blake growled.

Niall made a sound of agreement. "We'll go back. Now."

"But we have to be careful." Blake folded the letter, but didn't bother shoving it back in its envelope as he marched to his suitcase to fish out the bank draught and instructions. "He's likely already put something in place to double cross us."

"I believe you're right," Niall said grimly. "So we'd best tread carefully."

They bundled up in their already wet coats and headed out into the rain again. Night was falling, which, combined with the rain, lent an aura of gloom and desperation to the evening. Shell Cottage didn't look any less abandoned when they reached it, but at least there was a thin trail of smoke coming from one of the chimneys when there hadn't been earlier. In addition to that, a plain, black carriage was parked in front of the garden gate.

"That's them," Niall said, equal parts relief and anger as he picked up his pace and approached the carriage.

Before they could come within twenty feet of it, the carriage door opened and Ian stepped out. "The medallion and the money, if you please," he said without introduction.

Blake took the envelope with the bank draught and the box with the fake medallion from his coat pocket and held them up, but said, "Give me my children first."

Ian scowled, shifting restlessly. "They're in the house."

Blake nodded and stepped forward to hand him the envelope and the box, but Niall thrust out a hand to hold him back. "Prove it," Niall said.

Ian snorted, but his shoulders bunched anxiously. "You think I'm lying? That I'd go back on my deal?"

"Yes," Niall said.

"He's not lying." Annamarie scooted to the carriage door, but rather than climbing down, she stood, hesitating as her traveling dress filled the doorway. She picked at her skirts and grimaced up at the rainy sky, as if loath to ruin her clothes.

"Forgive me if we don't believe you," Niall told her.

Annamarie made an offended sound and turned up her nose at Niall. "But of course, a man like you wouldn't believe a decent woman. I'm certain you have no experience at all with good people, you perverted husband-stealer."

Niall huffed and rolled his eyes.

Blake ignored the interaction and marched closer to Annamarie. Ian flinched as though he would intercept him, and Annamarie yelped and braced herself in the door, as though Blake meant her harm.

"I just want the children, Annamarie," Blake said, pausing when he was still several feet from her and holding up his hands to show that he meant no harm. He wouldn't hurt her, but if she thought he might and it spurred her to return the children faster, then he would let her believe it. "Is Ian telling the truth about them being in the house?"

"He is," Annamarie insisted.

"And I say prove it," Niall repeated.

"Oh, Ian, they aren't going to leave us alone unless you show them," Annamarie whined.

"Fine," Ian grumbled, then marched to the gate. He

311

threw the gate open so violently that it rattled on its hinges, then marched up to the window beside the front door. He rapped on it angrily and shouted, "Show your faces, you little wretches."

Fury like nothing Blake had known roared in his gut, and he started toward Ian, intent on throttling the man, if he could. He stopped dead after only a few paces when the curtain parted to reveal Greta and Jessie, or at least their heads and shoulders. The window was too high to see all of them, or to see Alan, but it was most certainly them.

"Darlings," Blake cried out, picking up his pace.

"Wait!" Annamarie shouted as he rounded the front of the carriage. She hopped down, squealing at the rain, and dashed around the carriage to meet Blake. "I...." her mouth hung open for a moment as her gaze traveled past Blake to Ian. As Ian marched forward to join the interaction, Niall did as well.

"You've seen them," Ian said. "Now give me what I asked for."

Blake held the envelope and box out to Ian, but Annamarie threw herself into Blake's arms before Ian could take them. The gesture was a shock and threw Blake off balance.

"I know you're a good man, Blake," Annamarie said, her eyes shining with tears and regret. "If you had only loved me the way I wanted you to, this whole thing could have been avoided."

"But, you see, I could never love you that way," Blake

said, his heart feeling oddly sympathetic for the woman who had caused so much trouble in his life. He glanced over his shoulder to Niall. "I always have and I always will love Niall, whether you understand or approve or not."

Annamarie gasped and took a large step back, then sniffed. "May God have mercy on your soul," she said, her face turning stony. A moment later, her expression softened. "You will let me see the children from time to time, won't you?" she asked, her face changing yet again to an odd sort of anxiety. "I may not be the maternal sort, but they are my girls. And girls need their mother, especially as they grow older. I...I feel horrible about parting with them." She sent a worried look to the house, where the girls still watched from the window, and then glanced to Ian and bit her lip.

Blake sighed. "It would be wrong of me to keep them from you indefinitely. But I'm afraid you'll have to earn my trust again before that will be possible."

"I...I understand." Annamarie lowered her head and twisted her gloved hands together. "Oh, I simply cannot bear this rain."

She tore past Blake, possibly even bursting into tears as she did, though Blake didn't have a chance to follow her to see if that was the case. Ian marched forward and plucked the envelope and box with the medallion from his hands so fast that he knocked Blake to the side. As soon as he had them, he nearly ran for the carriage.

"Come on." Niall burst forward just as fast, grabbing

Blake's arm and wrenching him toward the cottage. "I don't trust him as far as I can see him. We need to get the kids out of here, out of Blackpool, now."

Blake nodded. The carriage's driver snapped his reins over the horses, sending the carriage careening down the road at a dangerous pace. Blake didn't care where Ian and Annamarie went next. They could go to hell as far as he was concerned. He had his children back.

Greta and Jessie were shouting something on the other side of the window, their eyes wide with terror and their faces pale. They banged against the glass, shouting, "Papa! Papa!" and other things Blake couldn't make out.

"The door is locked," Niall said as he rattled the handle.

"Girls, can you open the door?" Blake shouted through the window.

"Mama!" Greta banged against the inside of the glass, pointing at the carriage. "Alan! She has Alan!"

"I need you to open the door from the inside, darling," Blake instructed her.

Only when she dashed away from the window did her words begin to sink in. Blake tore to the front door—which Niall was now attempting to knock down by ramming his shoulder into it. He pushed Niall out of the way, trying the handle himself.

It took a few more, maddening seconds before Greta managed to unlock the door from the inside and wrench it open. As soon as she did, Blake leapt into the house, gathering both of his girls in his arms.

"Thank God," he groaned, hugging them for all he was worth and coming close to bursting into tears. "Thank God you're safe."

"Where's the boy?" Niall asked in a far darker voice. "Where's Alan?"

"Mama still has him," Greta said, voice hoarse, nearly beside herself. "Mr. Archibald called him a bargaining chip."

Blake's heart dropped to his bowels. He continued to hold his girls close—or rather, they continued to cling to him, burying their faces in his wet coat, as though their lives depended on it—while glancing around the cottage as if Alan would pop out of the woodwork.

"She's right," Niall said, guessing Blake's thoughts immediately. "He isn't here."

"I want to go home," Jessie wailed. When she lifted her face to him, Blake was struck dumb with a moment of blinding rage at the angry red bruise that covered half her face.

The corners of his vision went black and he began to shake. "What happened to you?" he asked, holding her tighter.

"Mr. Archibald struck her when she tried to fight him to get Alan back," Greta said, her eyes wide and streaming with tears. "Mama didn't see him do it."

"I want—" Jessie started, but dissolved into wails and sobs as she clutched Blake so hard he didn't think he would ever be able to pry her away. Not that he wanted to. If he had his way, his girls would never leave his sight again.

"We have to go after them," Niall said, starting for the door. "As fast as possible. That ship leaves tomorrow."

"Mama and Mr. Archibald are going to Grandfather Cannon's house in New York," Greta confirmed the suspicion Blake had had all along. "And they're going to take Alan."

"We can't let them go." Blake shifted his girls so that he held their hands and followed Niall out into the rain. He hated forcing his girls to run through the chilly downpour with his whole heart, but it was better for them to get a little wet now so that they could save Alan from being taken away and prevent the entire situation from getting more complicated.

But before they were even close to the hotel, Blake saw the problem in their situation.

"We can't leave the girls alone in the hotel," he called to Niall, who rushed on by his side, holding Greta's hand. It was a good sign that Greta trusted him enough to take Niall's hand, but Blake would dwell on what that meant later.

"There's no telling how far Ian and Annamarie have gotten already in that carriage," Niall added.

"Or what time the next train for Liverpool departs," Blake agreed. "They're going to get away." It broke his heart to admit as much.

"We might still have a chance," Niall said. They were closer to the center of Blackpool now, and several people stared at the odd group they made as they hurried on. "We were counting on Ian not realizing the medallion we gave him is a fake, but that might be what saves us in the end."

"If he wants it that badly, he might not leave England until he has it," Blake said, following that line of logic.

"I'm not sure we can count on that, though," Niall said. "We need to be in Liverpool, monitoring the departing ship."

"And I need to send a telegram to my bank not to honor that draught," Blake added.

"But I want to go home," Jessie wept.

Blake winced at the choice in front of him. Whatever they did, they would have to bring the girls with them. He would go to Liverpool to intercept Ian and Annamarie and get Alan back, but he wasn't sure the girls trusted Niall enough to return to Selby Manor with him. Especially not Jessie. She was as likely to think Niall would be cruel to her the way Ian had as not. She didn't know him. By that same token, if he stayed with the girls and sent Niall to Liverpool, even if he did intercept Ian and Annamarie before they boarded the ship, Alan didn't know Niall. And if the police got involved, they would give Alan to Annamarie and not a seemingly random stranger. If they all went to Liverpool, that would only prolong the trauma his girls were experiencing with no guarantee they would catch up to Ian and Annamarie.

"I don't know what to do," Blake told Niall as they reached the hotel and stepped into the shelter of the lobby. The girls instantly clung to him again, proving even further that he couldn't and wouldn't separate himself from them. "I have to choose between my daughters and my son and heir," he went on, the full horror of the situation hitting him.

Niall scowled. "I'm sure that's what Ian had in mind from the start." He wiped a hand over his wet face, studying the girls with a look of compassion. For a moment, Niall was silent, as if he were running through the same options Blake had. At last, he said, "We'll have to contact the police in Liverpool to inform them of the situation. They're the only ones who can stop Ian and Annamarie from getting on a ship with Alan."

"You're right." Blake nodded, feeling more at ease with Niall there to help. "In the meantime, we need to get the girls home to—no." He glanced from Niall to each of his girls. "We need to take the girls somewhere Ian and Annamarie or anyone who might be in league with them won't find them."

"Because if Ian feels like he needs to hold on to Alan as—what did you say Mr. Archibald called him, Greta?" Niall asked.

"A bargaining chip," Greta answered, eyes round.

Niall nodded, looking back at Blake. "He wants something more from you, or at least to ensure that you live up to your end of the bargain. Which you aren't doing because of the medallion. Chances are he won't return Alan until he has all of his money and our reputations are ruined."

"And he probably knows the medallion is a fake now," Blake added. The situation was beginning to make sense, though it was still wretched. He studied his daughters for a moment before saying, "We have to return to Selby Manor, at least at first. It's the only place Ian would know where to find us with further demands."

"We need to go to London as soon as possible after that," Niall said. His face broke into an almost nonsensically ironic grin. "I have a show that opens in just over a week. I nearly forgot."

It was mad. The entire situation was utterly mad, but there was little they could do about it.

"We'll go to Selby Manor, then," he decided, squeezing his girls closer. "We'll have every police officer in this country searching for Ian and Annamarie and Alan. We'll get Alan back, but we'll go to London and find a safe place for the girls, where Ian and Annamarie won't be able to reach them, before we do."

CHAPTER 21

The journey back to Selby Manor seemed to take ten times as long as any of the previous trips Niall and Blake had made because of the girls. Niall was impatient the whole time on Blake's behalf, but he couldn't begrudge the girls their need for naps and snacks and awkward trips to the ladies' facilities that were their own kind of puzzle, considering neither Niall nor Blake were permitted to enter a public toilet for ladies, but Greta and Jessie were too young to go by themselves. Not that Blake wanted to let them out of his sight anyhow. He was nearly arrested in Liverpool for accompanying his girls into a facility, even though they'd waited until it was empty and Niall had stood guard by the door.

"Let's hope that's the only encounter we have with the police," Blake said after arguing with an officer at the Liverpool train station. He held each of his girls' hands and sped through the platforms as they rushed to catch a train.

"I've definitely been accosted by the police for less savory reasons," Niall agreed with a grim look.

"You have?" Blake asked, brow lifting, as he let go of Jessie's hand at the platform long enough to fish out their tickets for the porter.

Niall waited to answer until they were past the man and settled in their first-class compartment. "It's unavoidable in London, particularly when one is part of the theatrical set. But they leave us alone for the most part, unless someone does something foolish."

Blake focused on making sure the girls were comfortable, but the look on his face was wary. "I only hope the officers at Liverpool's central police office took my pleas seriously and plan to keep an eye out for Ian and Annamarie at the dock today."

"They will," Niall said, though he wasn't so sure.

They'd stopped off at the central Liverpool police station first thing upon arriving in the town that morning. The officers had been sympathetic to Blake's fears about Annamarie taking Alan out of the country, but even though Blake was a duke, without orders from a court or papers from a solicitor, all they'd been able to promise to do was watch. To complicate matters, Blake had been less than discreet about his dependence on Niall, which had raised eyebrows. Niall loved Blake with all his heart and his life felt right again, now that they were together, but even in London, their life together wasn't going to be easy, considering the way Blake wore his heart on his sleeve.

Niall had just about resolved to bring the subject up and educate Blake on the various ways men like them could keep a low profile while still living as they wanted to when the carriage they'd hired in Leeds to take them to Selby Manor pulled up to Blake's front door.

"We're home," Greta said, nearly weeping with relief.

"I want to give Sarah a big hug," Jessie added, leaping toward the door and trying the handle before the carriage had fully stopped.

"Her doll," Blake explained, holding the door handle firmly so that Jessie couldn't do herself harm. Enough harm had been done to her already, and Niall shared the rage he saw in Blake's eyes every time he looked at the bruise Ian had left on the sweet girl's face.

In spite of the fact that the girls clearly felt their trials were over when Blake finally opened the door, climbed out of the carriage, and lifted them down, Niall had the terrible feeling their problems were only just beginning when Xavier burst out through the front door and rushed to meet them.

"Sir," Xavier began, standing in Blake's path to stop him from racing after the girls, who had darted ahead into the house as Charles held the door. "The police are here."

Blake shook his head and blinked at Xavier, but dread filled Niall's gut.

"For what reason?" Blake asked as the three of them headed up the terrace stairs and into the house.

"They arrived an hour ago demanding to question the staff and to know your whereabouts," Xavier reported. He glanced to Niall. "Both of your whereabouts. They are particularly interested in whether you are together." The sharp look in the young man's eyes hinted there was more to the word "together" than physical proximity.

"Ian," Niall hissed, acid in his gut. "This has to be part of his plan."

"It would fit," Blake sighed wearily, rubbing a hand over his face. He hadn't had time to shave in days, which had him looking rough and roguish. Under any other circumstances, Niall would have found his appearance irresistible and dragged Blake off to let the man have his way with him. "Where are the officers?" Blake asked Xavier at last.

"In the Egyptian parlor, sir," Xavier answered. "It's the farthest from here, so I thought it would give me a moment to explain things."

"Good idea." Blake thumped Xavier's shoulder, then started down the hall, calling, "Let the nursery maid know the girls are back."

"You're not going to confront the police immediately, are you?" Niall rushed after Blake.

Blake glanced at him, a determined spark in his eyes. "You may know the way of things in London, but things work differently in Yorkshire. I know how to manage local police officers."

He added a wry grin that was almost enough to give Niall confidence that they'd make it through the confrontation unscathed.

That confidence faltered when they entered the Egyptian parlor and were faced with two Metropolitan Police officers from London. They were examining curiosities around the room, but turned to frown at Blake and Niall when they entered.

All the same, Blake kept his smile in place as he greeted them with, "Gentlemen, I'm sorry you were made to wait. I've only just arrived home from an emergency trip to Blackpool to retrieve my children. My wife and I had a disagreement, and I had reason to believe she intended to take my son, the future duke, and my daughters out of the country."

A burst of pride filled Niall at the clever way Blake began the encounter. In one, quick comment, he'd reminded the officers he was a duke, a married man, and a father, and that Annamarie was in the wrong. All the same, Niall hung back to observe how things would go next instead of drawing attention to himself.

The officers gaped and stammered, immediately on the back foot.

"We received reports of, um, acts of gross indecency taking place here, your grace," the taller of the two officers said. He glanced in Niall's direction.

Niall stood near the cabinet where he'd found the necklace they'd given to Ian to serve as the medallion, hands behind his back, shoulders squared, face implacable, looking as masculine as possible.

Blake laughed as though the idea were ridiculous. "Who made these reports?" he asked, but rushed quickly to, "Please have a seat, gentlemen. I see my excellent staff have already provided you with tea." Indeed, a tea set sat on the table under one of the windows.

"No, thank you, your grace," the tall officer said, his brow knit into a frown. "We cannot divulge where we received our reports, only that we were charged with investigating and making arrests, if warranted." He turned to Niall. "Are you Mr. Niall Cristofori?"

"I am," Niall answered without moving from his position.

"We were told that you are a known sodomite," the second, stouter officer blurted, scowling at Niall in disgust.

Niall shrugged. "Who told you that?"

"Mr. Archibald said—"

"You are known to associate with all manner of men through your theatrical connections, are you not?" the first officer cut the second off.

Niall grinned, in spite of the fact that his heart raced with danger and fury at Ian. At least they had proof of who was behind the whole thing now. "I am a renowned playwright," Niall answered with a shrug. "I am friends with a dozen or more actresses with interesting reputations as well. Does that make me a rake?"

"Er, it's just that—"

The first officer scrambled to come up with a way to counter Niall's statement, but he was interrupted by a woman's raised voice from the hall, saying, "I know they've just returned. It was a happy coincidence that I arrived moments after they did. I must speak with Lord Selby. To apologize, you see."

"Oh, God," Blake blurted, pressing his fingertips to his temples just as Lady Inglewood marched into the room, a hapless Charles trailing behind her.

"I'm so sorry, your grace," Charles hissed, but it was too late.

"Lord Selby, please allow me to extend my deepest, deepest apologies to you for the other night." Lady Inglewood swept into the room, hands outstretched toward Blake, ignoring the officers. "I'm afraid I was in my cups, as the saying goes, and grossly in the wrong to come here. Though I was flattered by the way you welcomed me." She arched an eyebrow and cast a coquettish grin to Blake's trousers.

Niall nearly snorted into laughter at the sudden turn of events. Lady Inglewood was a menace, but she was also exactly the Deus ex Machina they needed at that moment.

"You were here the other night?" the first officer asked, thoroughly confused.

"I'm afraid so," Lady Inglewood answered with a low, sheepish laugh.

"It was a private incident," Blake said, taking Lady

Inglewood's hand and patting it. He went so far as to gaze fondly at her to help the narrative along.

Both officers stood where they were, mouths hanging open, looking as though a prank had been played on them that they had yet to fully figure out. Niall thanked God that he didn't have to say or do anything to help Blake prove his innocence. The more he stayed out of things, the better. And while he was at it, he made a few mental notes for scenes in future plays.

"There must have been a misunderstanding at some point," the first officer said at last, standing straighter and tugging at his jacket as if to save face. "The matter needs further investigation, but—"

"Where are they?" a new shout sounded from the hall. "Selby, you bloody, cheating sod, where are you?"

Shock at hearing Ian's voice rattled Niall. He had just enough time to step back before Ian charged into the room. Once again, Charles trailed behind the new arrival, red-faced and desperate, as though he'd let another situation completely escape his control.

"You lying thief," Ian continued to shout as he marched up to stand toe to toe with Blake. Lady Inglewood yelped and rushed to Niall's side, as though he could protect her. "What is this?" Ian raged on, holding up the necklace they'd attempted to pass off as the medallion.

"It's the medallion you wanted." Blake jerked away from Ian, maintaining a look of utter bewilderment, in spite of the fact that they absolutely *had* cheated Ian out of what he wanted. In fact, underneath his pretend shock, Blake looked overjoyed.

"This is a piece of rubbish," Ian growled, throwing the necklace to the floor. "I want Professor Carroll's medallion."

"What is Professor Carroll's medallion?" Lady Inglewood whispered as she clutched Niall's arm.

Niall didn't get a chance to explain.

"That's it." Blake gestured to the necklace on the floor, then added with perfect, feigned innocence, "Isn't it?"

"No, you buggering bastard, it isn't," Ian exploded. "Where is the real thing? That's what I want, or you'll be sorry."

"Where is my son?" Blake demanded, taking a step into Ian. "Did Annamarie and Alan sail without you?"

"No, we were prevented—" Ian stopped, his face pinching as if he'd made a mistake. "Give me the medallion."

"Give me back my son," Blake demanded, the light of victory in his eyes. "Or would you care to explain to these officers from Scotland Yard why you are holding my son hostage against his will?"

Ian took a few stilted steps away from Blake, glancing to the officers.

"We weren't aware there was a kidnapping involved in this case," the tall officer said, his expression going flat.

"I hope you see now that the accusations that were made against the Duke of Selby were false and born out of a personal grudge," Niall said, hoping to turn the tables completely. "Mr. Archibald is the one who should be arrested."

"He's the criminal." Ian pointed at Blake.

"What accusations?" Lady Inglewood asked at the same time.

"Lord Selby and Mr. Cristofori have been accused of gross indecency," the second officer answered, though he no longer looked certain.

Lady Inglewood gaped at Niall, then at Blake, then burst into laughter. "Oh, good heavens, what a ridiculous notion." She clutched her chest as she laughed. "Lord Selby is a married man, sir," she told the officers, looking down her nose at them. "And he has sired three children. Everyone knows that *that* sort of man is infertile."

Niall's brow shot up before he could school his expression. He'd all but forgotten that was a common misconception that had existed for centuries about their sort.

"And as for Mr. Cristofori," Lady Inglewood went on with a cheeky grin. "I wager Miss Yates would tell a different story about his proclivities." She lowered her voice to a whisper. "Rumor has it that she spent the evening here after making Mr. Cristofori's acquaintance at a supper party last week."

"She was rather nice," Niall said, grinning, heat rising to his face, but not for the reasons Lady Inglewood or, hopefully, the officers, would suspect.

"What?" Ian barked. "This is ridiculous. And it's a

waste of time." He turned back to Blake. "Hand over the medallion or you'll never see your son and heir again."

"Did you hear that, gentlemen?" Blake stepped toward the officers, fury bright in his expression. "Mr. Archibald has just threatened my son."

The officers exchanged a look, as if deciding whether to act on Blake's words.

"It was not a threat." Ian's face lost all color, and he backpedaled toward the parlor doorway. "The boy is with his mother. She has every right to take him to visit her family in America."

"But she has not left yet," Blake rounded on Ian, marching toward him. "Has she?"

"No, but—"

Ian stopped, seeming to realize he'd tipped his hand at an important moment. Blake looked both triumphant and ready to murder him.

"You will not take Alan out of the country," he said, marching to stand toe to toe with Ian again and lowering his voice to a hiss. "If you so much as dare to look at a ship, I will move heaven and earth to make your life a living hell. If Annamarie returns Alan to me, I will grant her a divorce with whatever sort of settlement she wants, provided the two of you leave England forever once it is finalized. My children will stay with me. All of them. Do I make myself clear?"

Ian cowered as Blake spoke, but once Blake finished, he straightened and cleared his throat. "I want that medallion. Hand it over now and I'll have Alan sent back immediately."

Blake's confidence faltered. "I don't know where it is."

"You...what?" Ian barked.

"It was given away years ago, to a traveling theater company," Blake admitted. "It could be anywhere."

Ian gaped at him, his face going red. At last, he snapped his mouth closed and growled, "Then you'd better hope you find it before I do. I'll trade your stupid boy for the medallion, but if I find the medallion before you do, Annamarie and I will be on the first ship to New York." He leaned closer to Blake and murmured just loud enough for Niall to hear from where he and Lady Inglewood stood, "And you'd better hope the lad is a good swimmer."

The threat was so evil that Niall gasped and balled his hands into fists as he surged toward Ian, intent on beating the man senseless. Blake lunged for him, but Ian anticipated the move and dodged out of his way. He didn't stop with one lunge, and turned to flee from the room as if he knew full well he'd gone too far.

"Go after him," Blake ordered the police officers. "The man just threatened the life of my son."

"He didn't exactly—" the second officer started with a wince.

"We don't have jurisdiction here," the first officer said with a guilty look.

"You were threatening to arrest Lord Selby and

myself for gross indecency, but you don't have the jurisdiction to stop a kidnapper?" Niall demanded, marching
up to the first officer.

"We were sent with a specific mission," the man
replied, shrinking away.

Niall shook his head in disgust, then turned to follow
Blake, who had rushed after Ian as soon as he saw the officers wouldn't.

Ian managed to stay just enough ahead of them as he
dashed down the hall, out the front door, and into the
carriage that was waiting for him. Blake attempted to run
out in front of the carriage—as though he could stop a
team of horses with his bare hands—but Niall pulled him
back and held him steady.

"You heard what he said," Blake roared, attempting to
shake out of Niall's grip. "He intends to harm Alan. And
he didn't even tell us where he and Annamarie are
hiding."

"He won't hurt your son," Niall tried to reassure him,
even though he was just as furious and would have flown
after Ian with pistols drawn, if he could. "Remember
what Greta said. He views Alan as a bargaining chip. He
won't harm your boy, or risk Annamarie's wrath by doing
so, until he has what he wants."

Blake whipped to face him as the sound of Ian's
carriage faded into the night. "We have no idea where the
medallion is," he said through a clenched jaw.

"We'll find it." Niall grabbed the sides of Blake's face,
forcing him to calm down and look into his eyes. "We'll

find it," he repeated, "like we found each other again after all these years. Nothing, not even ourselves and the mistakes we've made, could keep the two of us apart. We are meant to be together. You know that."

Some of the struggle went out of Blake's tense muscles. He swayed closer to Niall, letting out a breath and bowing his head when Niall moved his hands to Blake's shoulders. "I know," Blake said. He rested a hand on Niall's waist for a moment before giving up whatever resistance he had and pulling Niall fully into his arms. "I know," he repeated, then buried his face against Niall's neck.

Niall was vaguely aware that they were being watched from the doorway, likely by Lady Inglewood, the officers, and who knew how many members of Blake's staff. He hoped the high stakes of the situation would be enough to explain away the embrace. In case it wasn't, he took a step back from Blake, but held his gaze when Blake glanced up and met his eyes.

"We'll go to London immediately," he said in a low voice so that no one overheard. "We'll take the girls and put them somewhere safe. I don't trust Ian not to come after them if he thinks he can use them to get what he wants from you as well."

Blake nodded, desperation in his eyes, but also trust. "You're right." He paused and shoved a hand through his wild hair. "We can't stay at Selby House in London. Ian will expect us to be there, and God only knows what he'll try to throw at us if he knows where we are."

Inspiration hit Niall. "I have friends. Lots of friends. The Brotherhood will be able to help us with everything."

"The Brotherhood." Blake nodded. "You mentioned them before. They're...they're men like us."

"They are," Niall said. "There are places where we can stay hidden and where we can be together without anyone so much as raising an eyebrow. We'll be able to keep the girls safe there as well. We can call on old friends to help find that bloody medallion and to ferret out Ian and Annamarie. You remember John Dandie and David Wirth?" Blake nodded. "David and his partner, Lionel, are able to accomplish impossible things for our sort all the time. They can help. And John has just returned to London to open a law office, but he has contacts all over the country. Between the two of them, we will beat Ian at his own game, I swear."

Blake let out a breath and grabbed Niall's hands, squeezing them tightly. "Niall, I don't know what I'd do without you." He stepped closer, his gaze dropping to Niall's lips for a moment before darting over Niall's shoulder to their audience. He glanced back to Niall and said, "I love you."

"And I love you," Niall whispered tenderly in return. "Come what may, I'm never leaving you again, whether you want me to or not." His mouth twitched into a grin and deep affection filled his heart. "We're going to make a life together. You, me, and the children. We'll defy the odds to make a family, no matter what it takes. Between your title and my fame, they won't dare to question us or tear us apart. Never again."

"Never," Blake agreed, twining his fingers through Niall's. "The world is changing so much these days anyhow. Why not change it to suit us?"

"You know I would kiss you right now if I could," Niall replied with a saucy grin.

Blake grinned in return. "Then let's get rid of Lady Inglewood, make sure the girls are in bed, then go to bed ourselves," he whispered.

Niall was all for the plan. It was as mad as could be, and the two of them were likely to land in every sort of hot water in the years to come, no matter what they did, but it would all be worth it now that they were back in each other's arms.

EPILOGUE

The scene backstage in the Concord Theater after the premier performance of *Love's Last Lesson* was one of utter chaos. John Dandie had to dodge chorus girls in enormous dresses, stagehands carrying enormous set pieces, and Everett Jewel's enormous ego to reach the dressing room where he was told he would find Blake and his girls. The mood was excited and jovial after the smashing success of the performance. Niall had sent John a ticket to the sold-out show and requested his presence backstage afterward to help with a thorny problem, and after what he'd just seen, John was certain every paper in London would be singing Niall's praises in the morning.

But John knew he wasn't there to sing anyone's praise. He'd been paying attention to the events of the past fortnight, gleaning information when and where he could from friends and professional connections. As soon as he'd heard the news that Castleford Estate had been sold to Danny Long and would be converted into a convalescent home for members of The Brotherhood suffering from nervous exhaustion, he knew Niall's mission in the north had been successful and Blake was back in the fold. He wasn't at all surprised when he turned the corner into the dressing room to find Blake and his daughters playing cards at a small table, Blake's son nowhere in sight.

"You haven't changed a bit, your grace," John said with a broad smile as he strode into the room.

"John." Blake put down his cards and leapt up from the table, crossing to close John in a friendly hug. "It's been too long," he said when he took a step back, smiling. "And don't bother with the whole 'your grace' bit. I never liked it when my friends were that formal. And besides which, we're supposed to be in hiding."

"We're hiding from Mama and that horrible Mr. Archibald," Blake's older daughter said as she and her sister watched John suspiciously from the table.

"I won't breathe a word," John promised them.

He studied Blake for a quick moment. It'd been ten years since he'd last seen the man. He'd aged, but not badly. In fact, Blake was even more handsome than John remembered him to be. More than that, in spite of the dire circumstances John had heard about, Blake looked happy and content.

The reason for that look of happiness walked into the dressing room a moment later. The second Niall entered the room, Blake lit up like the sunrise. His girls relaxed as well.

"John. You made it." Niall walked over to shake John's hand, then said to Blake, "I told you he would come."

"I never had any doubt." Blake grinned and shifted to stand by Niall's side, resting a hand on Niall's back.

John fought not to grin at the obvious affection between the two, just as they had been at university, only more confident.

"Congratulations on a truly excellent performance, by the way," John said to Niall. "Another triumph."

"We saw it yesterday, during the dress rehearsal," Blake's younger daughter said. "Jane and Katie and all the other girls came to see it too."

John's brow flew up, and he sent a questioning look to Niall.

"Stephen Siddel's girls," he explained. He glanced to Blake, swaying toward him and taking Blake's hand. "We've taken up residence in Darlington Gardens, Earl's Court, two doors down from Stephen and Max's orphanage. Greta and Jessie have become fast friends with some of the girls."

"And I trust Stephen and Max enough to leave my girls in their care when business has taken us elsewhere," Blake added, his expression turning more serious. "Which is why we've asked you to meet us here tonight."

"I'm aware of the situation," John said as Niall gestured for the three of them to move to the far end of the room while the girls resumed their card game. They could likely still hear what the adults were saying, but they didn't seem to care. "I've been given to understand that Ian Archibald has run off with Lady Selby and the current Marquess of Stanley, your son."

"He has," Blake said, letting out a shaky breath. John thought highly of Blake for being so obviously concerned about a child, his child. Not every duke cared as much. "We're terrified that they'll go to Annamarie's family in New York and that we won't be able to get Alan back because of it." He glanced to Niall.

John smiled at the way the two men so obviously cared for each other. He would have given everything he had for a partnership like that. He thought he'd had something close twice before, but real love felt desperately out of reach.

There wasn't time for his own heartbreaks and longings, though. He took in a breath and clasped his hands behind his back, thinking hard about the problem in front of him. "So your primary concern is finding Ian, Lady Selby, and your son before they can leave England."

"Correct," Blake and Niall answered together.

John found it sweet. "And you have no idea where they are?"

"None at all," Blake sighed.

"And what about—"

He was interrupted by an almighty crash as one of the actors stumbled into the dressing room with an armful of decorated parasols that had been used as props in the show. He dropped several with a gasp of, "Oh! Sorry."

"Mr. Piper, Mr. Piper!" Blake's girls seemed over-joyed at the interruption and leapt out of their chairs to scramble for the parasols Martin Piper had dropped.

"Can we play with the parasols?" Blake's younger daughter asked, glancing adoringly up at Martin.

"Well, er, um, that is, they're for the play." Martin sent an apologetic look to Niall. "I was just going to store them in here, since Jewel wants his room cleared of props."

"Of course, he does." Niall rolled his eyes. "Put them wherever you'd like."

"Yes, sir." Martin attempted a comical salute, drop-ping more parasols in the process. The girls giggled as though it were a game and jumped around, picking them up. "Once a property master, always a property master, eh?" the cheery man told Niall.

John watched Martin for a moment, shaking his head, before facing Blake and Niall again. "Back to business. I've been given to understand that there's some sort of Egyptian artifact at play in this whole thing as well?"

"A medallion," Blake said with a nod. "Remember the prize I won at graduation? Professor Carroll's medallion?"

"Vaguely." John stroked his chin and frowned. "That's what Ian wants?"

"Yes. And he's adamant about it too," Niall said.

"But why?" John shrugged.

"Either it's a matter of pride or the medallion is worth far more than any of us suspected," Blake said.

"Which was what Ian kept trying to claim before the exam," Niall added.

"Whether it's valuable or not is irrelevant as long as Ian thinks it is," John figured. He glanced to Blake. "And you have no idea where it is?"

"None." Blake shrugged. "The most we've been able to find out is the name of the theatrical troupe it was donated to, but the troupe was defunct years ago."

"What were they called?" John asked.

"The Shakespearian Society of Yorkshire," Niall said.

Another small crash sounded from the corner of the room where Martin was attempting to store parasols in a cabinet while the girls played with them. "I used to work for the Shakespearian Society of Yorkshire," Martin said.

John, Niall, and Blake all stared at him.

"Were you with them when they performed *Anthony and Cleopatra* in Leeds four years ago?" Blake asked, stepping closer to him.

"Yes, I was in charge of—"

A sharp knock on the open dressing room door stopped Martin's explanation cold. They all turned to find a short, devilishly handsome man with dark hair and blue eyes watching them all like a hawk. He was dressed nondescriptly, as if not to draw attention to himself, but John found him immediately arresting.

"I was told Martin Piper was in here," the man said, taking a step into the room.

341

"That's me." Martin started toward the man, stumbling over a parasol on the floor as he did.

John stopped him from crossing the room to the unknown man by holding out a hand. "And who are you, might we ask?"

"Detective Arthur Gleason," the man said, coming forward, hand outstretched.

Wariness pooled in John's gut, along with a feeling like he wouldn't mind investigating more about Gleason... in private. "And what is your business with Mr. Piper?" he asked.

Gleason narrowed his eyes at John. "Not that it's any of your concern, but I've been hired to ask Mr. Piper a few questions about his previous employer."

Judging by the sudden alarm that came to Blake and Niall's eyes, they'd instantly reached the same conclusion John had. Gleason had to have been hired by Ian, and Ian must have figured out the medallion had been donated to the troupe Martin once worked for.

"I'll tell you anything you want to know," Martin said with a shrug, glancing to John as if John might try to stop him again. "But truthfully, I don't know much." He ended with a self-deprecating laugh.

"Don't tell him anything," John cautioned Martin.

"I beg your pardon." Gleason glared at John. "What gives you the right to interfere with a private investigation?"

"I suspect the man who hired you is a criminal himself, guilty of kidnapping," John said.

"Do you now?" Gleason smirked at John. The gesture was as aggravating as it was arousing. But before John could do a damn thing about it, Gleason nodded to Martin. "Perhaps we could speak privately."

"Um...." Martin glanced to Niall, broke into an apologetic look, then started forward. "Alright?"

"Careful what you say," John murmured as Martin passed.

Gleason sent John one more grin—as if he'd won a hand at cards against him—then left with Martin. In an instant, John was determined to win the game, whatever the game was.

"He's working for Ian, I know it," Niall said once they were alone.

"He has to be," Blake agreed. "Who else would be looking for the medallion?"

"We can ask Martin all about it as soon as Gleason is done with him," John said, shifting into business. "In the meantime, we need to find Ian."

"But how?" Blake shoved a hand through his unruly hair. "They could be anywhere. It's been weeks, and he hasn't so much as tried to contact us yet."

John frowned in thought and rubbed his chin. An idea came to him quickly.

"Edward Archibald is Ian's older brother," he said.

"Edward Archibald the MP?" Blake asked.

Niall's expression lit with inspiration as well. "He's a member of The Brotherhood as well as a Member of Parliament."

"He might know where his brother is hiding," John said, nodding to let Niall know he was on the right track.

"But would he be willing to divulge his brother's whereabouts?" Blake asked.

"I don't think they're close," John said. "I was friendly with Edward at university, and I seem to recall there was no love lost between the two of them."

"Then would he even know where his brother is?" Niall asked with a frown.

John let out a breath and dropped his shoulders. "At the moment, it's the best lead we have. We need to make contact with Edward Archibald, and we need to corner Martin as soon as we can so he can tell us what he knows about the medallion, if anything. We have to find that medallion before Det. Gleason does."

Blake glanced anxiously across the room at his daughters, who were still playing with parasols. John stepped forward and clapped a hand on his shoulder.

"Don't worry, Blake. We'll find them," he said. "I give you my word, I won't rest until your son is back in your arms. I'll leave no stone unturned, and I'll enlist every bit of help from The Brotherhood that I can."

And if Detective Arthur Gleason got in his way, John would give the handsome devil a run for his money. He was looking forward to it.

I hope you've enjoyed Niall and Blake's story! I loved every minute of writing it, but I actually have to give credit for the story idea to my good friend, Laura Stapleton. It all started with a conversation about...well, I won't want to implicate either of us or who we were talking about, but Laura said the magic words, "What if...", and here we are.

As for my other inspiration for this book and its characters.... So there's a song that I first heard in the 90s, "Cristofori's Dream" by David Lanz. Not only is that where I got the idea for Niall's surname, it's also the song that I imagine Blake playing at various points in the book. I cannot urge you enough to pop over to YouTube or Spotify to look it up and play it for yourself! It's such a beautiful piece of music, and it totally captures the spirit of Niall and Blake's relationship.

But what about Alan? This might be a happily ever after for Niall and Blake, but Blake's son is still missing. Never fear, though! John Dandie is on the case, and he has help. Find out if Edward Archibald knows where his brother is...and if Martin Piper knows what happened to the medallion...and what sort of mayhem and craziness happens when a stodgy MP who is desperately careful about concealing who he is ends up joining forces with an affable, clumsy, adorable actor in *Just a Little Madness*, coming in January! Keep clicking to get started reading Chapter One!

· · ·

AND AS FOR JOHN DANDIE.... SPARKS WILL certainly fly between him and Detective Arthur Gleason. In fact, those sparks might be around for several books as the two of them work against each other...and possibly together...to find both the medallion and Ian, Annamarie, and Alan! There's much more of The Brotherhood to look forward to!

BUT BEFORE THAT, YOU'RE GOING TO GET A CHANCE to catch up with all of the couples from The Brotherhood series so far in the next book, *Just a Little Christmas*! This novella is my little gift to you. It's light-hearted, fun, and sure to put a smile on your face and leave you fanning yourself.

AUTHOR'S NOTE: I JUST HAVE TO SHARE THIS with you too.... Forms of address are complex and controversial, especially among Romance writers, and I really hate them. It's one reason why I try to avoid writing about the higher ranks of the nobility completely. My personal belief is that, while there *were* rules in place, behind closed doors and in the privacy of one's own home and among one's friends, no one gave a you know what. Yes, Blake, as a duke, would have been referred to publically as "your grace". But among his friends? At home? That's a whole other kettle of fish. However, I did have one head-scratcher as I wrote this. How would Xavier, Blake's valet, address him? On the one hand, Xavier is a servant. On the other, he's Blake's closest friend.

So I went to the hive mind and asked the question in a Facebook author group I'm part of. And as I should have expected, the answers ran the gamut from "He would absolutely call Blake 'your grace'" to "Body servants called their masters by much less formal names, like 'sir'". After much discussion (with authors sharing links to online resources left and right and getting into fistfights on the subject that would have been funny if I hadn't been in the middle of them) it all came down to one VERY important point: A duke is called whatever a duke wants to be called by the people closest to him. Because he's a freakin' duke. Good point! That's why I chose to have Xavier refer to Blake as "sir". In my mind, Blake would have preferred for Xavier to just address him as "Blake", but given his personality, Xavier would never dare. Calling Blake "sir" is about as informal as Xavier is willing to go. (P.S. You'll get to know Xavier much, much better soon, as he's one of the heroes of *Just a Little Mischief*, coming this spring!)

Now, all that being said, as part of this long and ponderous discussion, my bestie, Caroline Lee, actually had the best answer to the question "What would Xavier call Blake?" It was such a good answer that I'm sharing it with you in its entirety:

· · ·

"So there you go, Merry. His valet can call him whatever the Duke says he can call him.

Please, please, have the Duke drunkenly declare "you can call me Ducky McCheeseface for all I care, Xavier" and then the valet calls him Sir Ducky for years..."

Xavier would be appalled.

Wanna keep in touch with me in the fastest way possible without having to check your email or go on social media? Text TEMPTATION to +1 215-486-0270 today!

If you enjoyed this book and would like to hear more from me, please sign up for my newsletter! When you sign up, you'll get a free, full-length novella, *A Passionate Deception*. Victorian identity theft has never been so exciting in this story of hope, tricks, and starting over. Part of my *West Meets East* series, *A Passionate Deception* can be read as a stand-alone. Pick up your free copy today by signing up to receive my newsletter (which I only send out when I have a new release)!

Sign up here: http://eepurl.com/cbaVMH

. . .

ARE YOU ON SOCIAL MEDIA? I AM! COME AND JOIN the fun on Facebook: http://www. facebook.com/merryfarmerreaders

I'M ALSO A HUGE FAN OF INSTAGRAM AND POST LOTS of original content there: https://www. instagram.com/merryfarmer/

AND NOW, GET STARTED ON JUST A LITTLE MADNESS...

LONDON – JANUARY, 1891

THE THEATER WAS ONE OF THE ONLY PLACES IN London that a man like Edward Archibald could truly hide. Of course, it was rather like hiding in plain sight, because everyone with even a shred of sense knew that the world of the theater was and always had been full of inverts, women of loose morals, and every other sort of unconventional personality to be found under the sun. Society was willing to overlook certain aspects of the character of theatrical types as long as they were entertaining and put on a good show, which playwright Niall Cristofori and star of the stage Everett Jewel always did. Almost no one batted an eyelash over the personal lives of those two men and their ilk, the lucky bastards. Members of Parliament weren't so lucky, as Edward most certainly knew.

Edward rose along with the rest of the audience to applaud the end of *Love's Last Lesson* from his seat near the back of a box in the second balcony. He'd seen the show six times since it opened in the fall and considered that night's performance one of the best. The rest of the crowd thought so as well, as attested by their enthusiastic applause. They clapped particularly loudly for up and coming comedic actor Martin Piper when Jewel shoved the man forward to take a second bow.

Edward tried his best to ignore the thrill in his chest and the way his breath caught in his throat at Martin Piper's affable, smiling face and strong, lean form. He absolutely refused to acknowledge the way his trousers suddenly didn't seem to fit properly as the man blew kisses to his adoring public, landing one relatively near him, before giving way so Jewel could take his bow. Jewel's prowess on the stage and magnetic appeal were a given, but Edward had been taken with Piper from the very first time he'd seen the play. His gaze stayed on the man once he resumed his place with the ensemble as Jewel preened and bowed. Piper made Edward laugh, and precious little made him laugh anymore.

Before the applause had fully died down, Edward scooted his way to the exit at the back of the box. He was not an actor. He was the very opposite of the theatrical luminaries who could get away with murder as long as they were charming and entertaining. He was a back-bencher in the House of Commons. His job was to represent his constituency in York by staying as quiet as possible, never drawing untoward attention to himself, never, ever landing in the papers as part of a scandal, and shouting out "Aye" when his party told him to. Which was why he found sitting in the dark at the back of a crowded theater, not a soul in the world aware of his existence, merely looking on as other, better people than him shone like diamonds, to be the most enjoyable thing he could possibly imagine. And it didn't hurt that the male chorus for Cristofori's show was made up of some of the finest specimens of masculinity he'd ever—

"Archibald, is that you?"

A familiar voice startled Edward out of his indulgent thoughts, driving home the fact that his trousers still didn't fit right after an evening of feasting on the sight of Martin Piper and his like.

"Lord Chesterfield." Edward jerked to a stop in the middle of his flight through the lobby and turned to his fellow parliamentarian with an uneasy smile. God, the man could probably see the state of his lower regions as if he were standing up like a sequoia. A man like Chesterfield would know exactly what he was thinking and exactly who he was thinking it about. The whole world could see right through him, and he would be damned for it. He cleared his throat. "What a pleasant surprise."

"Likewise." Chesterfield approached him with a broad smile and extended a hand. He had to drop the arm of the attractive lady—who was years too young for him and who was most certainly not his daughter—to do so. "Smashing show, didn't you think?"

"Yes, it was rather droll," Edward replied with as bland a look as possible. He smiled and nodded to the woman with Chesterfield, debating whether he should appear to find her alluring so as to avert any suspicion his thoughts might cause.

"I never thought I'd see such a doggedly conservative man like you haunting a place like this," Chesterfield went on with a laugh. He turned to his companion and said, "Archibald never steps a foot out of line. He's the most boring and flaccid member Parliament has." He followed his comment with a raucous laugh.

Edward smiled warily at the comment. He heard that and much worse on a nearly daily basis, but it was better to be called boring than to be called out for the truth. "I was just on my way home," he said, swaying forward and trying to indicate to Chesterfield that he didn't want to chit-chat.

Chesterfield ignored his move, leaned forward, and lowered his voice. "Have you heard the latest about the raid in Marylebone? They broke up a very interesting party, you know." He leaned back and tapped a finger to his nose, then darted a sideways glance to his companion before touching his fingers to his lips in caution.

"Yes, I do believe I heard something about it in passing," Edward replied.

In fact, several prominent members of The Brotherhood—an underground organization of men who loved other men that Edward was a part of—had been arrested and were currently awaiting trial. It was all The Brotherhood had been able to talk about in the last few days. The party was of a sordid nature—the sort of thing Edward was both repulsed and reluctantly fascinated with—and its organizer, Walter Borne, had accidentally invited a blackmailer. The blackmailer in question had spent months befriending the men in order to be invited to something like that, and he had jumped bringing the police with him, at the first opportunity. The Brotherhood was livid, and David Wirth and Lionel Mercer were up to their eyeballs, pulling out every legal stop they could to exonerate the unfortunate bastards who had been caught up in the whole thing. The net result was that every invert in London was even more on his guard than usual. And Edward was *always* on his guard.

"That sort is a blight upon England," Chesterfield went on, puffing his chest up. "Their sort should be rounded up and thrown in the fire like the fags they are before they can corrupt the morals of the young. Why, my wife and her friends are intent on raising funds to do something about it. I believe they're meeting about it this evening, the blessed things." He turned to his companion —who was most certainly not his wife. The young lady giggled and cooed, hugging Chesterfield's arm and leaning into him in a way that exposed her ample bosom. "Come on, dearie," Chesterfield went on. "We'll be late to Monroe's soiree, and I hear he's had some of the good stuff imported from Burma." He laughed and kissed his companion's cheek before nodding to Edward and marching off.

Edward waited until Chesterfield had his back turned to scowl in frustration. A blight on England indeed. The hypocrisy of men like Chesterfield, with their mistresses, oriental narcotics, and who knew what other vices, insisting that men like Jewel—who just wanted to show off—or like Niall Cristofori and Blake Williamson—who only wanted to reunite Blake's family so that they could live in domestic peace for the rest of their days—was appalling.

The anger those thoughts brought with them burned in Edward's gut as he crossed the Concord Theater's lobby to retrieve his coat and hat from the booth near the front, then headed out into the frigid night. Maybe Walter had the right of things and he should make hay while the sun was shining, as the phrase went. Perhaps bending over backwards to avoid notice and deny the urges that were sometimes so demanding he couldn't sleep wasn't the way to go. He wasn't a total monk, after all. He should be bending over forwards with a strapping companion behind him. He'd been cruising in St. James's Park a time or two to find what he needed in the moment, which had never amounted to more than an impersonal hand, or even more rarely, a mouth, in the dark. Though he always felt miserably and dirty afterwards. But dammit, man was not meant to be made of stone, and he certainly wasn't.

His restless, winding thoughts took him around the side of the theater to the alley where the stage door stood. Already, a crowd of men and women huddled together in the cold and the dark, waiting, no doubt, for Everett Jewel to make his appearance. Edward grimaced at the pull he felt toward that crowd, walking forward to join them even as he warned himself he should go home and stay safe. The impish voice at the back of his head whispered that there might be a likely fellow loitering in the crowd who could do him a favor in a dark corner and end the relentless throbbing in his groin. When was the last time he'd had anyone, other than himself, do something about that merciless need? Months at the very least. One harmless little fumble wouldn't do him any harm. No one would have to know.

Edward glanced carefully at the men waiting for Jewel, keeping his eyes peeled for that particular look or a wink or any of the numerous signs their sort had to indicate they were game. He spotted a handsome young fellow with a wide mouth and teasing eyes leaning against the wall of the building beside the theater. The man's smile widened when Edward met his eyes. He touched the back of his hand as a signal. A rush of bittersweet excitement pulsed through Edward, and his cock stirred to life. With a mouth like that, he might get exactly what he needed from the man. He inched closer.

The stage door opened, and there was a roar of applause and adoration as Everett stepped out to greet his admirers. Edward noted the ever-present form of

Everett's lover, Patrick Wrexham, with a smirk. Anyone who thought they could get a piece of Everett for the evening would be sorely disappointed. Everett and Patrick were devoted to each other—a fact that had Edward's heart aching in his chest. What he wouldn't give for a man to adore and protect him the way Patrick and Everett looked out for and loved each other? When Patrick spotted him in the back of the crowd and nodded, Edward nodded back with a wistful grin. They knew each other from The Brotherhood, of course, and Edward had secretly envied Patrick and what he had for months.

That only increased his mad determination to get at least a modicum of pleasure that evening. And who knew? Perhaps a wicked assignation in the dark could lead to a lifetime of happiness. Men had met in stranger ways. He focused forward again, turning his hopeful grin to the young man leaning against the wall.

The young man's smile widened, and he stood straighter. He pushed away from the wall, walking with purpose toward the mouth of the ally and the street. Edward knew the signs well. The man probably had rooms nearby, or at least knew of a relatively private area, like a public toilet, where they could complete their transaction. Edward's heart thumped against his ribs in anticipation as he followed the man, taking care to keep behind him enough to deflect any suspicion, but close enough so that the man would know he was following.

They walked halfway across Covent Garden that way. The young man was definitely heading toward one of the public toilets. Edward was tense with expectation and arousal, though a large part of him felt tainted and gross already over what he was about to do. He told himself that he was only human, that he had every right to steal a moment of pleasure if he wanted to, and that both parties would be willing and eager. There was nothing wrong with what he wanted or what he was doing.

"Got a match?" the young man said, stopping near the entrance to the public toilet.

Edward reached into his pocket for the coins the man likely wanted to see before heading into the toilet.

"Charlie! Thank God. There you are."

Edward nearly jumped out of his skin at the shout from behind him. He whirled around, expecting to see someone who knew the young man. His heart dropped to his feet and his hands went numb at the sight of none other than Martin Piper striding toward him with a smile and something like determination in his eyes, as illuminated by the streetlights. For a fraction of a second, he was convinced Piper knew the young man, but a moment later, he realized Piper was marching straight toward him.

"You didn't have to come all this way to use the toilet you know, Charlie," Piper said, grabbing Edward's elbow and steering him away from the young man. He barely nodded to the fellow, then dragged Edward off toward the main street. "You could have used the one at the theater."

"Oh...I...sorry. Um, that is to say...." Edward stammered, no idea what was going on. He glanced over his shoulder at the young man, who had pulled up the collar of his coat and was rushing away. "Er, my name isn't Charlie," he finished.

"I know," Piper whispered, urging Edward to pick up his pace as well. He glanced around anxiously before letting go of Edward's arm and rubbing his mittened hands together. "You're Edward Archibald, MP. And that bloke was Jerry Rivers, one of the very worst black-mailers you'd ever want to come across."

Edward's nerves frazzled so fast and so hard that he missed a step. "Good God," he hissed, pausing to lean against a lamppost for a moment so his legs didn't give out from under him entirely. If he'd been caught cruising in Covent Garden...the scandal that would hit the papers by morning...his reputation, livelihood, and life ruined.... He didn't even want to think about it.

"Patrick spotted you at the theater door, saw Rivers hook you, and sent me after you before you could do yourself a harm," Piper explained. When Edward dared to look the man in the eyes, Piper's face brightened into a charming smile, and he held out his hand. "Hello. Martin Piper."

The tightness in Edward's groin flared to life again at the kindness in Piper's eyes and the genuine happiness in his smile. He straightened and took the man's hand. "Edward Archibald," he returned the greeting.

"But I already knew that," Piper finished as though that was what he was about to say. "Come on. Let's get you home, safe and sound." He thumped Edward's shoulder once they were finished shaking hands and steered him toward the main road. "Where do you live?"

Edward blinked and shook his head slightly, unable to believe that *the* Martin Piper was walking him home after rescuing him from disaster. "Er, just on the other side of Birdcage Walk, off of St. James's Park."

"Ooh, fancy." Piper's eyes lit up even more. "Close to the halls of Westminster, I see."

"Yes, something like that." In fact, Edward had taken a small flat there in a fit of wickedness, as St. James's Park was one of the most fruitful and notorious cruising grounds for men like them. Whenever he couldn't stand denying his urges for a moment longer, there was always a likely fellow to be found in the park after dark.

WANT TO READ MORE?
PICK UP JUST A LITTLE MADNESS TODAY!

Click here for a complete list of other works by Merry Farmer.

ABOUT THE AUTHOR

I hope you have enjoyed *Just a Little Heartache*. If you'd like to be the first to learn about when new books in the series come out and more, please sign up for my newsletter here: http://eepurl.com/cbaVMH And remember, Read it, Review it, Share it! For a complete list of works by Merry Farmer with links, please visit http://wp.me/P5ttjb-14F.

Merry Farmer is an award-winning novelist who lives in suburban Philadelphia with her cats, Torpedo, her grumpy old man, and Justine, her hyperactive new baby. She has been writing since she was ten years old and realized one day that she didn't have to wait for the teacher to assign a creative writing project to write something. It was the best day of her life. She then went on to earn not one but two degrees in History so that she would always have something to write about. Her books have reached the Top 100 at Amazon, iBooks, and Barnes & Noble, and have been named finalists in the prestigious RONE and Rom Com Reader's Crown awards.

ACKNOWLEDGMENTS

I owe a huge debt of gratitude to my awesome beta-readers, Caroline Lee and Jolene Stewart, for their suggestions and advice. And double thanks to Julie Tague, for being a truly excellent editor! Thanks also to my fabulous assistant, Cindy Jackson.

Click here for a complete list of other works by Merry Farmer.